ANCHOR POINT

AJ BAILEY ADVENTURE SERIES - BOOK 13

NICHOLAS HARVEY

HarveyBooks

Printed in the United States of America

First Printing, 2023

ISBN-13: 978-1-959627-00-5

Cover design by Wicked Good Book Covers

Back cover illustration by Efa Finearts

Mermaid illustration by Tracie Cotta

Author photograph by Lift Your Eyes Photography

This is a work of fiction. Names, characters, businesses, places, events and incidents are either the products of the author's imagination or used in a fictitious manner unless noted otherwise. Any resemblance to actual persons, living or dead, or actual events is purely coincidental. Several characters in the story generously gave permission to use their names in a fictional manner.

DEDICATION

This is for my uncle, Mike Golding.
Thank you for the love, support, and opportunities you've always
given me.

PREFACE

Whenever I'm asked which one of my books is my favourite I usually answer, "The one I just finished." I believe it's because I become so immersed in the story and characters, I find myself mentally living in their world.

Anchor Point was all that - and more.

Cheryl and I have been visiting the Cayman Islands for over twenty years; we've owned property there and consider it our second home. But this was the first novel I've written whilst staying there. I was writing about the area known as Anchor Point while diving the very spot. We were spending time with our friends who I include in the story – Casey Keller from the DoE and Lisa Collins the photographer – as well as eating lunch at Heritage Kitchen, and standing on Reg and AJ's dock in West Bay – with Chris and Kate of Indigo Divers, the actual owners.

It was a similar feeling to when I wrote *Wrecks of Key Largo* whilst living in The Keys. If I wanted to research a location, I simply drove there and figured out how to make it fit into the plot.

It was also time for AJ and Reg to spend more time together. Boy are they fun to write. Their banter falls out of my head, and I hear the two of them good-naturedly jabbing each other – actually I hear my audiobook narrator Kim Bretton's voice as she captures them both so perfectly.

The other reason I enjoyed *Anchor Point* so much is the dual timeline story. I love writing this way, and it gives me an opportunity to mix a new set of characters into an historical plot based partly in real events from the period and partly from my own imagination. I became a great friend and admirer of Vin and Wil Crowe, feeling like an invisible partner along for their tumultuous ride, three centuries ago.

I hope you enjoy this story and find the location and characters as engaging and fascinating as I did. *Anchor Point* is very special to me.

1

LOS CAYMANAS

1704

Fate once more had dealt us a fair hand.

If several of the crew were to be believed, that is. Tired, hungry, and grumbling as men often were after time on the open seas. I gave credit to our captain's fine navigation, but in my thoughts alone. I was a lowly ship's boy whose opinions weren't sought nor offered.

Navigating the oceans with little more than a compass, a vague map, and the notes from a prior captain made finding destinations a combination of skill and good fortune. Bringing us into the intended bay on an island five miles wide at the east end and no more elevation than the tallest tree provided on the flat land required an abundance of the former. But again, this was my unshared and admittedly biased opinion.

Being the captain's son was a precarious position. Never completely trusted and rarely included in off-duty gatherings. I'd work alongside these men each day, then be discarded like a stray dog. But it didn't bother me. Soon we would be free of this predicament.

Boatswain Hinchcliffe yelled orders from the bowsprit as we edged slowly closer to the island's sandy shore, the clear waters negating the need for lead line as the bottom was now visible. With a final cry and wave from the boatswain, the men released the anchor, which took a firm hold on the reef below us.

The softly ebbing tide would pivot the *Royal Fortune* about the anchor, and we would see if the boatswain's call would keep the rudder free of the sandy shallows. Our three-masted carrack drew less water than the larger, modern galleons preferred by most, merchantmen and privateer alike. She was also nimble and had outrun, when required, every ship our path had crossed. A record undoubtedly destined to come to an end at some point in time.

Los Caymanas were uninhabited by man as best I knew, although a few of the crew had heard rumour of a community being established on the west side. But the islands were home to an abundance of turtle and caiman – a large reptile akin to an alligator, according to the captain. The crew had restocked on the island before, under the leadership of a previous captain. That was the unfortunate one before the equally unfortunate Mr Rochefort. The memories the crew shared of their earlier visit were dominated by the swarms of mosquitoes which unmercifully feasted upon bare flesh. I found myself already scratching my legs in anticipation.

Captain Rochefort had taken over the *Royal Fortune* only months prior when the long-serving captain and owner of the ship had succumbed to an awful fever. Blessed that the sickness hadn't spread to the rest of the crew, the men had readily agreed that Rochefort, as navigator, should succeed as captain. He understood the privateering agreement with the Crown known as the letter of marque under which they sailed, and they had no reason to suspect he would be timid in his leadership.

Rochefort indeed showed himself to be an able captain, but while the carrack had haste and agility, it lacked firepower. Six cannons were not enough against the newer galleons of Spain and

Portugal, who now often sailed in guarded convoys with their New World plunder. He'd scored minor successes with a few smaller merchantmen who had given up without resistance, but the *Cielos de Oro* was a different story.

The *Royal Fortune* alone was no match for the Spanish galleon, but as fate would have it, we weren't alone. A privateer ship under the English flag had attacked the lone galleon north-west of Jamaica when we arrived shortly after dawn. It was a fierce battle. Rochefort attempted to assist the English ship with intentions of dividing the spoils, but before he could line up to fire, the privateer ship took a mortal cannon shot below the waterline.

Seeing them rapidly sinking, Rochefort feared we would suffer the same fate from the Spanish cannons and ordered a hasty retreat. The men jeered, eager for battle - even a one-sided affair - and stood firm. The navigator, Vin Crowe, saw an opportunity and heaved on the wheel, barking orders to the men who enthusiastically obeyed once they realised the *Royal Fortune* was lining up to attack.

When the smoke of battle finally settled and a white flag waved, it was the Spanish captain who chose to relinquish his ship and threw the fate of his remaining men into the hands of our crew. To my distress, our own captain had perished in the conflict. I considered him a good man, despite his occupation.

Vin Crowe, who was quiet, slight in size yet decisive in action, had been faithful to Rochefort and had not intended to undermine the man's command. But with the battle won and the captain dead, the men quickly assembled and voted Crowe as their new leader, a role Vin had neither sought after nor desired.

In a brief moment created by another man's oversight rather than Crowe's ambition or design, I became a captain's son. It made for a difficult situation, requiring great care and secrecy, and one I feared would lead us to ruin instead of home.

The *Cielos de Oro* would have made a grand prize herself had she not been blown to shreds beyond our capability of repair. Her captain was gracious in defeat and begged the lives of his men be spared. Crowe spoke enough Spanish to communicate, and an assurance was made.

Our new captain guided the carrack alongside the stricken larger ship and the men eagerly lashed the two together. None of us expected to find what waited below decks. Hoping for gold and silver, but knowing it was more likely to be sugar and tobacco, Boatswain Hinchcliffe shouted for Crowe to come below. Bolts of fine silk and other textiles lay stacked between barrels of exotic spices from the far east.

When questioned, the Spanish captain confessed they'd stumbled across a lone English East India Company ship, the *Brackley*, returning to Portsmouth after a long passage around the Cape of Good Hope. The ship had surprised them by surrendering after minimal cannon fire. They learnt the hapless Englishmen were almost out of ammunition, fresh water and food after being attacked several times since becoming separated from their convoy during a storm. The *Brackley* had also sustained considerable damage from which the crew had patched together repairs as best they could.

The *Cielos de Oro* had been less than a week at sea on her way to collect sugar from Cuba, so the captain was left in a quandary. If he claimed the English ship, he'd be forced to split his crew. If he turned back with both vessels, he'd add weeks to an already delayed trip. In the end, he moved all the bounty he could fit into the hold of the *Cielos de Oro* and set the English ship free to continue home. He would drop the exotic cargo in Spanish-held Cuba then continue home with a hold full of sugar as planned.

Captain Crowe ordered the men to take all the spices and bolts of fabric we could cram into our smaller ship. As we moved the bounty, space was made in the Spanish hold, and about the time the *Royal Fortune* was bursting at the seams, Crowe discovered a wooden chest hidden behind the remaining goods. The boatswain raised the lid to reveal scrolls of company papers, which he threw aside in anger and disappointment.

Undeterred, Crowe reached into the chest, lifting a false bottom aloft. Below were several bags of precious rubies and diamonds, along with a cutlass unlike any they had seen before. The locket and chape of the scabbard were decorated with ornately engraved gold, and the hilt of the sword itself appeared to be solid gold. The curved blade was bronze with a fine engraving along its length. The uniquely disc-shaped pommel behind the grip was adorned with a ring of brilliant rubies, and the button was a dazzling single red stone. Every detail in the hilt, including the knucklebow and sculpted quillons of the crossguard, were meticulously shaped and engraved.

Handing the bags of jewels to the boatswain, our new captain immediately laid claim to the cutlass. Its value would be deducted from the captain's double share once all their bounty had been sold.

But that was more than a month back, when the crew were overjoyed with their new captain, along with the most lucrative haul they'd seized to date. Before we'd sailed away from Jamaica. Before we'd anchored in the small bay off the north-east coast of Los Caymanas. Before the mosquitoes began to bite. How quickly times could change.

The decision to press on to Los Caymanas in favour of returning, windward, to Jamaica had received a majority vote… after the captain had made a persuasive argument. The spices, tea, and rolls of silks filling our hold would fetch a far better price in British America than in Kingston, the captain assured the men. But the farther the *Royal Fortune* had sailed west, the more an uneasiness built over the ship like a black cloud.

Kingston offered the debauchery these savage men craved, where their portion of our plunder would be readily squandered. Now, faced with this mosquito-infested island, void of plentiful rum and women for purchase, some regretted agreeing to the captain's plan, and were now souring the mood of the others.

Under Hinchcliffe's orders, several ordinary seamen unlashed one of the cockboats and lowered it to the water. I remained on the quarterdeck behind the helm, hoping not to hear my name called.

The north-eastern breeze kept the evil insects from the open water, but those chosen to go ashore would not fare so well.

Mercifully, my name had not passed his lips, and I watched the six unfortunate men stroke the oars towards shore. I knew too well they'd be gone for hours, hacking their way through the dense mangroves and thickets in search of fresh water. The other cockboat had been lowered, and a crew of four hunted turtles in the bay. In truth, 'hunted' was a misleading term as the hard-shelled beasts were so plentiful the men simply dragged them from the surface into the boat.

While all was quiet aboard the *Royal Fortune*, I took the opportunity to retire to the captain's cabin, which we shared. Knocking softly with three raps and a delayed fourth, I heard the order to enter. Located in the stern, the captain's berth was below the quarterdeck, and while not lavish by any means, was far nicer than the ordinary seamen's bunks. A full-size cot, small writing desk, and a chest of drawers filled the space, and best of all, a window opened, allowing a breeze to dampen the balmy heat.

The captain stood before the wooden furniture, stripped to the waist, washing from a bowl of fresh water. "Wil, I'm glad you're here. I need your help."

Modesty was a luxury not afforded to a pirate at sea, and we'd both accepted that our lives depended on our willingness to push our bashfulness and sense of propriety aside. Handed a well-worn roll of cloth, I reached around my mother's chest and used the strapping to flatten her breasts as best I could.

2

BALLS OF CONCRETE

Present Day

A hollow concrete cone bobbed in the water like a Swiss cheese version of a space capsule. Inside, a bright orange lift bag kept the strange grey object afloat while the divers manoeuvred it into the desired position. With delicately precise movements, AJ Bailey and Reg Moore, the two professional divers on scene, released air from the bag, allowing the 3500lb bulk to begin its descent.

From the Department of Environment boat anchored in the sand nearby, cameras clicked and video rolled as they lowered the first Reef Ball to be situated in Bluff Bay off the north coast of Grand Cayman. A pneumatic line ran from a bank of air tanks on the boat to the lift bag, and AJ held the control valve in her hand.

"Go down, Reg, and guide me, all right?" AJ said, her English accent nasal behind the dive mask.

"Don't drop it on my bloody head," he replied, his deep, gruff voice sounding equally strange.

"Well, don't hang about underneath it, you silly bugger," AJ replied with a wry smile.

Reg rolled his eyes and put his regulator in his mouth.

"You two are on video for the world to see," Casey, their friend from the DoE, reminded them. "And hear."

Reg gave her an okay sign and descended below the surface. AJ giggled to herself, bled a little more air from the bag, then stuck her mask in the water to see where they were aiming. As the mass of concrete descended, the air inside the lift bag would be compressed by the increasing pressure of the water above. AJ needed to feed more air into the bag to maintain control. Too much, and it would bob back to the surface. Too little and it would accelerate out of control to the ocean floor, potentially shattering the moulded form.

She gently opened the valve and listened to the hiss of air, closing the valve when the Reef Ball slowed almost to a stop. She popped her reg in her mouth and hit the purge valve, clearing the mouthpiece of salt water. The mass eased downwards and when its speed picked up, AJ gave it another blast of air to slow it down once more. It was a painstaking process, and they had a dozen Reef Balls to place, but this wasn't a race and they'd be able to refine their technique with each successful placement.

Another diver appeared ten feet away, pointing a fancy under-water camera rig at AJ with bulbous strobes mounted either side on long spindly arms. AJ wanted to stick her tongue out or give her friend, Lisa Collins, a two-finger salute, but she had a regulator in her mouth and her hands full.

She blinked a few times, having made the mistake of looking at the powerful strobes when they fired, then noticed Reg gesticulating from below. He was pointing to her left, telling her to move the mass that way. AJ moved around to the right side of the six-foot-wide bulk and kicked her fins. The current was almost non-existent and the surface chop light, but the ocean was still a lot more powerful than she was, and it took several strong full leg kicks to reposition the Reef Ball. Of course, then it didn't want to stop, and Reg began waving again, this time the other way.

Sod it, she thought, let's get it closer to the floor and then I'll get its exact location sorted, else I'll be swimming around like an idiot. Reg continued waving and pointing but AJ ignored him until the base of the Reef Ball was four feet off the sand. Reg folded his arms and tilted his head, glaring at her through his mask. AJ laughed, which wrinkled her cheeks and flooded her own mask.

She popped a little more air into the bag so it hung neutrally in the water, then let go of the valve and reached down, pulling her fins off. They'd once performed a similar task, placing a bronze statue called Angels of the Deep on the sea floor off Seven Mile Beach, and losing the fins helped them push against the bottom instead of paddling against the water.

Unfortunately, on that occasion they'd carefully put the concrete base in position, ready for Simon Morris's beautiful sculpture of a mermaid, turtle and stingray, when someone blew it up with Semtex hidden in the turtle shell. Thankfully there were no injuries, and the perpetrator was arrested, but the bronze sculpture didn't fare so well. Simon was now busy creating a second version of Angels of the Deep.

Reg followed suit and removed his fins before the two of them pushed and shoved the Reef Ball over the mark in the sand they'd made earlier. AJ began releasing more air and the concrete cone slowly descended with a billowing cloud of stirred-up particles, ruining most of Lisa's pictures.

Finally, the cone settled into the sand and AJ released the rest of the air in a long stream of bubbles racing to the surface. Once it had deflated, she pulled the lift bag through one of the large holes dotted over the surface of the Reef Ball. Putting their fins back on, they then rose smoothly towards the sparkling surface above.

"Why did you wait till it was all the way down to shove it over?" Reg griped as they handed the lift bag up to Casey.

"'Cos you were waving your arms like a copper in the middle of Piccadilly bloody Circus and these things are a bugger to move about," AJ replied. "It was much easier once we could dig our feet into the sand."

"Yeah, that wasn't so bad," he admitted.

"Fine for you two, maybe, but knackered my shots," Lisa complained, resting her camera rig on the swim step.

"Oops. Sorry Leese," AJ said.

Her friend beamed her usual smile. "Got some good stuff on the way down and next time I'll know what's coming."

"Oi," Casey whispered from above them. "We've got eleven more of these things. How about you get up here so we can move on?"

"Listen to Drill Sergeant Keller," AJ joked as she climbed the ladder.

"That's more like it, young lady," Casey countered as she held the top of AJ's tank while the diver waddled with the heavy gear to a bench running down the side of the aft deck, guiding her into one of the tank racks.

AJ looked out at eleven more concrete cones bobbing in the bay, tethered together. Diane Davidson from CCMI, the Central Caribbean Marine Institute based on Little Cayman, sat down beside her.

"Go okay?" she asked.

"Easy peasy," AJ replied. "I'm glad we're doing it with the lift bags. It makes it pretty simple."

"Good to hear," Diane said, letting out a long breath. "Saved us a lot of money over a barge, but I was sweating until we actually used them."

AJ shrugged out of her buoyancy control device, or BCD as the vest-like piece of equipment was known. The scuba tank strapped to the back, and the BCD contained an air bladder with which the diver controlled their buoyancy in the same manner the lift bag worked.

"Could you give the press a quick debrief on how it went?" Diane asked and AJ groaned. She was happy and comfortable giving dive briefings on her own boat for her Mermaid Divers customers, but outside of that, public speaking wasn't something she enjoyed.

"Don't suppose you'd have the old man do it, would you?" she said hopefully, looking at Reg towelling his mop of salt and pepper hair and scraggy beard.

"Umm... You're a bit less..." Diane whispered, struggling for the right words.

"Intimidating?" AJ suggested.

Diane chuckled. "He does have a rather forthright manner."

"Fine," AJ conceded, looking across the deck at Reg, a former Navy hard hat diver and a bear of a man. He grinned at her.

She shook her head. Behind his gruff London accent and King Neptune appearance, he was one of the sweetest people AJ had ever known. Reg and his wife, Pearl, had been AJ's island family since she'd moved to Grand Cayman, first to work for them, and then setting up her own dive operation. Her father and Reg had helped AJ get started and now her business thrived alongside Reg's three-boat Pearl Divers operation. The Cayman Islands are a scuba diving Mecca, so there were plenty of customers for the good outfits.

AJ unzipped her wetsuit and pulled her arms from the sleeves of the 3mm neoprene, letting the upper half drop to her waist. It was her habit between dives as the wetsuit gave her a layer of protection in the water but was stiflingly hot in the fierce Caribbean heat. She instantly felt self-conscious wearing a sports bra top and revealing her full-sleeve tattoos to the waiting huddle of press, but her long-sleeved sun-shirt was in the enclosed cabin of the DoE boat. She quickly towelled herself dry, furiously rubbing her shoulder-length purple-streaked blonde hair and steeled herself for addressing the small crowd.

"Everything went as planned," she began. "The lift bag system worked well and as you can see, the Reef Ball is in place."

"There seemed to be a lot of sand stirred up on the bottom," one of the journalists pointed out, a scrawny guy who didn't look comfortable on the gently rocking boat. "Are you worried about disturbing the reef or the environment in any way?"

Several of the other journalists looked at the guy like he was an idiot, and AJ took a breath before replying. She thought about how her young Norwegian friend, Nora, would answer, and made sure to take a different tack.

"We chose the location because of the perfect depth and sandy area well clear of the existing reef, so no, we're not disturbing the sea floor any more than a stingray foraging for food would do."

"Thanks AJ," Diane quickly intervened before the idiot could ask another question. "Shall we move to the next site?"

Casey started the diesel engines on the DoE boat, confirming they were moving on, and AJ turned to Reg.

"You're doing the next one," she whispered.

"I'd have punched that little shit," he replied.

"See," she replied, giving him a slap on his brawny arm. "That's why I have to do all the bloody talking."

3

SALT CAY

1702 (two years earlier)

Father was no seaman. In the month it took to sail from the docks of London to our destination on the Turks island of Salt Cay in the eastern Caribbean, he'd lost considerable weight and survived almost exclusively on water and dry biscuits. Mother, on the other hand, had been raised on the coastal waters of southern England and thrived during the journey. While Father lay slumped over the edge of the poop deck, Mother showed me and explained in detail the workings of all aspects of the two-masted brig. I was wide eyed and fascinated.

Both the ship's captain and navigator seemed happy to answer all our questions, although Mother appeared to know as much about sailing as the pair of them combined. Her father owned a fleet of merchant vessels on which he'd often taken his family along on shorter trips.

Of course, everything was different now. Queen Anne had taken the English throne, and we were once again at war with the Spaniards, this time with the Dutch as our allies. Atlantic crossings and the Caribbean Sea were dangerous enough from weather alone, but now our lookouts had to stay vigilant for enemy masts.

My father, Lord Montgomery Crowe, would once have been a fine prize for a Spanish captain to claim, but with the change in monarchy also came a reshuffle in government which left Father without a seat in Parliament. So, we were on our way to an obscure island across the ocean.

We arrived at Salt Cay, not to an established harbour and welcoming committee, but a mooring offshore and a cockboat ride across the shallows to what appeared to be a tiny uninhabited protrusion above the water. Upon reaching the sand, three men came out of the stands of palms and other exotic trees to greet us. They led us a short way to what we hoped would be a town. It was not. Nor could I describe it as a village, or even a hamlet.

Three wattle and daub dwellings sat along the edge of a large, shallow interior lagoon. Bands of white bordered the brackish waters and any small mounds which broke the surface of the lagoon. Salt: a precious and valuable commodity, and the reason my father had been sent all this way.

The men explained that they'd arrived from Bermuda many years ago and made their living collecting and selling the salt deposits. A ship came by each month to transport and pay for the goods, which were sailed to Jamaica and the Thirteen Colonies.

I looked across the water to the south, seeing a few more homes in the distance, and wondered why they would choose to be separated.

"I was told there were Negro slaves," my father said, pointing to the other homes. "Is that where you keep them?"

A tall Englishman named Helms, who appeared to be the man in charge, shook his head. "They are Negroes, sir, but they are not slaves. These men came from Bermuda too. They work for us."

I was twelve years old, so it was all a grand adventure for me. I'd heard talk of slaves and seen headlines in the newspaper, but their plight had remained outside the perimeters of my world.

Intrigued, albeit a little nervous, I was keen to meet a Negro in person.

My father wiped his brow as the relentless tropical sun beat down upon us. "I see," he said, and I recognised the impatience in his voice. "I must inform you I am here on behest of Queen Anne of England to secure a bountiful and consistent supply of salt for the needs of Her Majesty's Royal Navy."

Helms looked at my father and then to the dozen sailors who were labouring through the narrow woods with our possessions. If he was of a mind to challenge the authority of the lord before him, he chose to contain himself while the numbers did not favour an advantage. "There's enough salt for all, but if you're concerned, you'll find plenty more on the neighbouring islands."

Father didn't press the point, but looked around at the meagre huts. "Are accommodations available, Mr Helms?"

The man sighed and looked from my mother to me. "No, sir, but we'll make them so, for your family's sake. My house is the far one. Give me until sundown to make arrangements, then it'll be yours until you build your own."

From Helms's tone of voice, I expect he intended his words in the literal sense. He had no way to know my father had never reduced himself to physical labour, or intended to do so. As usual, Mother and I stayed quiet, as was our place in the order of things.

During the overseas passage, I'd steadily grown used to the heat and humidity. We'd left a cool, rainy London, and the temperature slowly rose as we'd made our way west, and then south. I did envy Helms and the other men in their lightweight linen trousers and billowy, loose-fitting shirts. I prayed Father would allow us similar tropical attire.

We spent the afternoon in the shade of the trees circling the huts, which we learnt had been ambitiously named Balfour Town. If Father's directive to grow the island into a productive resource for the Crown came to fruition, the place might well flourish into its name.

My mother, Davina Crowe, sat on a clothes chest and fanned

herself, lost in her thoughts. At five feet, six inches tall, she was but a forehead shorter than my father, with broad shoulders for a woman but a slender figure. While Father preferred to spend his days seated in Parliament or in his office at our house in London, Mother, whom her friends called Vina, was always active.

When the weather allowed, she would take me outside for my lessons. Sometimes we would walk the London streets while she had me do arithmetic in my head. English could be taught in the park, and when it rained or was too cold to go outside, she would invent number games often involving the many flights of stairs in our four-storey townhouse.

She was also a practical woman, commonly repairing things around the house herself rather than calling a carpenter or seamstress. Of course, she would tell Father a fib if he enquired how much the repairman had charged. He wouldn't stand for his wife to be doing such menial tasks. She'd wink at me when she was forced to lie, then later, when we were alone, explain that Father had too many pressures to concern himself over trivialities such as this.

Lord Montgomery Crowe indeed had pressures and far too much work on his shoulders. Or so he claimed when Mother would ask him to join us at the park, or read an essay I'd written for English, or visit Mother's family. It bothered me when I was younger, but I'd grown used to the company of one parent, and while visiting her family in Portchester, Mother taught me to ride a horse, swim, and row, and my uncle gave me fencing lessons.

If my preference had been a consideration in my father's eyes, I would have lived with Mother's family in their country estate a few miles north of the bustling docks of Portsmouth. My absence would slip by unnoticed, but he'd never allow Mother out of his sight for any length of time.

"I thought there was a town here, Mother, and..." I looked around us at the flat, triangular-shaped island no more than two miles across, echoing the words Father had told us for the past two months. "And people."

She smiled at me. "It appears that is not the case, Wil."

"Are we going home?" I asked, hoping we wouldn't leave immediately.

"I'm not sure what your father will choose to do," she replied, standing and resting a firm hand on my shoulder. "But whatever it shall be, we'll make the best of it, won't we?"

I nodded, and although not thoroughly convinced, along with feeling homesick and isolated, I trusted Mother would find a way to make our circumstances better.

Father trudged across the sandy soil covering the limestone rock below, a scowl on his face. When he reached us, he paced about, sweat pouring down his face.

"I've sent a letter," he finally declared, "explaining the situation here is in stark contradiction to the details of my appointment." He looked at Mother. "And completely unsuitable for my family, of course."

"Are Mother and I going home?" I blurted, before I could stop myself.

He wheeled around. "You'd like that, wouldn't you?" he growled in a low voice, wagging his finger at me and then, in turn, at Mother. "The pair of you would dearly love to abandon me here, damn you."

"That's not at all what Wil meant, Monty. Of course we'll be wherever you are," Mother quickly intervened. "If you're staying, then we shall, too."

"Damn right you are," he replied, glaring at her. "You'll not shame me."

I wished I'd stayed quiet, but Mother had a gift for ignoring the man's wrath as though his words merely glanced off her person and fell to the ground. Sometimes, her calmness made him more mad, and that's when she'd stop trying to settle him with words and find something to do for him instead. Usually pour him a stiff drink and leave him be.

My father had never struck me, not even a rap across the backside. Mother had, when I was younger and deserved it, but I never feared her. I was terrified of disappointing her, but not of her harming me, even though her smacks stung like the devil. But there was something about my father's eyes which made me wonder what he was capable of if provoked. In a few years, I would likely match his height. He was a physically unimposing man whose expensive clothes hung from his frame in a limp and lifeless fashion, but it disturbed me to sense such caution when his temper flared.

"I have made arrangements for three men from the ship to remain with us until the first merchantman arrives in two months' time," he continued in a calmer tone. "They will build us a home while I see about hiring some of these local men to collect the salt under the Crown's employ. I've also requested workers of our own be sent in all haste."

"There," Mother replied with confidence in her voice. "You've already organised everything. We'll be fine."

Father scoffed as we all watched Helms carrying his possessions to another man's hut. "I'll be damned if they'll have the satisfaction of seeing me run back to England with my tail between my legs. But believe me," he raged on with more finger wagging, "once there's more blasted salt than the ships can hold, I'll be off this godforsaken island."

He stomped towards the vacated hut and left Mother and me alone for the time being. Two things struck me with concern as I watched him go. His use of the singular when it came to leaving Salt Cay was the first, and the second was how on earth the stack of furniture we'd dragged across the Atlantic would fit in the tiny hut.

4

COAL FOR CHRISTMAS

Present Day

They set the next five Reef Balls in the sand without incident, the placing of each subsequent one going a bit smoother and faster each time. AJ and Reg alternated roles to stave off the monotony and Lisa took a few pictures every time, then wandered off to photograph more interesting critters. After the fourth Reef Ball, she climbed back on the boat and excitedly showed everyone a picture of a seahorse she'd found.

"How the bloody hell did you see that tiny little fellow?" Reg laughed. "I can hardly see it when you zoom in. I could pass by a hundred of 'em down there and wouldn't know it."

Lisa pulled a magnifying glass from her BCD pocket. "I use this," she chuckled. "I find a spot that looks like a suitable home for one, then I search until I see something worth photographing, or I move on to the next place."

"Speaking of next," Casey said, shutting down the engines once her mate had secured the anchor.

"Yeah, yeah, yeah." AJ grinned. "Isn't it lunchtime yet? I'm famished."

"One more before I'm feeding you," Casey replied, pulling on the line, bringing the giant string of concrete domes closer.

AJ looked at the journalists chatting with Diane, sandwiches in hand. "I think we need to form a union, Reg. Have a representative to negotiate our rights to have sarnies when everyone else does."

Reg scoffed. "What you need is a stint in the Navy. That'll teach you to do what you're told when you're told to do it."

"I don't think I'd like the Navy."

"I didn't say you'd like it," Reg replied, slipping into his BCD. "I said it would do you good."

"They make you get up early, don't they?"

"Yup."

"I wouldn't like the Navy," AJ said, pulling her wetsuit up. "I bet it's fun to shoot the big guns, though, isn't it?"

Reg stood up, fins in hand. "Not when the buggers are shooting back."

"Fair point," AJ said, slipping her arms through the straps of her BCD and standing up next to him, cinching the waistband.

"These are good," Casey said, and they both turned. She was eating a sandwich. "I was going to wait for you two, but seeing as you're taking forever, I decided to have one."

"I'm calling my union rep," AJ said.

"I'm getting in the bloody water," Reg grunted.

"Che Guevara!" AJ said, holding up a clenched fist as she stepped into the clear water behind Reg.

It was AJ's turn to wait on the sea floor and guide the Reef Ball into place while Reg lowered it by controlling the lift bag. They'd figured out, once the lower half of the concrete mass was underwater, they could drop it relatively quickly until it hovered a few feet above the sand. The trick was to get the blast of air just right to halt the descent without sending it zooming back towards the blue sky above.

AJ stayed well clear while Reg let out a little air to start the Reef Ball on its journey to the bottom of the sea, 30 feet below. They'd used a dive weight wrapped in bright yellow cloth to mark the chosen sites, which they retrieved once the Reef Balls were in place. She noticed this cone was dropping a bit too close to shore and began to worry they'd be shoving the mass a long way along the bottom, so she swam in and pushed it as best she could. Reg threw his arms up, asking her what she was doing.

There followed a manic series of hand signals proving the two of them could bicker back and forth underwater nearly as well as they could above. When Reg blew air into the lift bag, the Reef Ball came to a stop 18 inches above the sand, and the bright yellow marker was right below him instead of the concrete cone. AJ pointed as if to say, *See, I told you!*

Ditching her fins, she dug her feet into the sand and pushed again, the hefty mass slowly moving towards Reg, who kept an eye on the dive weight through one of the holes in the cone. When they'd lined it up, he dumped air from the bag and the Reef Ball dropped into place with a waft of powdery sand billowing up all around.

AJ looked around in the silty haze for her fins and spotted a dark area in the pale yellow sand. Reaching down, she wrenched her hand back when she felt something firm and crusty rather than the expected smooth rubber. Waiting, she let the murk thin out for a few minutes while Reg retrieved the deflated lift bag and the dive weight. She hoped she hadn't accidentally grabbed a stray piece of living coral, and the nerdy reporter's words echoed in her head.

Finally, with Reg signalling he was ready to surface, she spotted her fins which lay next to a clump of dark-coloured rock. Curious, she dropped to her knees and looked more carefully. She could see it wasn't coral but an object with the years of concretion growth she'd seen on other artefacts. AJ carefully picked it up and Reg swam down beside her. They both looked at the object and then at each other. Reg shrugged his shoulders, then tapped two fingers on his mask and pointed his thumb towards the surface. *Look at it on the boat.*

A bright light flashed, and AJ blinked a few times, clearing her vision. Lisa gave her an okay sign, then left on her slow ascent to the surface. Reg followed. AJ put the object down, slipped her fins on, picked it back up, and followed them to the boat.

"What you got there?" Casey asked, as AJ handed her the object on the swim step.

"Probably a piece of junk, but it's been down there a while," AJ replied, climbing the ladder.

Over the years she'd seen and brought up enough items from the sea floor to know it could be something of historical value from as far back as Christopher Columbus, who first named the uninhabited islands Las Tortugas in 1503, or a worthless piece of scrap metal tossed over the side of a fishing boat thirty years ago. By the amount of encrustation, she guessed the item had been down there a lot longer than thirty years, but it could still be junk.

The other two divers were already aboard, so Casey pulled the ladder and tied it in place. AJ slipped out of her BCD and pulled on the leash on her rear wetsuit zipper, shrugging her shoulders out of the neoprene. Casey handed her a plastic bucket half full of seawater with the artefact sitting in the bottom.

"Perfect, thanks Casey," she said and stared at the object.

It was around six inches long and oval in profile, both ends somewhat blunt, although the entire surface was bumpy from limestone deposits.

"What is it, then?" Reg asked with his mouth full of sandwich.

"It's a piece of coal, so I'm giving it to you for Christmas," AJ replied without looking up.

Reg chuckled, which sounded more like a train rumbling through a tunnel. "You should be able to knock some of that rubbish off with a hammer or a screwdriver."

"What if it's a tiara, or a jewel-inlaid crown?" she said. "You'd have me smashing it to bits."

"Do you think it's a bloody tiara?"

"Don't be daft. No one has a head that shape," AJ said, grinning. "But my point is, it could be something delicate, yeah?"

"Give over," he replied. "Casey? Got a screwdriver?"

"Slotted or Phillips?" Casey asked.

"Slotted is better, but doesn't much matter. Bigger is better."

"If you break my priceless piece of Spanish treasure, I'll chip the crustiness off you with a screwdriver," AJ threatened.

They both chuckled as Casey arrived with a large, slotted screwdriver, which looked like it had been in the toolkit for some time from the rust coating. Casey handed it to Reg, who handed it to AJ.

"Chicken," AJ mumbled and picked up the artefact.

She played it around in her hand for a minute, feeling its weight and looking for a good spot to chip a little concretion away. Finally, she picked a ridge and gave it a poke with the screwdriver. It left a small mark on the surface, but nothing more. AJ smacked it harder, and a tiny piece flew off.

"Blimey, girl," Reg grumbled. "We'll be here till Christmas if you keep tickling the bloody thing."

"Hush, you. I'm strategically analysing the correct fracture to work on."

Casey joined Reg in laughing and AJ couldn't stop herself from joining them. She gave the lump a much harder whack, and a sizeable chunk fell out of the middle, splashing into the bucket.

"Oh, bugger," AJ yelped and looked up at the others.

The first thing she noticed was Lisa behind her camera, grinning like a Cheshire cat.

"You got that, didn't you?" AJ asked, cringing.

"Oh, yes," Lisa chuckled. "Wished I'd shot video, but I got a nice sequence."

AJ also noticed the journalists were also crowded around and now keenly watching.

"Do you think you knocked the tiara into the bucket, or is that the part you're still holding?" Casey asked, trying her best to keep a straight face.

AJ set the remaining outer part aside and picked up the lump she'd dislodged. She couldn't see any signs of metal or ceramic showing. She chipped away carefully, and small pieces and splinters came loose, dropping into the bucket. AJ continued poking, prodding, and tapping at the hard growth, but still nothing revealed itself.

After reducing the chunk to half its former size, she put it back in the salt water and returned her attention to the outer section. With careful examination, she noticed one very small, smooth, mottled green surface.

"Look at this, Reg," she said, holding it for him to see.

Reg put a pair of reading glasses on and twisted and turned AJ's hand.

"Probably shouldn't knock that about anymore, love," he grunted. "That looks like copper or bronze to me."

"Yeah," she replied. "That's what I thought. Perhaps even gold."

5

MARCUS

1702

Salt Cay was a beautiful island. Within the first week, I'd walked the perimeter along the sandy beaches and ventured into the woods where I was able. There were several more lagoons, similar to the one we'd seen, but the others were all smaller. Each had salt deposits around the edges where the scorching sun evaporated the brackish water.

Helms, the other two white men, and a workforce of six Negroes, worked in and around the lagoon every day. They used rakes, spades, and rudimentary wheelbarrows to collect the salt and form large piles closer to the shoreline. It was hot, sweaty, manual labour. Before we'd arrived, the men worked five days a week, but Father had negotiated to purchase gathered salt from Helms for the first few months until his own labour force arrived, so they increased their hours and added one more day.

In the meantime, Father passed the day by sketching the lagoons, planning a more efficient manner of collecting salt, and complaining. The three sailors firstly constructed themselves a crude shelter, and then began on a home for us. There was not an abundance of trees suitable for construction wood, but even more scarce were the tools with which to fashion planks. The men had brought a few items from the boat, and borrowed more from Helms, but my father's request for an elaborate two-storey home was quickly rejected, and work began on a simpler dwelling.

Stone was plentiful if the limestone base of the island was quarried, but the task proved back breaking and time consuming. With labour in short supply, another compromise had to be made, and the stone foundation Father had planned was scrapped.

Helms strongly recommended elevating our home off the low-lying ground, which the existing huts were not. They'd experienced several powerful storms since they'd arrived, and each time their small huts had flooded, requiring repairs. While they had still not set aside time and resource to build themselves raised dwellings, the man was kind enough to offer us the advice.

At first, Father dismissed most of what Helms and the other two men told us, but when time after time his own ideas proved impractical or impossible under our circumstances, he quietly bowed to their ideas. After five weeks, we finally had a habitable structure, and Mr Helms reclaimed his own hut. Ours was larger than the existing huts, had three rooms divided by woven mat walls, and a wooden floor as it was three feet above the ground.

Throughout our time so far on Salt Cay, I had observed the dark-skinned men from a distance as they worked, but ventured no closer. At the end of each day, the men returned to their own huts, and although the three white men seemed happy to work alongside the Negroes and chat with them during the day, they never mixed after work.

From our new house, raised as it was, I had a better view across the lagoon and could see several women in their camp along with children. The three white men were alone on the island, only Helms being married. He claimed he would send for his wife and two daughters once the island became more established, which possibly explained his passivity in allowing us to settle there.

"Let's go for a walk," Mother said from across the room.

I turned and suspected she'd been watching me for a while. Outside, although it meant facing the tropical sun, was more appealing than the arithmetic problems I faced in the morning's lesson, so I eagerly obliged. Father had remained a stickler on the dress front until he himself could bear the heat no longer and finally succumbed to more appropriate garb. Needless to say, we hadn't packed anything remotely suitable, but Mother sacrificed a linen sheet from which she fashioned lightweight shirts, and trimmed a pair of trousers below the knees for me. Father refused anything so crude in the trouser department, but eagerly accepted the shirt.

We walked through the band of trees to the beach and strolled south, gingerly walking over the rugged bare limestone in sections between the beaches. Mother cut through the trees once we were past the lagoon, and I realised she was leading me to the Negroes' camp. Filled with a mixture of trepidation and excitement, I followed in her bold footsteps. As we approached, chickens scattered in our path and two dark-skinned women looked up from the half barrel they were doing their washing in. My own apprehension was reflected in their faces.

"Good morning," Mother called out. "I'm embarrassed we haven't been by sooner to introduce ourselves. I am Davina Crowe, and this is my son, Wil."

Father would be furious if he'd heard Mother omit her title of 'Lady', but regardless, the two women appeared dumbfounded. They looked at each other and slowly stood, wiping their hands dry on their fustian frocks.

I knew black people lived in England, but not in our neighbourhood. This was the closest I'd ever been to a dark-skinned human being. The features of their faces were more rounded, and light glimmered from their perspiring flesh, showing their colour to be more bronze than black.

"Do you speak English?" Mother asked with a warm smile.

The larger of the two women nodded. "Yes ma'am," she replied, her accent like no other I'd ever heard.

"What are your names, my dear?"

As the woman considered her reply, I spotted a boy peeking from the doorway of one of the huts. He was staring right at me.

"Smith. Bess Smith," the first woman replied, "and this here is Nelly, ma'am."

"It's nice to meet you both, and please call me Davina. No more of this ma'am business. I think we can drop formalities as we're all in this together."

Bess and Nelly had no idea what to make of my mother. I had no way of knowing what their prior experiences with white women had been, but I presumed it was not like this.

"I see you have a young son. Perhaps he'd like to meet Wil?"

My heart jumped. He might have liked to meet me, but I wasn't sure I was ready. Bess waved the boy over and said something to him in a language I didn't know. She spoke quickly, but her tone had a musical quality.

"Dis is Marcus," Bess said as the boy arrived by her side and put an arm around his mother.

I guessed him to be several years younger than I was, and by his expression, more scared of me than I of him.

"Hello. I'm Wil," I said, taking my mother's lead.

The boy looked curiously at me, but didn't say a word.

"He ten, sir, and he mighty shy," Bess replied for her son.

Mother crouched down. "Just Wil is fine, Bess," she said, and smiled at Marcus.

For a moment the boy clung to his own mother's hips, but slowly his curiosity won over and he took a short step forward.

"Wil here is twelve, but it appears you two are the only boys on the island," Mother said. "Perhaps you'd like to explore together?"

Marcus's eyes widened, and he looked from Mother to me. There was an intensity in his stare, as though he were searching me, studying my intentions. His look reminded me of something I'd encountered before but couldn't place.

"I would like that," I said.

Without warning, the boy stepped past Mother and, in two bold strides, stood right before me. He was shorter than I was, but in loose linen knee-length trousers and no shirt, I could see his body was lean, with a muscular frame developing even at his young age. I sharply inhaled, unsure whether I was being attacked or greeted.

"I can show you," he said, his voice sounding older than his years.

He stepped around me and walked towards the trees behind their camp. Mother got to her feet and nodded towards the boy, encouraging me to go with him. Marcus was swift despite his bare feet, which seemed impervious to the rough ground, and I had to quicken my pace to catch him. When he reached the treeline, he ducked through a gap I couldn't even see, and disappeared into the woods.

For several moments I stood there unsure how to proceed until the boy's face appeared between the foliage. He beckoned me, and I pushed through the leaves and small branches to follow him. Most of the trees were low and wide rather than tall, and thick shrubs filled the gaps between the limbs at the edges of the wood. But once inside, the ground cover thinned, and we ducked under low branches and weaved between the tentacle-like tree trunks.

Marcus moved effortlessly through the maze and seemed to know exactly where he was going. I, on the other hand, had become completely turned around. If the boy abandoned me, and with the sun overhead, I'd have been hard pressed to find the camp again. I reminded myself that the island was only a few miles long, so if I walked in one direction for long enough, I'd find the ocean.

The brush and ground cover thickened once more and the sound of the soft waves brushing the shoreline became louder. I followed Marcus out of the woods to a rocky outcrop overlooking the ocean. We stood by the edge and looked down at the crystal-clear water six feet below. Colourful fish flitted between sea fans and sponges scattered over the reef for 20 yards or more from the shoreline. Farther out, the water turned a bright turquoise for a wide section over an expanse of sand before darkening to a navy blue where the sea floor dropped away.

Marcus nimbly stepped down the jagged rock to a shelf just above the waterline. He turned and looked up. "This is good fishing."

"With a spear or a net?" I enquired.

"Spear," he replied. "Da net get all tangled in da reef."

Both the Negroes and white men fished by spear along the coastline and used nets from the two small rowboats they kept at one of the beaches. Chickens, eggs, and fish were the main source of food, with rice and whatever vegetables anyone could get to grow in the island's sandy soil.

"Do you spear?" I asked.

Marcus looked at me with that same penetrating stare. "Of course."

I had been out on the rowboat with Mr Helms several times, but Father didn't really approve. He'd categorically said no when I'd asked to go spear fishing. 'We're gentlemen, not common fisher-men,' he'd told me. I looked around us. We were the only two human beings in sight. I carefully stepped down to the rocky shelf.

"Can you teach me?" I asked.

Marcus nodded, and for the first time, I caught a hint of a smile.

6

HOLY GRAIL

Present Day

After a short lunch break, Reg and AJ were back in the water, and a boat picked up the journalists, returning them to the Morritt's Resort dock inside the reef-protected Colliers Bay. From there, the minibus which had brought them out that morning made the 23-mile drive back to George Town along the two-lane coast road.

The two divers felt more relaxed with the press out of their hair, and Lisa was a friend, so her strobes firing off every few moments didn't bother them. The object AJ had found was in the saltwater bucket on the boat, and while they were setting each Reef Ball in place, Casey sat on the bench and delicately chipped more of the crud away. Between every dive, AJ and Reg studied her handiwork, and they all made guesses as to what it might be.

As more of the smooth metal surface could be seen, the object was beginning to take on a defined "D" shape. The curved part was three or four inches wide at one end and tapered along its radius to less than two inches wide at the opposite end. Some pieces of concretion fell away to reveal the metal surface underneath, but others enthusiastically clung to the object they'd spent decades - perhaps centuries - adhering to.

"It's a handle for something," AJ suggested, taking a wild stab in the dark based on the shape.

"Part of a ship's bell?" Casey guessed.

"Could be a little statue, or a candleholder," Diane, who'd stayed on the boat, said.

Reg turned the object over in his hands. "Do you know why this area is called Anchor Point?" he asked, gesticulating at the surrounding ocean.

AJ raised her hand as though she was in school. "Because boats anchored here," she said with a chuckle.

"Correct," Reg replied. "Which boats in particular?"

The three women looked around them. The shoreline had a short sandy beach leading into mangroves and woods. To the east around the low, tree-covered headland they knew were a few homes but otherwise the area was deserted.

"It's like a lot of the places they named bays," AJ said. "It's not really a bay, is it?"

Reg pointed to the headland. "Right, but the point out there offered some protection from the easterly and nor-easterly winds and seas. It also allowed ships to sail from anchor and continue west. On this side of Hispaniola, the sailing ships heading for Florida or back to Europe had to sail west with the winds and currents around Cuba to take the Gulf Stream back east on the Straits of Florida. So the name comes from centuries back in the Age of Sail."

"So this could be 17th century?" AJ commented.

Reg laughed. "It could be the Holy Grail," he said, tossing the object to her. "But it's not."

AJ caught the mysterious lump of metal and organic crud. "Careful, you bloody great oaf! You could be throwing the lost chalice of something or other about like it's a dog's toy."

She picked up the screwdriver and carefully chipped away at

the wider end of the artefact. A few small chips splintered away, and then a larger clump fell free.

"Blimey! Look at this," she said, turning the object around to show the others.

"That's rust," Reg grunted. "No way the rest of it is ferrous, or it'd be brown dust by now. But something iron or steel was part of this thing."

Casey took the artefact from AJ. "You two still have three more Reef Balls to set, and I don't want to be taking the boat home in the dark, so get on with it."

"All right, all right," AJ protested. "But you be careful with King Arthur's bedpan."

Setting the final Reef Balls went without incident, and they made it back around the island to George Town harbour just as the sun was setting. Reg and AJ threw their dive gear in the back of AJ's fifteen-passenger van, then she drove them to Reg and Pearl's house in West Bay. AJ's Ducati Multistrada was parked in the driveway beside Reg's old Land Rover, so she knew her boyfriend, Jackson, was already there.

The front door opened and Coop, Reg's Cayman brown hound mutt, flew outside and ran excitedly between Reg and AJ, unsure who he was most pleased to see. AJ won when she scratched his ears and he rolled over to give her the privilege of rubbing his belly.

"Hello, loves," Pearl greeted them at the door in her London accent, throwing her arms around her husband.

Reg leaned down and kissed her. Pearl had just turned sixty, but no one would guess she was a day over fifty. Short and curvaceous, she had a smile which brightened the room, and a singing voice which entertained everyone a few Fridays a month at the Fox and Hare pub.

"How'd it all go?" she asked.

"No bother," Reg grunted, opening the fridge and taking out two bottles of Strongbow cider.

"I found the Holy Grail," AJ said, before hugging the much taller Jackson and giving him a kiss.

"The Holy Grail of what?" Jackson asked, his Californian accent and manner calm and smooth.

"*The* Holy bloody Grail," she replied, holding up the bucket, which was beginning to smell a bit ripe.

Jackson peered inside. "I didn't expect the most sought-after artefact in the world would smell this bad."

"It's covered in a few thousand years of growth," AJ said. "So you'll have to forgive its odour."

Jackson carefully plucked the object from the murky seawater. "Not very goblet shaped, is it?"

"Holy Grail is one of the theories in play," AJ confessed. "It's a non-ferrous metal so it could be gold or silver."

"Or bronze," Jackson added. "They used a lot of bronze back in the day. It might be a part from an old ship."

"Gonna make you rich, is it? That smelly bucket." Pearl chuckled as she returned to frying battered fillets of fish.

"The *Geneva Kathleen* wreck, or what's left of her," Reg said, "is just around the point at Barefoot Beach. She was an old wooden ship. Good chance it's a piece of hardware from her when she ran aground."

Jackson placed the object back in the bucket and AJ set it outside the front door, then washed her hands in the kitchen sink.

"Isn't there just a big winch left in the sand?" she asked, taking her Strongbow from the counter.

"I haven't been there in years, but pretty sure that's all there is," Reg replied, taking a seat at the dining table. "It's a snorkelling site from the shore as it's shallow and the pieces are sitting in the sand. All the wood was blown ashore or carried out to sea aeons ago."

"When did it sink?" Jackson asked, helping Pearl carry all the taco fixings to the table.

"About a hundred years ago, if memory serves," Reg replied.

"1930," AJ said, looking up from her mobile. "Wooden sailing ship carrying lumber from Gulfport to Curacao, according to the World Wide Web. Where's Gulfport?"

"Mississippi," the only American in the room replied.

"Any chance a lumber ship sailing through the Caribbean would be carrying the Holy Grail with them?" AJ asked with a grin and took a swig of cider.

"About as much chance as your lump of rubbish is worth more than its weight in scrap," Reg said, laughing.

"We'll see about that," AJ shot back. "I'm taking it down to the museum in the morning to see what they say."

"Does that mean I'm taking the boat out again?" Jackson asked.

"If you wouldn't mind," AJ said, giving him her best persuasive smile.

"Wait a second," Reg interrupted. "If I remember correctly, the director of the National Museum isn't one of your biggest fans."

AJ looked shocked. "Gladys Wright? She's a lovely lady. We get along like a house on fire. She's just a little prickly with everyone."

Reg roared with laughter, his broad chest heaving. "Prickly? She'll never forgive you for that business with the Cross of Potosí."

"I think the issue was more about AJ associating with Jonty Gladstone," Pearl added, handing out tortillas to everyone.

"Don't get me started on that plonker," Reg grumbled.

AJ sighed and stroked Coop, who'd rested his head on her leg, knowing she was the easy mark for treats. "Maybe I'll just call Buck Reilly and ask him what to do next."

Reg thumped the table with his beefy fist and laughed all over again. "He'll fly straight down just to play with *your* artefacts!"

AJ blushed, and Jackson grinned. Buck was a friend and an expert in the treasure hunting business, but he was also rather fond of the ladies.

"If he shows up, I'll make sure Nora's with me," AJ said, referring to her tall, slender Norwegian friend, who was also a local police constable. "She knows how to handle Buck's advances."

"You mean, lead him around by his..." Reg started, but Pearl slapped him on the arm. "You know what!" he continued. "That's all I was going to say."

"She does have the man wrapped around her little finger," Jackson added.

"Without even saying a word," AJ chuckled. "She shuts him down every time, but always gives him a slightly less frozen Nordic look before he leaves."

"So," Pearl asked, "are you going to call him?"

"Yup," AJ replied. "But I'll tell him I'm in Australia and just found the Holy Grail on the Great Barrier Reef."

That set Reg off laughing once more. Jackson leaned over and kissed AJ.

"That's my girl," he whispered.

7

NEW RULES

1702

One of the fish separated from the school and neared the orange sponge below me. The silver and yellow fish with the sloped noses were bigger than most that came this close to the shore, and good for eating. It was difficult to time their movements in the surge by the rock outcrop, but my aim was improving. The fish turned around the sponge and bit at a morsel on the coral. The moment it paused, I thrust the spear down and pinned the fish to the reef.

"Got 'im!" Marcus yelped next to me.

I carefully raised the spear, and Marcus kneeled down, sliding his hand under the water and cupping the fish, making sure it didn't writhe from the barbed tip. Plucking the fish from the spear, Marcus threw it in the basket with the other seven we'd caught that morning. On the first day he'd shown me how to use the spear, I'd contributed nothing to the basket, but now, two weeks later, we'd speared four apiece.

Looking up, I shielded my eyes from the hot sun, noting it was higher in the sky than I'd guessed it to be. We were late.

"We need to go," I said, handing Marcus the spear and grabbing the woven basket.

We scrambled up the rocks and ducked into the woods following the trail, which was much clearer than the first day I'd tentatively followed my friend. We'd spent three days with machetes, hacking at branches and dragging the clippings aside until an easily passable path emerged. At either end, we'd left foliage disguising the entry points so no one else could find it.

I couldn't think of any good reason why we were hiding our trail, beyond the fact that we were boys, and boys loved to have secret hideaways. Peeking through the branches until no one was looking, we stepped from the woods and ran to the camp.

"What you bring me today?" Bess asked as I held the basket out for her to see. "You did good," she said, nodding her approval. "But best you be off 'fore you keep your mama waitin' too long."

Handing her the basket, I looked at Marcus, who in turn was staring up at his mother.

"Go on now, you can go wit him."

Before she changed her mind, we ran down the well-worn trail along the south end of the lagoon towards the narrow band of trees separating the inland body of water from the ocean. Three minutes later, out of breath and covered in sweat, we arrived at the shady spot where Mother had set up a makeshift table and bench from driftwood and rocks. For the past month, this had been our ocean-front classroom.

"You're tardy, Mr Crowe," Mother said firmly. "And it appears you've been a bad influence on your friend."

"I'm sorry, Mother," I said, sitting on the bench.

She cracked a smile at us both, and Marcus laughed.

"I'm sorry too, Mrs Crowe."

"You can redeem yourself by reciting the alphabet for me," she responded with a wry smile, taking a wooden-framed slate and holding it for Marcus to see. Each letter of the alphabet was depicted on the slate in order. Davina waved her hand at me. "You can finish the arithmetic problem from yesterday." Returning her attention to the young Bermudian, she instructed him to begin.

Bess had been reluctant at first to let her son take lessons when Mother offered, more from concern of being a burden than not wanting her son to be educated. Marcus's father, Nathaniel, shared her worry, but Mother was convincing and assured them she would be discreet. Of course, they didn't know that her primary reason for covertly schooling the young lad had far more to do with her own husband.

As Father stayed in or close by our hut all day, busying himself with plans and schemes for when his workforce arrived, it was simple to avoid his interest. Until curiosity lured him out to the coastline.

To our south was a small outcrop covered with trees which obscured our view in that direction. The trees formed a semicircle around our spot, also hiding the beach to the north. The narrow band of woods behind us screened us from the camp to the east, so it was only from the ocean we could be seen. When the men fished, they would often wave, but as Father never spoke with the other men unless he needed something, Mother didn't worry about them saying anything.

I could tell by the way the three sailors he'd hired looked at Father that they did not care for his demeanour. He spoke to them as though they were common workers, well beneath him. Mother conversed with everyone in the same way she spoke to me or Father, unless he was present, and then she tended to not say anything at all. I'd soon noticed that everyone paused to chat with my mother, but avoided Father whenever possible. With less than twenty people on the island, I couldn't comprehend why we wouldn't all get along and help each other.

We heard Helms and several other men excitedly talking from the beach but couldn't make out the source of their attention. No ship was due for several weeks, so we assumed it might have been a favourable catch from the rowboat. Mother urged us both to pay attention to our studies, and the chatter from the men continued, so I did my best to ignore them.

Paper was in short supply and not something we could readily replace, so much of our arithmetic and spelling was done on a pair of slates with slate pencils. We were under strict orders not to lose, break, or press too hard with the slate pencils as replacements were also months away. I was working on a new algebra problem and Mother was helping Marcus master the idiosyncrasies of the letter Q when the trees rustled close by.

"What is going on here?" my father's voice boomed as he appeared in the clearing.

Behind him, Mr Helms stood motionless, looking just as surprised as we were.

"I'm conducting Wil's lessons for the day," Mother replied in a remarkably calm voice.

Father's eyes finally left Marcus and turned to Mother. His face was glowing red. "Why must you insist on bringing shame to this family?" he spat in a low tone. He sounded like each word took great effort and pain for him to speak them.

"William, go to the house," he snapped without looking my way.

Marcus and I glanced at each other. I nodded towards the woods and his path home. Marcus didn't need convincing. He'd disappeared before I'd even reached the treeline past my father. Mr Helms was also retreating, a regretful look on his face. I paused once I was out of sight, and tiptoed back closer to the clearing, staying low behind the shrubs.

"What did I tell you about fraternising with the Negroes?"

Father had moved closer to where my mother stood, next to our makeshift classroom she'd taken great effort to construct. Mother remained stoic and silent.

"Well?" he growled. "What reasoning can you give for disobeying me?"

I watched my mother's lips quiver, and I willed her to remain quiet. But words began flowing as though she could control them no more.

"I'm not one of your servants, Monty. Someone to order around like you own me. That boy deserves an education as much as anyone else, and I enjoy teaching. What harm can possibly come of this?"

Father's whole body appeared to shake, and his weight shifted repeatedly from one foot to the other. "Damn you, Davina! Do you understand what people would say in London? In Parliament? I'll be the laughing stock of high society. All because you want to teach a Negro alongside our son?"

"London!" Mother retorted, her own voice beginning to lose its passive control. "Do you see anyone here from London besides ourselves? How in God's good graces would anyone in London have any idea what is happening on this pile of sand in the Caribbean Sea?"

Father edged towards her. "What about the three men who'll be returning on the next ship?" he replied, struggling to keep from shouting. "They'll take great delight in telling everyone from here back to England how a Lord's wife is associating with slaves!"

Mother groaned in frustration. "They are not slaves, Monty. They are people on a distant island making the best of things, just like us."

"Like us?!" Father bellowed, thumping the table with his fist. "You compare me to a Negro slave? I should never have brought you with me. If I'd known you'd embarrass and betray me, I would have left you and the boy in London."

"That boy is your son, Monty. He has a name, and he'd enjoy time with his father occasionally if you could tear yourself away from whatever it is you occupy your time with all day."

I ducked lower as Father spun around and paced in a circle, muttering to himself. He completed his turn and leaned over the table, his face close to Mother's and his finger poking her shoulder.

"This is what will happen, Davina. You and William are to have nothing more to do with the Negroes. You will hold your lessons in or outside the hut, and William can play within sight of the camp."

"That's preposterous, Monty. Wil is a young boy stranded here with only one chance of a friend. If you won't spend time with your only son, you must let him play with Marcus."

Father's hand now gripped my mother's arm. "I'm done explaining. This is how things will be, so help me God, or I'll confine you both to the house."

"If you plan to treat us like criminals locked in a cell, then send us home on the next ship," Mother demanded, shaking his hand away.

"You'd like that, wouldn't you?" Father yelled in return without restraint. "Leave me here alone while you gallivant around London without a care in the world!"

Mother glared at her husband. "On my return, I could send your mistress back here for you…"

Her sentence remained incomplete as Father swung his arm and struck my mother across the cheek with the back of his hand. She teetered back for a moment, then regained her footing and lifted her chin. "I'll wait while you choose a switch. I'd hate to see you damage those delicate hands, Lord Montgomery Crowe."

Father let out a snarl and struck her again. I was on my feet and running across the clearing… except I wasn't. I was shaking like a leaf and remained motionless behind a screen of foliage. My chest burned and I willed myself to rush to Mother's aid, but fear gripped me and I remained quivering with tears running down my face.

I finally leaned forward and saw Mother wiping blood from her lip. She'd now chosen silence, but her chin was still high and she glared at the man before her with contempt.

"Get to the hut," he said firmly, and after a few moments locking eyes with her husband, she relented and walked past him.

Ducking my way through the trees, I ran inside the woods behind the beach, catching glances of them both walking across the sand, he following her by two paces. I reached the short path the men had cut through the band of trees from the beach to the camp and stopped.

They had both paused near Mr Helms on the beach and were staring out to sea. A ship I didn't recognise was sailing towards the island. If they were flying a flag, as all vessels were supposed to when approaching land, I couldn't see it.

8

FABRICATION AND SPECULATION

Present Day

AJ stepped out of the van, grunted something unintelligible to Jackson, and closed the passenger side door. Jackson grinned as he pulled away in the pre-dawn darkness, well accustomed to his girl-friend's hatred of early mornings. Unfortunately, the dive business was full of early mornings as the boats had to be prepped every day for customers arriving by 7:30am.

AJ trudged down the small, sloped car park to the tiny hut she shared with Reg. He was already there, leaning against the open door, watching his crew bring the boats into the jetty from their night-time moorings.

"Morning, sunshine," he greeted her.

"It is," AJ mumbled, dropping her rucksack and the stinky bucket inside the hut.

She retrieved her stainless-steel travel mug full of coffee from the side pocket and clutched it as though it was the elixir of life. Which, in AJ's opinion, coffee may well be.

"Didn't go to the museum then," Reg commented.

AJ grunted, which she intended to be a negative response, and Reg apparently took as such, as he didn't ask for clarification. She watched Thomas Bodden, her friend and sole full-time employee, bring *Hazel's Odyssey* towards the pier. She was about to walk down and help him tie in the 36-foot Newton custom dive boat, but seeing a couple of Reg's crew were there already, she left them to it.

Reg owned three of the similar Newtons, and when all four boats were running, the small jetty was a busy place. Moored stern to stern with the ocean-side boats' bows overhanging the pier, they could all fit without bottoming at low tide, but it had taken some trial and error to perfect the system.

Thomas's tall, lean frame sauntered up the dock like a long-legged bird. Born and raised on the island from lineage reaching back to the first settlers, he was one of the few Caymanians to choose the dive industry as a career.

"What did you find out east den, Boss?" he asked, beaming his ever-present smile.

"Did you tell him?" AJ asked Reg.

Reg shook his head. "Nah, he was already paddling out to your boat when I got here."

"How did you know?" AJ asked Thomas as he reached them.

Thomas held up his mobile. "On der internet dis morning," he replied.

"What?" AJ asked in surprise. "Show me."

Thomas unlocked his mobile and opened a web browser page. "Here," he said, showing her the article.

"Conservation effort reaps instant reward," AJ read aloud. "What the bloody hell is this?"

Reg peered over her shoulder. "I bet it's that wanker asking the stupid questions."

"Cayman News Blog," AJ read. "I've never even heard of it."

"Dat guy claims he gets da latest local news before anyone else," Thomas said. "I saw da link on Facebook dis morning."

"The idiot glosses over the Reef Ball program and says we

found 'a relic which could well be lost treasure from the pirate age'," AJ read. "What a complete bloody tosser."

"I'd definitely stay away from her ladyship at the museum now," Reg laughed.

"This isn't journalism," AJ moaned. "It's mostly fabrication and a bit of speculation, with zero facts except that we were placing Reef Balls in East End."

"What's the geezer's name?" Reg asked.

"Sean Carlson," Thomas said. "He's all over da social media."

"I don't do any of that bollocks," Reg grunted. "Pearl, bless her heart, handles it for the business."

"I post a diving pic or video every day," AJ said. "But that's it, really. We do have a private family group to post stuff for each other. I check that a few times a week." She handed Thomas back his mobile. "Hopefully, this bloke doesn't have too much of a following."

Thomas took the phone and tapped the screen a few times. "He got 45,000 followers."

"Strewth," Reg mumbled. "There's only 70,000 people on the islands. No way two-thirds of them are interested in this plonker."

"Means he has a lot of people overseas reading his bullshit," AJ said, and picked up her rucksack. "Bring the bucket, Thomas. Jackson will be back with the customers shortly."

The sky was brightening over the ocean and an orange hue glowed across the trees and buildings behind them to the east.

Thomas picked up the plastic bucket. "Oh, my good Lord. Dis stinks."

"Yeah," AJ admitted. "That crud has been stewing in there all night. Best dump it out and get some fresh, but don't throw out the Holy Grail."

"What ya got here, anyway?" Thomas asked again.

"Pirate treasure according to Sean Pain-In-My-Arse Carlson."

Thomas laughed. "Let's hope da man guessed right, den."

• • •

AJ's mobile rang as she cruised towards the dive site Big Tunnel, north of their dock. Caller ID told her it was Lisa Collins.

"Morning Leese," she answered, her perkiness rising with the sun.

"Hey, love. I'm glad I caught you. Did you see the article that Carlson bloke posted online?"

"Unfortunately," AJ replied. "What an idiot."

"Exactly. Well, I wanted to tell you he called me last night and asked for pictures of you finding whatever it was you found down there."

"I saw one of your pictures in his article, but it was of the Reef Balls on the surface," AJ replied.

"Yeah, I told him I was there to photograph the CCMI project. He'd have to get permission from you for anything else."

"You're a star, Leese, thank you. He didn't bother contacting me before he posted his rubbish."

"All right, love, gotta run. I have a class this morning," Lisa said. "And I'm meeting Diane for lunch, so I'll ask her not to invite that bloke along next time."

"Good thinking, thanks," AJ replied and ended the call as she throttled back and coasted towards the dive site buoy.

Thomas looked up at the fly-bridge from the bow where he waited with the boat hook.

"We doing Easy Street instead, Boss?"

AJ frowned, confused for a moment, then she looked along the shoreline and counted the buoys she could see.

"Bollocks," she muttered to herself. "Sorry, I had my head up my bum for a minute."

She gently pushed the throttles forward and continued to the next buoy a few hundred yards farther along.

AJ had asked Thomas to guide the first dive, but as he prepared to start the briefing, she gave him a nudge.

"Mind if I take this dive after all?" she whispered.

"I thought you had a call to make?" he asked.

"I do, but I need to clear my head first. That bloody article has me all wound up. If Buck starts being cheeky, I'm likely to bite his head off, and the poor bugger doesn't deserve that when I'm asking him for advice."

Thomas chuckled. "All yours, Boss. I was just tinking a nap sounded good."

AJ grinned. Thomas had the amazing ability of sleeping anywhere at any time, a talent she did not possess. She looked around the deck at her customers. They were all returning clients with experience who'd already been diving with her this week.

"Has anyone not been to Big Tunnel before?" she asked, and one couple out of the eight divers raised their hands. "But you dived Little Tunnels with us the other day, yeah?"

The couple both nodded.

"Big Tunnel is very much like Little Tunnels, except there's one and it's enormous," AJ said with a smile. "Like, drive a double-decker bus through it big."

The divers all laughed.

"Okay, everyone knows the routine. I'll take you through the big hole in the reef and we'll come out on the wall. Stay towards the top of the tunnel or you'll go below 100 feet, which will be our max depth for the dive. Based on current, we'll go one way or the other, and see what we can find. Top of the reef is about 60 feet here so dive time will be based on no-deco time more than gas left in the tank. If you stay about 10 feet above the reef, it'll get you a little extra bottom time and you can use the mooring line or chill in the water column for your safety stop. Everyone ready?"

With nods and okay signs from everyone, she and Thomas helped the customers into the water before AJ followed them in.

Forty minutes under water did the trick. By the time AJ was back on the boat with her customers talking excitedly about the eagle rays and reef shark they'd seen, her angst over the internet article had dissipated and her mood improved. She slipped out of her wetsuit, then chatted while she helped switch the customer's gear over to fresh tanks.

Thomas voted on Chain Reef for the second dive, and the customers agreed, so AJ climbed the ladder to the fly-bridge and started the diesels while Thomas freed them from the buoy. They'd be spending an hour on the surface between dives to safely allow the nitrogen build-up to work its way out of their systems, so she was in no hurry. Idling along, she replied to a few customer emails on her mobile, and once they were tied in at the second dive site, she dialled up Buck Reilly.

"If you've finally realised you can't live without me, your timing's terrible," Buck said in way of a greeting. "I'm a committed man these days."

"Nora will be most disappointed," AJ responded.

The line was quiet for a moment. "She will?"

Deliberately ignoring him, she moved on. "So, Buck, I was hoping you could help me with something salvage related."

"Oh, sure," he replied, gathering his wits back up. "What do you need?"

AJ took a deep breath. "Let's say someone happened to find an artefact while diving, and brought it up," she explained. "And that artefact turns out to be a few hundred years old. I know it needs to be reported or registered, but it's okay to bring it up to be identified, right?"

"Are you in the Cayman… I mean, is your theoretical person in the Cayman Islands?" he asked in amusement.

"Yes."

"And the artefact was recovered within Cayman waters?"

"Yes."

"Who did the artefact belong to originally?" he asked.

"I don't even know…" AJ began, then sighed. "I'm not very good at this cloak and dagger stuff, am I?"

Buck laughed. "You'll need to put some work in if you want to pull the wool over anyone's eyes, that's for sure."

"Well, I have no idea what it is yet, so I don't have a clue whose it was. I found it near Anchor Point down the East End, which was a popular mooring site for sailing ships passing through back in the 17th and 18th centuries. It could be worthless, but by the growth on it, I'd say it's pretty old. Oh, and it's non-ferrous."

"Do you have it with you?" Buck asked.

"Yeah," she said, looking down at the bucket by her feet.

"Stand by," Buck said. "I'll switch us to a video call so I can see it."

"Oh, okay," AJ stammered, realising she was in her swimsuit.

She set her mobile down and grabbed her long-sleeved Mermaid Divers sun-shirt and slipped it on.

"Hello?" came Buck's voice, and she picked the phone back up, smiling at Buck, now on video.

"Hold on a sec," she said and grabbed the artefact from the bucket, shaking off the water.

AJ held it up in front of her mobile so Buck could see.

"Okay, turn it around, slowly," he said.

She rotated the object and then showed him each end.

"What do you think?" she asked.

"How much concretion have you chipped away?" he asked.

"A bunch," she replied. "A big chunk fell out of the middle, but I'm nervous to keep bashing away at it. It seems like it might be a handle broken off a pot or vase."

"Show me the larger section with bare metal again," Buck asked, and AJ manoeuvred the piece as requested.

"Got an idea what it might be, Buck?"

"I do," he cautiously replied. "But I'll give you the standard disclaimer when viewing something still covered in muck via a small screen. This is just a stab in the dark based on shape and what I think the metal might be."

AJ nodded. "Yeah, yeah, don't worry, I won't give you a one-star rating if you're wrong."

Buck laughed. "Okay, in that case, I think it's the hilt of a sword or cutlass."

9

PRIVATEERS

1702

My knees stung from scraping across the rough ground beneath our raised hut. We'd stored excess building supplies and many things we'd brought with us but couldn't fit in the house underneath, making an excellent cover for Mother and me. Mr Helms had suggested we hide ourselves until the intentions of the new ship be known. Father had consented rather than agreed.

I'd been afraid at first as the adults around me seemed to be deeply concerned, but after waiting for what felt like hours, I was growing impatient. If the ship was Spanish or French, they might well slay us all, as our nations were at war. If it was English, they might have supplies or even manpower willing to work for my father. The idea that it might be a privateers' ship never crossed my mind.

Emerging from the trees behind the beach, Helms led a dozen men I'd never seen before. I was accustomed to sailors from military to merchantmen, and these fellows were dressed in the linens and wools of the average seaman, but something was different about them. Several wore silk scarves of bright colours around their heads and sashes over their shoulders. Each carried at least one pistol in the waistband, or tethered to the sash, and cutlasses hung at their sides.

The man I guessed to be their captain walked alongside Mr Helms. He wore a jacket with an impressive array of buttons and a sword with a decorative hilt.

My mother put a hand on my shoulder. "Stay silent, Wil."

I did as she said, but the men seemed to be friendly, despite their threatening appearance. As they reached our small semicircle of huts, they paused.

"As you see, there are just but a few of us on the island," Mr Helms explained.

"What of those dwellings?" the man asked, pointing across the lagoon.

Helms followed his gaze. "We have a handful of workers who labour the salt collection with us. That's their camp."

The man nodded and looked around, his deeply tanned and weathered face cleanly shaven, unlike most of his men.

"We have a man to bury, if you'd guide us to a suitable spot, sir. We usually bury at sea, but by the time the storm calmed we were in sight of land. I chose to wait so the man's final resting place can be marked."

"I'm sorry to hear of your loss," Mr Helms replied. "We are yet to suffer our own, so we have no cemetery chosen, but I have a place in mind. As you can see, the island is quite flat, but there is an area of slightly higher elevation. The storms tend to flood the lower land."

"Fresh water?" the man asked.

"We use a cistern system. The lagoons are salt laden, but we can spare a barrel if you have one to fill."

The man ran a hand through his hair and stared under our house. It felt like he was looking right at me, and Mother squeezed my shoulder.

"He can't see us in the shadows," she whispered. "Keep perfectly still."

I knew she was probably right, but his eyes lingered on our location for long enough to make me question the idea.

"I have more than one needs filling, Mr Helms, but I'll accept as much as you'll allow us."

Helms nodded towards the top of Salt Cay. "Grand Turk is the larger island to the north you would have sighted when you arrived here. There's plenty of fresh water there."

The leader turned to his men who had scattered about our camp, some chatting with our men, although Father stood to one side.

"Bring the captain's body ashore, boatswain," he addressed to a severe-looking man with long dark hair. "We'll bury him here."

"Aye," the man responded and nodded to several of the men who followed him back to the beach.

"How long do you plan on staying, sir?" Helms asked.

The man returned his attention to his host. "I dare say we'll move on tomorrow. Anything on Grand Turk, besides fresh water?"

Mr Helms shook his head. "More salt and people to rake it. Maybe twice the number here."

"No tavern, then?" the man asked.

"Not to my knowledge, sir."

The man grunted. "Probably for the best. Care to show me your cemetery site?"

Mr Helms nodded. "Certainly, sir." He started to walk, then paused, turning to the stranger. "I don't believe you mentioned your name, sir?"

"My apologies," the man replied. "Rochefort. Captain Rochefort as of last night."

"This way, captain," Helms said, and led him east into the woods.

. . .

"They don't seem dangerous, Mother," I whispered once the two men had walked away.

"These men are privateers, Wil. They cannot be trusted," she replied, looking to see where the unaccounted men from the ship had gone.

I was confused and eager to see their ship. "But privateers sail for England. Why would they hurt us?"

"Wil, they are pirates," she hissed, holding a firm grip on my arm. "Most of these privateers are nothing more than thieves and rogues. Who knows where their intentions lie?"

"Mr Helms seems to trust them," I said, my curiosity outweighing my willingness to accept my mother's words.

"He has no choice, Wil. What was the man to do? Tell them to pull anchor and leave? We have but a handful of muskets and blades between us. Your father has a pistol and nothing more. You saw those men. They could slaughter us all in minutes if the mood took them."

Finally, the gravity of the situation became clear. I couldn't recall ever seeing my mother scared of anything. On the passage over, she was on deck helping the men trim the sails during a storm without a second thought.

"Mrs Crowe," came a voice from behind, startling the pair of us. "Mama sent me. She say you can hide wit us if you want to."

Silhouetted by the light behind him, I could see Marcus was waving us over. Mother started crawling his way, then stopped.

"Mr Crowe. He'll not know where we went," she whispered.

"I'll stay and tell him, then join you," I offered confidently.

"I'm not leaving you, Wil. We'll both stay until we can safely get word to your father."

I now took hold of Mother's arm. "Go with Marcus, Mother. It's safer for me than it is for you. They'll not concern themselves with a lad."

My knowledge of the ways of the world when it came to men and women was limited, to say the least, but I knew from being around enough sailors that they weren't always a gentlemanly crowd.

"That may be so, but I can't leave you, Wil," she said firmly.

Without further contemplation, I released Mother's arm and scurried on my hands and knees until I reached the edge of the hut and stood up. I heard Mother gasp, then we all fell silent.

"Where did you spring from?" one of the seamen asked in the thick accent of a London commoner.

I hadn't noticed the man before, but he was standing in the shade of a tree by one of the other huts with three of his shipmates.

"What's your name, then?" he asked when I didn't respond to his first question.

"Wil, sir," I mumbled, my legs feeling weak and unsteady.

"C'mon over and meet the fellas, Wil," the man said, beckoning me his way.

"William!" my father's voice snapped from behind me.

I turned and saw him standing at the top of the steps in the doorway to our hut. I hadn't realised he'd gone inside our home and been directly above where we'd been hiding.

"Come inside," he ordered.

I froze for a moment, unsure. The pirates now knew I was here and nothing would change that. I'd never dared directly disobey my father before, but curiosity was burning inside me.

"William!" Father growled from the doorway, but he didn't pursue me as I walked towards the group of seamen.

"Hey lads, this here's Wil," the pirate said, slapping me on the back.

They introduced themselves to me. Lefty, who had several fingers missing from his right hand, Dutch, who spoke with an accent, Cook, who I wasn't sure whether that was his name or occupation, and Badger, the man who'd first spoken to me.

"Your ol' man's a bit of a toff, ain't he?" Badger said, nodding towards our hut.

I don't know why I lied to the man, but the words spilled out before I could stop them. "That's my uncle, not my father. My father's a sailor. He's away at the moment."

"Doubt he's an ordinary seaman like us," Badger said with a smirk.

"Navigator," I replied, digging a deeper hole.

The men seemed to accept my deception. They were jovial and asked me many questions about the island and what we were doing here. I answered as best I could, hoping the distraction was allowing Mother to make her way safely to the other camp. Marcus would lead her through the woods, but I realised they'd have to cross open ground to the west before reaching cover.

I began walking east. "I'll show you how we gather the salt," I explained and gave them a description of how the water evaporated, leaving the salt deposits which we then raked into piles, careful not to drag dirt with it. All the men followed me except one.

"Don't dilly-dally, Dutch," I said, waving to the straggler who was eyeing our hut.

The others burst into raucous laughter.

"Yeah, don't dilly-dally!" they jeered at their shipmate until he sneered but followed along.

By the time we'd reached the edge of the lagoon where the shallow, brackish water met firmer ground, I couldn't think of anything more to say about collecting salt. All I could do was pray Marcus and my mother had made it safely away from our camp while I came up with something else to talk about. It wasn't difficult. I was full of questions for these intriguing men. My fears had subsided, quelled by their casual and friendly manner.

"What's your destination?" I asked.

Badger smiled, his crooked teeth an array of varied colours and angles, many missing. "Where the fair winds take us," he said.

"Hispaniola is where the captain had us heading," Lefty added.

"Isn't that Spanish?" I asked.

"Aye, that's the point," Lefty replied with a laugh.

"The strait between Hispaniola and Cuba," Badger explained. "Good hunting for Spanish ships, thinking they're in safe waters."

"Good place for them to trap us, too," Cook groaned.

They fascinated me, and I listened to every word, but my eyes kept returning to the weapons strung about their bodies. Badger must have seen me looking as he drew his cutlass.

"Here," he said, "feel the weight in your hands."

Ten minutes prior, I would have gasped in fear if one of the men had drawn his blade, but now I didn't flinch and took the sword from him. It was heavier than I'd imagined and the grip too thick for my smaller hands, but the power of the weapon gave me a surge of excitement.

"Look at his bloody stance!" Badger cried, and I realised I'd set my feet and bent my knees as I'd been taught to fence.

"This ain't no gentleman's sword, lad, and it won't be a gentleman's fight, neither," Badger said, moving behind me. He held my right wrist and pulled my hand holding the cutlass in a slashing motion. "Now twist your hand and cut back, lad."

He released his grip, and I swung the blade back and forth, forehand to backhand across my imaginary opponent's body. The cutlass was too heavy for me, and I felt its momentum taking control away from my intended movements, then the sword came to a stop, and I stumbled to the side. Dutch had pulled a dagger from his sash and easily blocked my efforts. He sneered at me, and Badger laughed loudly, slapping me on the back.

"Need to grow them muscles, lad. The Spaniards won't go easy on you just because you're a nipper."

I handed him back his cutlass. "Thank you, sir."

"Find us two sturdy branches of a good length," Badger said, and gave me a wink.

Before he could change his mind, I ran into the woods and quickly returned with two of the straightest branches I could find. Badger swiftly trimmed them to size with his cutlass, and so began my first lesson on how to fight like a pirate.

10

HALF-WITTED PLONKER

Present Day

AJ sat on the bench under the shade of the fly-bridge and chipped away at the artefact. Thomas sat on the opposite bench eating his lunch he'd picked up for them from Heritage Kitchen, the little food shack down the road from the dock. AJ's food sat untouched as she feverishly worked to remove more crud with a sharp knife and a small pick they used for removing scuba tank O-rings.

Buck had recommended the tools, as they didn't have an air-scribe available. Apparently, the pros used the pneumatic device which operated like a tiny jackhammer, but even if they found one used for engraving on the island, it wouldn't have the right tip. So the slower method with a pick would have to do, which was fiddly, but she was making progress.

They were out of the sun but also sheltered from the breeze, and sweat ran down AJ's face, dripping onto what she hoped to be the hilt of a sword, as Buck had predicted. It was beginning to appear that he was right. The knuckle-guard was the curved and tapered part of the

'D', and now the grip was slowly revealing itself. The bare metal was green, except in a few spots where AJ had accidentally scored the surface. Below the tarnished exterior was a dark golden colour.

"Your lunch is gettin' cold, Boss," Thomas commented, eyeing the unwrapped fish sandwich.

AJ look up and brushed her hair from her face with her forearm. "Oh, right," she mumbled and stood up, handing the artefact to Thomas while she washed her hands under the freshwater spray plumbed into the rear of the Newton.

"Dis is startin' to look like someting," he commented, turning it over in his hands. He gripped it as though it were a sword. "So da tang of da blade woulda been inside here, right?" he said, holding the rusty brown cavity at one end towards AJ.

"Yup. According to Buck, some swords were made completely from bronze, but most had a steel blade. This one must have had a steel one which has rusted away to nothing. If we're lucky, some remnant of the tang is still inside the handle which we can use to help determine the age of the sword. Apparently, we can send a tiny sample of the metals away and they can narrow down the time period by the metallurgy."

Thomas stood and dropped the hilt into the bucket of soapy water. "I best be going."

"Say hello to Amphitrite for me," AJ chuckled.

"I'll give her nipples a polish for you," Thomas said as he stepped to the dock, laughing as he left.

They didn't have an afternoon trip, but two couples had asked for a guide to the mermaid statue, an underwater sculpture installation by Sunset House Dive Resort. The nine-foot-tall bronze had been created by the renowned sculptor, Simon Morris, who was also responsible for Angels of the Deep, the one which had come to an unfortunate end.

Amphitrite, to use the mermaid's official name, was synonymous with scuba diving in the Cayman Islands, and customers often asked to see it. The easiest way was from the shore at the resort, and AJ was happy for Thomas to guide the customers and let them pay him directly in tips.

AJ unwrapped her now lukewarm sandwich and took a bite, staring into the bucket of dirty water. *Hazel's Odyssey* gently rocked, air hissed, and people chattered as Reg's crew refilled the tanks on their boats and prepared one of them for an afternoon trip. It was all background motion and noise to AJ, who was lost in her thoughts about her find.

"Talk to Reilly?" Reg asked, stepping onto the Newton.

"Yeah," AJ replied, as she finished chewing a mouthful of sandwich. "He thinks it's the hilt of a sword."

"Seriously?" Reg answered suspiciously. He was used to AJ messing with him.

"Take a look," she said, nodding at the bucket.

Reg fished the artefact out and looked it over. "Blimey. I'd say he's right." He sat down and continued examining the bronze piece, now mostly clear of growth. "He have any idea from when?"

AJ shook her head. "I've cleaned it up a lot since he saw it."

"Is it worth anything?"

She shrugged her shoulders. "No idea. Might be if we can date it."

"Be of interest to the museum, if nothing else," Reg said, dropping the hilt back into the soapy water. "Did you contact them yet?"

AJ shook her head.

"Best you do sooner rather than later, girl," he continued. "You know how touchy they get about this stuff."

She scrunched up the empty wrapping and threw it into the rubbish bin. "As soon as I contact them, we'll be buried in red tape."

"True," he grunted.

"And I was thinking..." she said, squinting up at the big man.

"Oh shit," he groaned, "here we go."

AJ grinned. "I was thinking it might be nice to dive the spot again before we hand it over."

"You were now, were you?"

"Be a chance to use our magnetometer."

Reg scratched his scraggly beard. "You thinking of taking your boat all the way around?"

"Nah," AJ replied. "Shore dive."

"When?"

"This afternoon, if we can take one of your vans, or your Landy."

"Can't today. I've got a leak in the cooling system on *Blue Pearl.* Gotta fix it before the morning."

"Don't you have people for that these days?" AJ joked.

Reg laughed. "I do if I don't mind doing it properly once they're finished. Easier to do meself the first time."

AJ's mobile rang, and she looked at the caller ID. It was a 3-4-5 local number, but not one that was in her contacts list. "Mermaid Divers," she answered.

"Is this AJ Bailey?" a man asked.

"Speaking."

"Hi, this Sean, we met on the boat yesterday."

"Oh, hello," AJ replied politely before she'd processed who it was. "Wait, Sean Carlson?"

"That's right, thanks for remembering me," he responded brightly. "I had a few follow-up questions about your find yesterday. Do you have a minute?"

"I saw your article this morning," AJ began, trying to decide what tack to take with the journalist.

"Oh, great!" he said. "Thanks for following me. I was calling to see if you'd figured out what you'd found? I'm excited to update my readers."

"You're a bit late, aren't you, mate?" AJ snapped back.

"I am? Did you sell the story to the *Compass?* Or international?" he asked, sounding deflated. "Damn it, I wish you'd spoken to me first. I mean, I'm the guy who broke the story for you."

"For me?" AJ fumed. "That's rich. I meant you're a bit bloody late asking what we might have found! *You* should have called me before you printed anything at all!"

"Why, Miss Bailey? I was there, and I reported what I saw," he replied defensively. "That's what we do as reporters. We tell the public about things we witness and investigate."

"So, you think you saw us bring up a relic which could well be lost treasure from the pirate age?"

"By the speculation between all of you on the boat, that is what I concluded."

AJ took a deep breath before continuing. It took all of her self-restraint not to hang up, but then who knew what he'd write next? "What if I told you it was an old doorknob, circa 2010? What are you going to tell your readers about that?"

"I would tell them I was disappointed to discover that AJ Bailey of Mermaid Divers was mistaken in what she found."

"You complete tosser!"

"Excuse me?"

"You're the only one who's mistaken, mate," AJ raged. "You made the mistake of going off half-cocked and printing a load of bollocks without fact-checking any of it."

"Are you saying you lied to me?"

"I never said a word to you! You made all this rubbish up from what you thought you overheard."

The man was silent for a moment. "Okay, Miss Bailey, let's calm down. I'm happy to apologise if you feel aggrieved in any way."

"Aggrieved? I'd like you to apologise to me and all your readers for being a shitty journalist and printing stories you conjure from thin air. How about apologising for that?"

"50,000 followers say I'm not a shitty journalist, Miss Bailey."

"45,000," AJ corrected.

"45,826 as of an hour ago," he rebutted. "I rounded up."

"I shouldn't be surprised. Near enough is good enough for you, right?"

Another few moments of silence followed.

"Am I right in assuming you have not given this story to any other publication?" he finally asked.

"Yes."

"Have you talked to someone else?"

"No."

"But you said…" he started, then stopped himself.

"You really are useless at this, aren't you? You don't even know what you just asked," AJ ranted with glee, wishing Nora could hear her. She was sure her Viking friend would be proud.

Carlson laughed. "Fair enough. So, is it a doorknob?"

AJ groaned to herself and was glad Nora wasn't around to see her struggle now. She didn't like to lie, even to a half-witted plonker like Sean Carlson, but she was stuck in a no-win situation. Lie and he writes she's an idiot who didn't know what she'd found, or tell the truth and he'd keep the story alive. Which meant further scrutiny, when she really wanted a few days to enjoy her discovery and poke about for more.

AJ would go through all the proper channels and had little interest in making money from her find, but it was fun digging up artefacts, and there might be more in the sand near Anchor Point.

"I have experts examining it now," she said, looking at Reg. "It's not a doorknob, but too soon to tell exactly what it is. The archaeologists take their time with this sort of thing, so don't expect an answer anytime soon."

"Archaeologists, huh?" he replied. "I'll check in with you again, thanks," he said in an unnervingly excited tone and hung up.

11

A NEW CLASSROOM

1702

I spent the morning watching the privateer ship leave. As they sailed from anchor, I moved around the north-west tip of the island to keep them in view. Marcus joined me and we sat together in the shade of a tree as their stern grew slowly smaller.

"What does dat say? On da back," Marcus asked.

"Stern," I corrected. "Tell me the letters you see," I continued, taking the opportunity for an impromptu lesson.

Marcus read what he could see, but the ship was too far away to clearly make out all the letters.

"The *Royal Fortune*," I told him.

"Dat da name of da ship?"

"It is."

"Why it called dat?"

I thought for a moment, having not previously considered the meaning.

"They are privateers sailing under the flag of the Queen. I suppose it means they're gathering a fortune for the Crown."

"What's a priva… What dat word?"

"Privateer. It means they own their ship and have a letter from the Queen allowing them to engage the enemy on her behalf."

"Dat da Spanish?"

"And the French."

"I met a man from France one time. He not a nice man. He beat my papa."

"Let's hope the *Royal Fortune* crosses his path and teaches him a lesson."

Marcus grinned. "I'll pray for dat tonight."

The crew had stayed a day longer than planned and it disappointed me to see them leave. It also meant Mother could come home, which helped ease my despondency. Father barely spoke to me in her absence. I realised that was not unusual. It was simply that Mother always filled the void. If he'd heard me lie about being his son, Father had not let on.

As I sat watching these intriguing men of the sea leave our tiny island, I came to several conclusions. First, I wanted to continue sailing the seas. A life full of adventure was now calling loudly and clearly to me. Of course, at twelve years old, I didn't consider the awful living conditions, dangers, and endless monotony between brief moments of excitement.

My second conclusion was one I'd determined Father and I agreed upon. We'd each prefer life without the other. I had no idea what would make my father happy, as I'd only ever known him to be severe and distant. I would hear him laugh occasionally during dinner parties at our home in London, but even in humour he was reserved compared to the guests.

"What now?" Marcus asked, looking at me.

I sighed. The question had been on my mind since it had become clear the pirates meant us no harm. Before their arrival, Father had laid down his law, which I was currently breaking by sitting here with my friend.

"I don't know," I replied honestly. "I need to speak with Mother."

Marcus stood. "I'll tell your mama tis safe to come home."

Apparently, Marcus was as eager to discover our future as I was as he sprinted along the beach, his bare feet impervious to the rocky terrain.

Mother hadn't waited for Marcus to bring her the news. She was already in our hut when I returned. I paused outside when I heard my father's voice, low but fierce. His words were lost, but his anger was clear. I assumed he was aiming his wrath at my mother, but she kept quiet. That usually meant she'd given up on reasoning with him and was letting him exhaust his ire.

I loudly clattered up the steps and entered our hut. They both turned towards the door upon hearing me.

"Wil," Mother breathed and swept across the room to hold me. "I've been worried about you."

She squeezed me tightly, and it felt wonderful. Secure somehow. Her frame was lean and feminine, yet surprisingly strong. Despite the fact she'd been forced into hiding, I was sure I was safer in her presence than my father's.

"I've been fine, Mother. The men were friendly."

"I tried to keep him inside, but he insisted on gallivanting about with those rogues," Father seethed.

"We're all together now and the ship is gone," Mother said firmly. "I doubt we'll ever see them again."

She finally released me, and I looked up at her face. Her right cheek was red, and I wondered if he'd slapped her again. I fumed inside and stared at the man.

"You will heed me, boy, or there will be consequences," he announced, wagging a finger my way. "You'll take lessons in the afternoons from now on. The mornings you'll spend with Helms and the other men." He took a step towards me. "While we're stuck in this godforsaken place, I expect you to do your part. Learn every aspect of this business, so you can help implement the new methods when the workers arrive."

"Monty, he's a boy," Mother complained. "He's not a labourer under your beck and call."

"Davina!" he yelled without restraint. "I'm tired of you two running around like commoners, embarrassing me and my family name. If the boy has energy to run rampant with thieves and barbarians, he can put his efforts to good use for once." He turned away and sat at his desk, which took up most of the living space of the hut. "I've made my decision. Now I expect you both to adhere to my wishes. The boy starts tomorrow morning with Helms." He paused from shuffling papers on his desk and looked up. "You shall tutor him here in the camp. That way, I know you're not wasting your time trying to educate slaves and making a fool of us all. Now go," he said, waving towards the door. "Leave me in peace to work."

Mother shepherded me out of the door, down the steps, and through the camp until we were in the shade of the trees. She embraced me again.

"Oh Wil," she groaned. "I'm so sorry."

"It's not your fault, Mother."

"Oh, but it is. If I hadn't agreed to our family's arrangement..." She paused and considered her words. "But then I wouldn't have you, and life wouldn't be bearable at all without you."

I wasn't entirely sure what she meant, but assumed it had something to do with my two grandfathers introducing my parents, as was common in English high society.

"What about Marcus?" I asked, my concern shifting to my friend.

Mother let me go and stared across the lagoon. "I don't know what we can do, Wil. But best we let things calm down for a while."

"I told the pirates he was my uncle," I blurted.

"You told them who was your uncle?" she asked.

"Father," I admitted. "I was embarrassed because he hid away like a coward, and then I felt awful about it. But now, now I wish I hadn't told them we're related at all."

Mother drew me into her arms again. "Oh Wil, you mustn't say things like that, but I do understand. He wasn't always this way, you know." She released me and held my shoulders at arm's length. "Where did you say your father was?"

"At sea. I told them he was a navigator."

She smiled and chuckled quietly. "A navigator, you say? You'll make a fine navigator one day, but your father… I think we can say the seas are not for him." She dropped one hand and squeezed my shoulder with the other. "Your father's never been the life of the party, but he was sweet and attentive when we were courting and first married. The pressures of politics seemed to age him, and being sent here was the final insult. We must try our best to be patient with him, Wil. Promise me you'll try?"

I heard my mother's words, but I struggled to find the sympathy in my heart. Still, I nodded and told her I would try.

"It's not fair to Marcus, Mother. Father will be watching everything we do," I said, changing the subject back to my friend.

"That he will," she mumbled thoughtfully. "But perhaps we can improve our classroom situation," she said with renewed vigour and a crafty smile. "With planning and a little patience, we may be able to continue as we were."

It took some time to carry, drag, and reassemble our crude classroom furniture to the back side of our hut. The afternoon sun scorched us, and combined with the intense humidity, left us soaked with sweat. Our new location offered us almost no shade as the sun tracked from east to west, so based on that premise, we set about forming a shelter.

With axe and machete in hand, we entered the woods in search of elusive sturdy, straight branches with which to build a frame. Mother assured me our construction needn't be perfect, as she was confident it would be temporary. We chopped, hacked and dragged limbs back to the hut, where we noisily began assembling our makeshift cover.

Helms and several of the other men stopped by on hearing the commotion and offered to help. Mother politely declined their assistance. Father looked out the window opening in the back wall several times and finally dropped the flap to keep out the noise. I grinned at Mother, who winked back.

Using twine, we strapped a long pole across the back of the hut, just below the window opening. From that, we extended branches to a second long pole six feet away from the hut supported by verticals at either end. Mother took her time showing me the securest way of fastening the pieces together with the twine. I noticed she was speaking louder than normal when explaining everything and rested every branch against the hut with a thud.

Finally, Father could stand it no more. The flap swung open and his red face appeared, rivulets of sweat running down his face.

"Must you make so much noise?" he bellowed.

Mother paused from knotting the twine around two poles. "It will only be for a few more days and then the shelter will be complete, Monty. We could hardly spend all afternoon in the bright sun. We'd simply roast."

"There must be a simpler way, for God's sake."

"Our old spot had natural shade, Monty, but the hut doesn't afford us that luxury. I suppose we could move to the trees at the edge of the camp if that would trouble you less?"

"I want you within sight of the house."

"Quite so, my dear. You made that clear, so we'll be as hasty as we can be. Two more days, three at the most," she said in a pleasant tone and returned to her task.

"Which trees?" Father demanded.

Mother stopped fussing with the twine once more and gazed off into the distance towards the woods to the east. "I hadn't given it much thought. I expect we could form something appropriate just inside that treeline," she said, pointing.

Father leaned from the window opening. He would be able to see us from there, and from the front door, if he bothered to leave his desk.

"Take all this down, and do it quietly, Davina. You may set up by the woods, but make sure I can see you."

Father disappeared inside the house but left the flap open. I smiled at Mother and she winked at me again. Within an hour, we had deconstructed our partial shelter and dragged everything over to the woods. We both sat down, exhausted.

"This will be a better spot," I said, between gulps of fresh water from a leather costrel.

"I think so," Mother agreed. "We'll finish constructing the shelter, as we have most of the wood to do it. We can tie the back beam between two trees and use palm fronds for cover. It'll be nice to have a roof from the sun and the rain showers."

"How do you know how to do all these things?" I asked her. I'd seen my mother handle horses with ease, hold her own fencing with her brother, sail a ship, and shoot a musket more accurately than most. But most of the time she was the wife of a lord, in pretty dresses at dinner parties.

"Because I'm a woman?" she said in way of reply.

I thought about her words for several moments. I supposed she was right. My surprise was based on the fact she was female. Being competent at men's work wasn't expected from a lady. If her society friends could see her sitting here, filthy dirty in linen trousers and shirt with her hair a mess, they'd walk by pretending they didn't know her.

"It's unusual, is it not?" I said.

She smiled. "When there's nobody around to do things for you, one must be prepared to carry on, regardless. My father told me that when I was a young girl. He taught me to ride and hunt for food, as well as to prepare it myself. He also had me spend a week working with each section of our staff. I cleaned rooms for a week, mucked out stables, polished silver, prepared meals, and acted as my mother's lady-in-waiting.

"I learned many things during those times. One very important lesson was realising our servants were no different from us. They were happy, sad, and bled like we did. The only difference was their standing in life. It gave me respect and understanding for those who deserved it, instead of those who felt entitled to it." She held out her hand, and I gave her the costrel. "I also learnt to pay attention to things. Much of what I know is from quietly observing. Choose your words carefully and use them sparingly, Wil, and always keep your eyes open."

It dawned on me how much I'd babbled in front of the pirates, and I felt embarrassed. But I had also watched them carefully, and they'd taught me many things. Thoughts of the *Royal Fortune* brought me back to Marcus.

"Father will see if Marcus joins us here," I said, staring at our home, but fifty yards away.

"Not when he sits behind the partition we're going to make," Mother replied.

12

NO BAG OF JEWELS

Present Day

Twenty-four hours had never felt so long to AJ. She wasn't known for her patience, and being convinced a government official was about to stop by at any moment demanding that she hand over the bronze hilt had fuelled her anxiety. She drummed her fingers on her knees as they bounced along in Reg's ancient Land Rover, trying to come up with a dive plan to cover the widest area.

"Will you sit still?" Reg growled loudly to be heard over the wind rushing through the open windows. "You're making me nervous with all your twitching about."

"I can't sit still." She replied, her voice jolting with the bumps. "Your Landy has air-ride suspension."

"What are you talking about?"

"The suspension is so bloody bad, I spend half the time in the air," she said with a big grin.

"Ha, bloody, ha. This baby is a classic."

They rode along in silence for a while, heading north across the island on Frank Sound Road, the only way to access the north shore without going completely around the East End.

"This is a bit like the old days, isn't it?" AJ said as Reg turned right in Old Man Bay, joining the Queen's Highway going east.

He smiled. "I was thinking the same."

"We dived just about everything we could, my first year here."

Reg chuckled. "You were a pain in the arse back then, too."

"You loved it," she said, shoving his arm. "Even Pearl came with us some days."

"It was simpler back then," he said, and AJ realised what they were talking about was nearly fourteen years ago.

"You'd just ordered your second boat when I arrived," AJ said, thinking back. "It finally showed up in the autumn, perfectly timed for slow season."

"My timing was never too good," Reg laughed. "I started the business six months before Hurricane Ivan. Was just beginning to fill the boat most days, then bang," he said, thumping the steering wheel. "Worst bloody hurricane the islands had in modern history clobbers us, then all we had was a handful of local customers shared amongst all the dive ops for the next six months."

"That was before you had the dock, wasn't it?"

"Oh yeah," Reg replied. "Long before. Didn't even have the first Newton. I bought this old diesel inboard from a bloke who was moving back to America. Bloody thing was slower than molasses at the North Pole, and broke down every five minutes, but it survived Ivan and had me back in the water the following week."

Reg slowed and searched along the shrubs and low trees which blocked their view of the ocean less than 50 yards away. They came upon a small opening in the bush and Reg pulled over and stopped. A narrow pathway led into the woods towards the sound of water lapping against the shoreline.

"How's that for a good memory?" Reg declared, shutting off the engine.

"Like an elephant, you," AJ replied, getting out of the Landy. "A big, old, grumpy elephant."

Reg's low laugh rumbled from the other side of the vehicle as they both walked to the back door. With their BCDs on their backs and magnetometer case in hand, they shoved the branches aside and made their way to the beach.

Bluff Bay to their left was shallow reef protected, but the barrier petered out as the shoreline curved. Waves rolled in from the open ocean, and when the winds blew from the north or northeast, the spot wasn't diveable. At least from shore. But today, the winds were down and by the time the surf reached the short sandy beach, they'd lost all their strength, washing harmlessly over AJ's feet.

She scanned the water and then the shore in both directions. They were the only human beings in sight. To the east, the coastline wrapped around the point which separated them from Barefoot Beach. To the west, she could just make out the roof of a home half a mile away down Bluff Bay. She wasn't really sure where Little Bluff Bay became Bluff Bay and why they named any of it a bay in the first place. It was little more than an indent. Without much of a bluff. But for Grand Cayman, 30 feet of elevation was a major topographical feature.

"We'd better enter here and swim out beyond the shallow reef," AJ suggested. "Then head west to the Reef Ball, where I found the hilt."

"Sounds fine to me," Reg agreed, and the two prepared their gear.

AJ was diving in purple Mermaid Divers leggings and rash guard, while Reg wore board shorts and a Pearl Divers rash guard AJ had designed for him to sell to customers. Neither bothered with a wetsuit, as they'd be diving shallow where the water was warmest.

Once they were ready, the two divers walked into the water carrying their fins. They carefully picked their way out, doing the stingray shuffle to make sure they didn't surprise a critter lounging in the sand and get themselves a barb in the foot. With air in their BCDs, they waited until they were waist deep, then floated on their backs and pulled their fins on, taking turns holding the underwater metal detector.

From there, they surface swam out until they were over nothing but sand, and one large concrete dome.

"Bluff Bay number seven," AJ said, reminding Reg of the tag number on the Reef Ball they were looking for.

She wasn't sure which one they were above, but they'd placed them numerically, so it wouldn't take them long to find number seven.

"Ready?" she asked, and Reg responded by dumping the air from his BCD and dropping below the surface.

The Reef Ball was already alive with small fish taking refuge where the predators would have a harder time catching them. They flitted in and out of the holes in the concrete when the divers approached, wary of the noisy, bubble-making creatures. AJ found the tag and held up three fingers to Reg.

Finning west, they could easily make out the next dome through the crystal-clear water. They had staggered and spaced the Reef Balls forty feet apart. Their objective was to grow coral quickly, and not interfere with the existing reef or coastline, so the deliberate separation was to avoid creating any kind of breakwater.

AJ continued past two domes, then checked the tag on the next one. Bluff Bay number seven. She gave Reg an okay sign, and he turned on the magnetometer, then began his first lap around the base of the dome.

Looking on, AJ found she was always excited when they began searching with the metal detector. Invariably, the anticipation would wear thin and monotony would take over as the chore was a test of endurance and discipline more than instant gratification. Beer cans tended to be the most popular find, carelessly dropped over the side of boats or left on the beach to be snatched by the high tide waters. Her only consolation was the good deed of removing rubbish from the ocean.

AJ and Reg had gone halves on the metal detector about a year before. They hadn't used it as much as they'd hoped, but it had proved invaluable on the occasions they'd had cause to break it out. Although it was called a magnetometer, objects did not have to be magnetic ferrous metals to be detected. It used electrical conductivity, so it would find aluminium, copper, gold, silver, and bronze, which were all conductive. However, it wouldn't detect poor conductors such as stainless-steel, pearls, bone, or stone.

Reg made wider and wider circles around the Reef Ball, each lap taking longer as the circumferential distance increased. AJ kept her dive buddy in sight, but amused herself rummaging through the sand farther away, finding mainly bleached white dead coral pieces and nothing of interest. Every once in a while, Reg would get a hit and she'd fin over and dig up the can, fishhook, or chain link.

When Reg got another beep, AJ unenthusiastically swam over to investigate the location while Reg moved on. She took a small trowel from her BCD pocket and began digging down, trying to be slow and methodical so she didn't create a thick cloud of sediment and fine sand. A foot down, she hit something solid with the trowel and began carefully excavating around the object. It didn't feel like a can this time, which probably meant it was a small anchor abandoned by a fisherman after becoming lodged.

Brushing sand aside in the hollow she'd made, AJ could see a rusty metal tube. She grabbed it and tried to pull it free, heaving as best she could with her knees in the sand for leverage. It began to move, so she pulled and wiggled the pipe until it broke loose of the sea floor, scattering a haze of debris and sand particles all around her.

She held the tube in her hand and waited for the dust to settle. As best she could tell, it was a section of steel plumbing pipe and she groaned into her reg. AJ reached down to brush her sand pile back into the hole she'd made when she stopped and stared at the strangely shaped piece of dead coral, which must have come up with the pipe. As more of the haze cleared, she set the pipe down and picked up the lump of coral. It was the same bleached creamy white, but was smoother than the porous coral fragments.

AJ gasped into her reg and quickly dropped what she realised was a bone, watching it drop to the sea floor. It was not a bone from any fish or water mammal she'd ever seen. She decided it could be an animal bone, maybe a cow or horse, but it was too big for a dog or cat. The trouble was, it looked remarkably like a human femur.

Banging her stainless-steel carabiner on her dive tank, she finally got Reg's attention, and he finned over. He was preparing the metal detector to search where she was pointing, then he too saw the bone. He stopped, looked at AJ, then back at the object, which was more of a dirty ivory colour now AJ studied it. Reg pointed his thumb to the surface, and they both slowly rose the 30 feet to fresh air.

"That's a bloody leg bone," AJ blurted as she took her reg out and put air in her BCD.

"Too right it is," Reg agreed. "That's curtains on your little adventure, love. We have to report this now."

"I know," AJ said. "Couldn't be a bag of jewels we find, eh? Had to be part of some poor, dead bugger. Just my luck." She stuck her mask back in the water and looked down at the sandy bottom and the bone lying where she'd dropped it.

"Do we take it with us," she asked, picking her head up, "or leave it down there?"

Turning, she saw Reg was staring towards the beach where they'd come through the woods. A man was standing there, looking at them through a pair of binoculars.

"Who the hell's that?" she asked. "Better not be that little plonker from the internet blog."

"It ain't," Reg grunted. "But if it's who I think it is, we'll be wishing it was that little idiot."

13

LESSONS

1703

Months rolled by with events that seemed to blend together. The first ship had arrived, bringing only two workers. Father was beside himself for days. The three sailors he'd hired couldn't leave his employ fast enough, so now he was down one man and starting over with new people. Whatever grandiose plans he had for improving the process of gathering salt would have to wait. Father had also taken to using a cane, complaining of gout. The severity of the ailment appeared to come and go based upon the demands of the camp. It was always playing up when extra hands were required.

I'd had a birthday. The two new men, Gordy and Duck, weren't impressed to be shown the way of things by a thirteen-year-old, but they were surprised the son of a lord would work alongside them every morning, and they soon accepted me. Or perhaps merely tolerated, but either way, they became pleasant enough.

They were both rough types from London who'd by their own account bounced around from job to job wherever a wage was offered. Duck had a prominent scar which wrapped from his fore-head around his left eye and down his cheek. He never spoke of it, but Gordy told me when we were alone one day that the wound was from a glass bottle. He grinned as he explained how his friend's nickname had accompanied the scar as he'd failed to heed the warning Gordy had apparently shouted across the bar room.

Between the hard toil and my adolescence, my body began to develop. I'd shot up in height and my muscles were growing stronger each week. I already stood eye to eye with my father, and any softness in my flesh was now firm. Everything Mother put in front of me I devoured, and an hour later, I was hungry again.

Father made it easy for Marcus to join us each afternoon for classes. He rarely set foot outside the hut, and when he did, it was to relieve himself or call to Mother for her to do something for him. Marcus grew quickly in mind and body. He was nearly two years younger than me but only three inches shorter and a formidable opponent when we wrestled - which as young boys becoming men we did quite often.

I taught him everything the pirates had shown me about swordsmanship and staying alive in a fight. Mother caught us duelling with sticks one day, and to my surprise, not only encour-aged our practice, but joined us.

"If we die of old age having never used these skills, I'll be glad of it," she told us, "but if a day comes that we need them, they may well help us reach old age."

At first, I was tentative and careful when duelling my mother. The idea of hurting any woman, but especially her, couldn't bear thinking about. After losing successively for weeks, I slowly began fighting with more vigour and offence. She would constantly coach me and tell me to be more aggressive, and finally my ego could stand it no longer.

Bashing her stick aside, I lunged for a kill shot to the body. Instead of my blunt stick meeting my mother's midriff, I lay on the ground with stars circling my head.

"Wil! Wil, are you alright?" It took a few moments, but her voice came in clearer as my dizziness faded.

"What happened?" I mumbled, suddenly worried I'd hurt her.

"I'm sorry, Wil," she said, leaning over me with concern in her eyes. "I conked you on the head a little harder than intended."

I sat up and saw Marcus staring at me with wide eyes. "Your mama got you good."

They both helped me to my feet. "I thought I had you," I said feebly.

"You found your determination. Now you need to control it," Mother said, keeping a hand on my arm.

"I was tired of losing," I admitted.

She smiled. "If these were real blades and a true adversary, you would never tire of losing, Wil. You'll only lose once."

It took several more months before I could equal my mother. I noticed she was improving too with our practice, which didn't make it easier. Over time, we'd fashioned our weapons into rough facsimiles of cutlasses, but I knew they were lighter than steel and of course the edges were harmless.

One day, Marcus and I were duelling in the clearing well away from the camp when Mother arrived with Mr Helms. We'd grown to trust the man, and he knew about Marcus and our various activities away from camp, but it still surprised me to see him here.

"Mr Helms has kindly agreed to help you both," Mother explained.

A nervous excitement overwhelmed me. However much I tried to imagine a real contest with blades, it was a far cry from duelling with Marcus and Mother. We were all careful not to seriously hurt each other. An outsider to our threesome added a new element of uncertainty. Mr Helms asked Marcus and me to continue our practice while he watched silently from the shade of a tree.

After I scored a strike on Marcus's right arm, Mr Helms told us to stop. He asked for my wooden sword, and I handed it to him. In sweeping motions, he felt the weight and balance.

"Far too light," he said. "But it's a start."

He kept my cutlass and beckoned Marcus towards him.

"Take your stance," he told the boy.

Marcus set his lead foot forward with a slight bend in the knee and held his cutlass out front at 45 degrees facing his opponent. With a lightning-fast flick of the wrist, Mr Helms bashed the boy's sword aside and rested his tip against Marcus's chest.

"If you are training to fight for when you're both grown, your opening may be fine, but if you're preparing for what might come tomorrow, you must choose another strategy," Helms explained. He handed me back the wooden cutlass. "Lady Crowe tells me you've had fencing lessons."

"Yes, sir. With my uncle."

"I'm afraid most of what you learned won't help you stay alive on a battlefield," he said. "No one stands before you and allows you to prepare yourself. It's chaos, mayhem, and ruleless. If you're fool enough to challenge an individual, then gentlemen's standards may apply, but in war, there's only one rule to live by. It's exactly that. Stay alive."

I looked at Marcus, and he looked at me. No doubt my expression mirrored his. I felt like a child, frail and helpless. Our training had been nothing more than a game with no proper use or purpose.

"We are few on this island, Mr Helms," Mother said, and we turned her way. "If men with ill intent land here, every blade will count. Mine, theirs, Bess and Nelly's too. I am aware of my fate if I'm unable to defend myself, sir, and I'd rather die fighting than succumb to their barbarous will."

"I understand, Your Ladyship, but…"

"Damn it, James, call me Davina," Mother interrupted firmly. "We can't stand on airs and graces when there's but a handful of us."

Helm wiped his brow. "I don't think the Lord would care to hear me being so familiar, ma'am."

"I doubt he would. You are correct. In his presence, you may address me by my worthless title, but at all other times, please use Davina."

Helms nodded. "Yes ma'am. What I intended to say was, I agree with you. We should all do our part if we're left with no choice, and I will aid you in this endeavour to the best of my ability. But I strongly advise your wisest course of action will be to evade the assailant if at all possible."

Mother thought for a few moments before replying. "Thank you for your concern and wisdom, James. We shall apply ourselves to securing a suitable location to hide if necessary. But I urge you to teach us how we may best defend ourselves if evasion becomes impossible."

Mr Helms took a deep breath. "Let's begin with realising our assets and weaknesses."

Mother moved around so the three of us stood before our new tutor.

"Your biggest vulnerabilities are strength, experience, and intent," Helms began. "But you can turn some of that around to your advantage."

"Rest assured, Mr Helms, my intent will be to give no quarter," Mother told him.

"Indeed, Your Lad… Davina," he quickly corrected himself. "But you must understand, most foes you will face are not intelligent, educated, or often even trained. They are men who have chosen a pirate's way of life because they enjoy debauchery and violence. Killing is a pleasure they look forward to."

"The privateers who came by the island didn't seem that way, Mr Helms," I ventured, feeling slightly defensive of the men who'd been friendly to me.

"We offered them all we had of value, Wil," he replied. "I dare say their approach would have been different if I'd told them to turn back at the beach. Captain Rochefort was a reasonable man who could see no gain in violence against citizens of the Crown. If men arrive who would rather slay us than converse, you'll be facing aggressors who will see you as easy kills. But as I say, that will be to your advantage.

"In open ground, your foe will attack with strength and vigour, rushing you. For most, the intimidation is enough to render them useless, frozen in fear. A pirate uses his cutlass in bold slashing motions, across the body."

"They showed me that," I agreed, and swept my wooden sword in the manner I'd been shown.

"Correct, and you do that well. But that is an offensive move, which you're unlikely to be in a position to use. Your assets are size, speed, agility, and surprise."

"We sneak up on dem?" Marcus asked.

"If that opportunity presents itself, certainly. But I mean surprise when you're not the defenceless target they'd taken you for."

Helms looked around the clearing. "Wil, move to the trail over there," he instructed, and I did so.

I was 15 yards from them, and Mr Helms gave Marcus instructions in whispers I couldn't hear. He then turned and talked to me.

"Wil, I want you to run across the clearing and attack Marcus. Do not hold back or go easy on your friend. You're bigger and stronger than he is, so you should easily make a strike. Run fast and don't give him time to guess your move."

I felt butterflies in my stomach. We'd grown accustomed to bruising each other with the sticks, so I wasn't concerned about hurting my friend. I was more worried about making a fool of myself.

"Charge like a heathen, Wil!" Helms called out, and I took off running.

Holding my wooden sword aloft, ready to slash my victim, I bore down on Marcus, who stood his ground and held his sword in a defensive stance. I could either bash his sword aside and bowl him over, or aim for his shoulder and force him to parry. I was sure I had the strength to strike through his defence.

Three steps from my friend, I drew back my sword and, as my leading foot planted before him, I brought my blade across my body with all the power I could muster. I was sure my pace combined with a strong swing would send Marcus flying, but instead, my sword found nothing but air and I stumbled past his position. Feeling a sharp smack across my back told me what a fool I'd been.

"Perfectly demonstrated, Wil, thank you," Helms said with a smile on his face. "You drew on your strength, size, and determination to best your younger friend in front of your mother and me. Simply put, you underestimated your opponent." He turned to Marcus, who was grinning from ear to ear. "Well done, young sir. You stood your ground, which was key to baiting the trap. But be warned. When a pirate, a Spaniard, or an Indian comes charging your way, they'll be far more fierce and intimidating than Wil."

"You've fought Indians?" Marcus asked in amazement.

Helms didn't smile. "I have, and I hope to never meet that misfortune again."

14

THE HEADMISTRESS

Present Day

Reg and AJ were nearly to Old Man Bay before Reg did anything more than grunt the odd response. The stranger was long gone by the time they'd collected the bone - which AJ made Reg do - swum back to shore, then pushed through the trail to the Land Rover. AJ knew to leave the big man alone until he was ready to talk, but she was dying to ask a million questions.

"Maybe it wasn't who I thought it was," Reg finally said.

"Who did you think it was?"

"Someone I hoped to never see again."

AJ was glad he was talking, but so far she was none the wiser who this mystery man could be. She waited, letting Reg tell her in his own time, but she really wanted to shake him until the words fell out.

He drove slowly through the turns of the small town, then turned left on Frank Sound Road. When he cleared the homes, and trees and shrubs lined the road once more, he continued.

"His name's Stone Pritchard. He's a treasure hunter."

"I've heard that name before," AJ said thoughtfully. "Maybe you've mentioned him?"

Reg scoffed. "Doubt it. I'd rather chew on nails than utter the bloke's name."

"What did he do?" she asked, sensing the deep hatred her friend had for this man.

"That would be a long list, but I can tell you a few choice items. He screwed me over on a deal we were supposed to be partners in. Left me holding the bag with our investors. He's wanted for conning people out of money in Belize, selling the same haul of old Spanish coins to two different parties in Costa Rica, and the Bahamian police want to talk to him about a dead body."

"He's wanted for murder? Surely the Cayman officials would extradite him, wouldn't they?"

Reg shook his head. "They've never been able to pin it on him, but I can tell you if he sets foot in the Bahamas, his next stop will be jail and they'll take their time questioning him, too. They know he did it."

"Bloody hell," AJ sighed. "And you think it was him watching us?"

"I was sure when I first saw him," Reg replied. "But you know how it is. You start wondering afterwards, thinking your mind was playing tricks and all that."

"Why would this Stone fellow be interested in us? Sounds like it would be in his best interests to stay out of your way."

"I haven't seen hide nor hair of him in donkey's years, but just the other day, someone mentioned his name. Said he was working on a project in Little Cayman."

"That's it then, isn't it?" AJ replied with a wave of her hand. "He's been on your mind. That's why you thought it was him. Probably just a local resident wondering why your Landy was parked there."

Reg looked at her. "Possibly," he grunted. "But get this. The guy told me Pritchard had been snooping around the Little Cayman museum and asking people about this story from the early 1700s."

"Not surprising, right?" AJ countered. "You said he's a treasure hunter."

"A story about a famous sword that was lost," Reg said. "Bit coincidental, ain't it?"

AJ didn't know what to say. She frantically racked her brain for who knew about the sword hilt she'd found. The number of people who knew she'd brought something up was enormous thanks to Sean Carlson and his stupid article online, but only their inner circle knew what it was. And Buck Reilly, but she was confident he wouldn't have told anyone.

"No one knows we found part of a sword, Reg. It's suspiciously coincidental, but it has to be just that. A coincidence."

"Perhaps," he conceded. "But best we do a bit of digging of our own."

AJ unlocked her mobile and opened the internet app, typing in the journalist's name. It took several tries because her finger kept hitting the wrong letters as the Land Rover bounced down the road. After swearing a few times, she finally found Carlson's blog page and checked for an update.

"That total wanker," she fumed. "'Dive boat operator, AJ Bailey, informs me the artefact she and co-diver Reg Moore brought up from the sea floor yesterday is indeed an historical relic and has been sent out for professional archaeological examination.'"

"Strewth," Reg groaned. "When did the little prick post that?"

"Looks like yesterday afternoon. I'm surprised Thomas didn't see it and tell me, but I should have checked myself. I knew it wasn't good when he got off the call so fast."

Reg grumbled under his breath and scratched at his beard. "It was Pritchard I saw. I'm sure of it now."

"You think he saw this online?"

"I guarantee he has software doing that tracking, or data mining, or whatever the bloody hell it's called when it hunts the internet for certain words."

"Keywords," AJ said.

"Any words he wants tracked!" Reg growled.

"They're called keywords, you old goat. That's what he sets the software up to search for."

"Oh, all right. Keywords then."

"You can search for words, phrases, strings, all sorts."

"Yeah, that stuff," Reg continued. "I'm telling you, he's the type to have software like that. He has no problem showing up at someone else's site and pinching their find. The bugger saw that little shit's article and jumped on this morning's plane from Little."

"The article the other day mentioned where we'd placed the Reef Balls," AJ added. "So he wouldn't have a hard time finding us."

Reg thumped the steering wheel and AJ wondered how many times the poor wheel had been smacked by his big paw. He did it when he was laughing, and when he was pissed off. The steering wheel would probably just break in half one day, mid corner, and Reg would wonder why his car fell apart.

"We need to get the Maritime Heritage lot from the museum to mark off the area and put a Joint Marine Unit boat or at least a copper on the shore watching the site," Reg ranted on.

"And what exactly are we going to tell them?" AJ asked before he could carry on.

"What do you mean? We found some geezer's leg out there. They have to investigate."

"Yeah, I get that, but how do we explain that we found the hilt of a sword, didn't tell anyone, then went back out and plucked a thigh bone out of the sand before deciding to drop by and invite them to the party?"

Reg chuckled. "I don't know, love, but you better come up with a good reason, 'cos it's your name all over the internet!"

AJ thumped his arm, which made him laugh harder.

Reg parked on Shedden Road behind the businesses fronting the harbour, and AJ led him down a dark, narrow walkway between buildings and up a flight of outdoor stairs to a door on the first floor. A small sign read 'Cayman Islands National Museum Business Office'. Inside, a receptionist greeted them in a small entrance area.

"How may I help you?" the young lady asked, glancing up at the two people before her.

AJ was used to spending her days with damp hair, salty skin, and no make-up on or near the water, but she suddenly felt self-conscious looking so dishevelled in an office setting.

"We found this," Reg announced, and pulled the bone from the black rubbish bag he'd wrapped it in.

The young lady pushed her office chair back a few inches. "Oh, my…"

"It's all right, Miss," Reg added. "It won't bite yer."

"Is Mrs Wright here?" AJ quickly asked, before Reg scared the poor girl to death.

The receptionist nodded and scurried away down the hallway. Reg chuckled.

"Great start," AJ grumbled. "Can you not act like a bloody caveman when her ladyship…" The receptionist reappeared with an older lady in tow, and AJ briskly changed her tone. "Hello, Mrs Wright. It's lovely to see you again."

Gladys Wright looked them both over in disapproval, peering over her dainty reading glasses. "Miss Bailey. What have you done now?"

AJ felt like she was back in school, facing one of the frumpy old teachers who wished they could still use the cane. Reg held up the bone.

"Where did you take this from?" Gladys asked.

"We found it, and what we think is the hilt from a sword in Bluff Bay," AJ explained, trying to remain friendly. "We thought it best to bring the bone up from the bottom rather than risk it disappearing."

"Have you contacted the police?" she asked.

"No, we came straight to you," AJ replied, hoping the exact timing of the past two days wouldn't come to light.

"I believe you found the artefact two days ago, Miss Bailey, so *straight* to me isn't true, is it?" She didn't wait for a reply, and AJ cursed Carlson one more time. "Where is what you *believe to be* the hilt of a sword?"

"It's at Reg's house," AJ sheepishly replied.

Gladys let out a long sigh. "Well, the bone needs to be taken to the police, who will determine whether this is a law enforcement or archaeological matter, and the artefact is what you should have brought to me."

"Sure you don't want to have a butcher's at this first?" Reg said, holding the bone up in front of the museum director.

Unlike the receptionist, Gladys didn't flinch.

"Chain of custody, Mr Moore. There are strict rules to adhere to regarding human remains," she said, then turned to AJ. "As there are for artefacts found in Cayman Islands waters."

"Yes, Mrs Wright," AJ responded, looking at the floor.

"Be back here before 5:00pm with the artefact," she said sternly. "But not before you've been to the police station. Good day."

Mrs Gladys Wright turned and disappeared into her office down the hall, leaving the receptionist looking uncomfortable. Reg put the bone back in the bag and they thanked the girl before leaving.

"She still doesn't like you," Reg said as they trotted down the steps.

"She's got your number too, mate," AJ replied. "She already knew who you were."

"I noticed," he grunted. "But at least I didn't get summoned back to the headmistress's office."

15

THE STORM

1703

Mr Helms preferred not to discuss his time in the army, but over the next several months, we learnt more about the man, nugget by nugget, as examples came up in our training. He made it abundantly clear that his preference was always to avoid a fight and hoped we would follow that same creed. He often spoke of the burden and responsibility that came with taking another man's life. I heard and absorbed his words, but it would take time and events of a magnitude I couldn't have foreseen for me to truly understand his meaning.

My skills and strength continued to grow. We trained or practised most days for a short while, and Mother joined us when she could. We all enjoyed the focus on something other than the daily monotony of life on the island.

Often it rained for a short period in the late afternoons when the clouds built. Occasionally, we'd experienced strong winds and a day or two of rain, but nothing compared with the beating we took one day in the autumn. Angry dark clouds filled the horizon and cooler winds blew, swirling and shaking the trees.

Marcus and I joined Mr Helms and the other men at the beach, where we dragged the rowboats beyond the sand and fastened them to the trees with several lines. Mr Helms assumed the role of commander, with no complaint from anyone. He barked orders and directions, keeping everyone, black, white, male or female, on task.

We filled every available container with fresh water. We pulled lines to stakes in the ground from each corner of every hut. Furniture was shoved against the outside wattle and daub walls, which were already rattling and shaking in the wind.

When we'd secured the Negroes' huts, the three original huts in our camp, and Father's workers' newer raised hut as best we could, Mr Helms sent Mother and me home to make sure our own hut was secure. We rushed up the steps to find Father sitting at his desk. He'd dropped the window opening flaps. Nothing more.

"Monty! We have to secure the hut. Help us string the ropes outside," Mother urged.

"Nonsense," Father replied. "We've endured many storms. That idiot Helms has everyone stirred up in a fervour."

I looked at Mother, aghast.

"Are you mad?" she said, covered in dirt and sweat from our toils. "Look outside, Monty. We've never seen anything like this before."

Father leapt to his feet and thumped the desk with his fist, his cane clattering to the floor. "Do you take me for a fool, Davina?" he bellowed. "I know what's going on, damn you."

I was dumbfounded, and Mother appeared to be the same. We stood in stunned silence for a moment while the woven walls shook and the wind swirled around our home.

"What are you talking about, Monty?"

Father shook his head and started his finger wagging. "Don't lie to me, Davina! Do you think because I'm working all the time that I don't see what goes on outside this house? Well, I see everything!" he yelled, sweeping his hand around the room.

"What is it you think you've seen, Monty?"

Father was beside himself with rage. "It's your good fortune the death penalty no longer applies, but be sure I'll have you before a court on our return."

Mother threw her hands in the air. "I am at a loss to understand what on earth you're talking about, Monty. What is it I'm accused of?"

"You've made a cuckold of me, and I shall not stand for it!"

I had no idea what that word meant, so I was no wiser, but Mother clearly did, and her shock tipped over into anger.

"You damn fool, there's nothing going on inside or outside this house!"

"Helms!" Father screamed. "It's Helms, and I damn well know it!"

"That's ridiculous!" Mother countered.

Father stepped from behind his desk, and I saw his hand begin to raise. Mother didn't flinch, but I moved between them. Father tried to shove me aside, but he lacked the strength, and turned to me in surprise.

"Step aside, boy," he commanded.

"You'll not lay a finger on her, sir," I replied, surprised at the steadiness and resolve in my voice that had become deeper in recent months.

"You'll not talk back to me, boy. See, this is what comes from running amuck with commoners and Negroes," he shouted, pointing accusingly at Mother.

But he didn't try to push by me again. Instead, he returned to his seat and picked his cane up from the floor.

"Now leave me to work."

"You'll cast us outside our own home with this storm approaching?" Mother asked in disbelief.

Footfalls came from the steps and Mr Helms appeared in the doorway.

"Lord Crowe, we must secure your hut before the front reaches us. The men and I are here to assist you."

Father abruptly stood and glared across the room. I was unsure what would transpire next, and I'm ashamed to admit that I hoped Father would challenge Mr Helms. But he didn't.

"Do whatever you see fit," he growled, and sat back down.

Mother shook her head. "We'll help."

She followed Mr Helms, and I joined them outside. The winds were increasing and rain now fell, stinging our faces as it blew across the island. Gordy was already up a ladder, fastening a line to the corner of our hut. I couldn't believe my father was sitting inside, allowing everybody else on the island to make preparations. Even Marcus and his father, Nathaniel, were helping.

"You must push the furniture to the walls, Davina," Helms shouted over the storm. "You're going to lose your roof at some point. When that happens, the walls will be torn apart. Hunker down behind the heavy wooden furniture and pray God's hands keep us all safe."

I was helping pull a rope tight while Nathaniel hammered the stake into the ground, but I saw Mother look towards the hut. I wondered if Father would allow us to move his precious desk and guessed similar thoughts were crossing his wife's mind. She nodded to Helms and helped tighten the next rope.

With all we could do outside completed, I slapped Marcus on the back and wished him luck. He and his father disappeared into the hazy mist of the rain now falling hard.

"Your huts will flood," Mother pointed out to Mr Helms.

"Indeed, they will," he agreed. "But we'll be fine."

"Take refuge with us," she replied. "At least we're off the ground."

We all looked at the rivers of water already running through the camp and knew it would soon cover the ground completely.

"If it gets too bad, we'll join Gordy and Duck in their hut," Helms replied. "Now get inside and move your furniture."

"If he lets us," I said.

"It must be done," Helms insisted.

"We'll make sure of it, James. And don't worry about us. Wil and I will take care of each other."

We all shared a knowing look before Helms nodded and trudged through the water and mud to his hut. Mother and I returned to ours. Rain was already leaking through any crack or hole it could find and dripped mercilessly down on our floor. Father had cleared his desk of paperwork.

"We must move the desk, chests of drawers, wardrobe, and beds, Monty," Mother said.

Father looked up, his jaw clenched. I was sure he would continue his mad tirade, but instead he stood and moved to one end of his desk. I took the other end, and we slid the heavy oak desk to the west wall. In turn, we manoeuvred each piece of furniture to the walls, trying to leave only small gaps between them.

The roof, which was densely woven palm fronds over wooden rafters, was beginning to pant as though a giant's hand was pumping on it from above.

"We need more rope," I blurted, and ran to the door.

"Don't go outside!" Mother yelled, but I was already fighting the door closed from the steps.

The storm had gathered more strength and the rain now fell in sheets of water, which cascaded from the rooftops to be whipped in a frenzy across the camp. I squinted against the stinging spray and crawled under the house. Water covered my legs, and I prayed the men had sought shelter in the second raised hut. Marcus, his family, and the people in the other camp would not be much better off. They'd constructed their huts in a similar style, except they were raised a foot or more on a rock foundation. They'd be lucky to stay dry.

I fumbled in the water until I found the last length of rope we possessed. Scurrying out, I struggled to stand against the wind. This was not a day I wished to be on the high seas. Sunset was still hours away, yet I could barely see the other huts around us. Branches, leaves, and other debris flew past me and disappeared into the murky distance.

Fighting with the wooden door to our hut, I managed to slip inside and fasten it behind me with help from Mother.

"A chair," I said as I uncoiled the rope.

Father brought a dining chair to me and I stood upon it, stretching to reach the ridge beam of the roof. It took some effort to force the line between the wood and the palm thatch, but once it was through, I jumped from the chair and handed one end to Mother, who now understood my plan. I wished for some form of anchor through the hefty floor joists, but settled for strapping the rope to the furniture.

Cutting the excess line, we repeated the operation at the other end of the hut, where the dividing wall split the tiny bedrooms. I couldn't imagine the woven palm leaves would hold, but perhaps we could save the frame and avoid the roof being stripped away as one.

Each time into the evening and night I decided the storm could not possibly worsen, it did. The fronds began disappearing from above us, unseen in the darkness. Once the wind could penetrate the hut, the front door and the window flaps were wrenched free. It was wetter and louder with them gone, but I noticed the structure shook less when the wind didn't have to fight to reach us.

The roof frame held, and in the middle of the night, the storm abated, leaving a firm wind and occasional rain showers. Soaked through and completely exhausted, we slept until daylight shone through our decimated roof, causing steam to rise from every waterlogged surface.

I quietly stepped to the doorway and surveyed the damage in awe. The roofs were gone from every hut except ours. The first dwelling on the end was a crumpled ruin, but the other two were standing. Across the camp, our workers' raised hut was roofless but otherwise intact. The water level had already subsided, leaving the sodden ground littered with natural debris.

Hearing the sounds of someone stirring in our hut, I turned. Mother softly moved across the room and stood beside me.

"Looks like we have a busy day ahead," she said, resting a hand on my shoulder.

My eyes wandered to the back of the hut from where Father had not yet appeared.

"Don't worry about him," Mother said. "I'll sort everything out."

I managed a smile. I believed she would, because I believed my mother was capable of taking care of everything.

16

SHORT PEOPLE

Present Day

Detective Roy Whittaker was a tall, thin man, with close-cropped salt and pepper hair, glasses, and light brown skin. Born and raised on the island, he'd been a policeman since the day he'd graduated from college. Now in his late fifties, he could take retirement any time he chose, but he found himself perpetually saying 'next year', and that year hadn't happened yet.

If Mrs Wright was hoping the police would be as tough on AJ and Reg as she'd been, she was mistaken. The two divers were often called in to help the police when underwater work was involved, especially tech diving, so they were all well acquainted with each other. Whittaker and his wife were also Pearl's biggest fans and rarely missed her Friday night performances at the Fox and Hare.

"Afternoon, Roy," Reg greeted his friend, and the detective stood from behind his desk and shook the big man's hand, then AJ's.

"Good afternoon," he responded brightly, "I have to say, your phone call has me intrigued. What can I do for you?"

"We found something you might want to have Rasha take a look at," AJ said, and Reg placed the plastic bag on Whittaker's desk.

When AJ had called from the car to make sure the detective was in his office, she'd avoided giving any details, preferring to present their story face to face.

Whittaker peeked inside the bag. "Is that what I think it is?" he asked, looking up at AJ.

"If you're thinking it's a human thigh bone, then yes, that's what our guess is," AJ replied.

Whittaker hit the speaker button on his desk and dialled an extension. It rang a few times before an English woman answered.

"Hi Roy, what's up?"

"Rasha, do you have a minute to come to my office? I have something for you, courtesy of AJ and Reg."

There was a brief chuckle over the line. "Is it whatever they found a few days back?"

The detective looked at AJ and Reg in puzzlement.

"No," AJ replied. "But we think it could be related."

"Well, this report I've been working on all day isn't going anywhere," Rasha replied. "So yes, I can come upstairs. I'll be there in a minute."

"Thanks," Whittaker responded, and hung up.

"Half the bloody island knows, thanks to that gormless prat, Carlson," AJ muttered.

"I must be part of the other half," the detective said with a smirk. "What are we talking about?"

AJ took a deep breath, then told Whittaker all about their find, Buck Reilly's preliminary identification of the sword hilt, and their subsequent dive that day. She left out the part about Reg's suspected Stone Pritchard sighting, and Reg didn't offer it up. As she finished telling their story, Rasha, the head scene of crime officer or SOCO - the island's version of CSI - walked into the office.

"What have you two been up to now?" she said with a grin.

"Why does everyone think we've been up to no good all the time?" AJ said, laughing.

Rasha and the detective looked at each other and chuckled. "If the shoe fits, my dear..." Whittaker said, "...if the shoe fits."

He slid the black rubbish bag across to the edge of the desk, and Rasha slipped on a fresh pair of nitrile gloves. She opened the bag without hesitation and held the bone up for examination.

"Don't suppose you've kept your mitts off this, have you?" she asked.

"Bit difficult, love," Reg replied. "We brought it up from 30 feet underwater."

"Was there any more of this unfortunate person down there?" Rasha asked.

Reg shrugged his shoulders. "No idea. Once we found part of him, we figured it was time to come see you."

"Is it human?" Whittaker asked.

Rasha nodded. "Thigh bone." She looked at Reg. "Why do you think it's male?"

"I don't," he replied after considering the question for a moment. "I suppose I was making an assumption. Is it female?"

"Hard to tell sometimes, especially in older bones," Rasha replied, turning the femur over in her gloved hands. "We go by weight, length, head diameter, and sometimes females have a third trochanter."

"So you think it's old?" AJ asked excitedly.

Rasha nodded. "We'll carbon date to get a better idea, but yes, I'd say it's quite old and has been underwater for a while, or more accurately, buried in the sand for a long time."

"Blimey," Reg grunted. "How can you tell all that?"

Rasha grinned. "Because if it had been above the sea floor, it would be sanded down by years of movement, or more likely decomposed completely. Same on land, unless it was buried in neutral-pH soil or sand. But that's all supposition. It'll take me a while to confirm anything concrete, and I'll need to confer with our forensic pathologist in the UK."

"Do we have good reason to open an investigation, Rasha?" Whittaker asked. "Or do you think this is old enough that we're talking about an archaeological project?"

"I wouldn't open a new case based on what I see here," she replied, slipping the bone back into the bag. "More than likely, this belongs to a local who was buried in one of the cemeteries near the water. Probably flushed out by a hurricane at some point; we've lost more than a few bodies that way."

"I dare say you're right," Whittaker agreed.

"It's not that big, is it?" AJ observed. "Do you really think it could be female?"

Rasha slipped the gloves off and dropped them into a rubbish bin next to the desk. "Depends on the age of the person and the time period. In the Middle Ages the average person was the height we are now, but in the years between, that number went down considerably and then increased again. The current trend suggests we're getting shorter once more."

"I'm skewing the data that way," AJ complained. She was five foot three.

Rasha laughed. "Me too." She was about the same. "The island didn't have too many residents until later into the 1700s, and at that time, a man who was five foot six would not have been considered short. A woman of that height would, however, be referred to as tall. It's possible that without more of the skeleton, we might not be certain of sex. Where's the artefact you found? Was it from the same place?"

"It's at Reg's house," AJ admitted. "Bluff Bay on the north side. We found the two things within 50 feet of each other."

"What is it?" Rasha asked.

"We think it's the hilt of a sword," AJ replied. "But we'd prefer to keep that quiet."

Rasha grinned. "Probably shouldn't have told that reporter bloke about it then."

AJ groaned. "He's making shit up. I didn't tell him anything."

Reg grunted and looked at AJ with an eyebrow raised.

"What? I didn't tell him! I just didn't lie to him. He made it up from there."

"So I assume he made up the part about it being sent out," Rasha said, "seeing as it's at Reg's gaff."

Reg laughed and AJ punched his arm.

"Okay, so I stretched the truth about that, but that's probably what will happen once we hand it over to the museum."

"Speaking of which," Reg said, tapping his watch, "it's gone four."

"Bugger," AJ groaned. "We have to go. I have to deliver the hilt to her ladyship over at the museum by five."

"Mrs Wright?" Whittaker asked.

"The one and only," Reg said, getting to his feet. "If AJ here doesn't hand her homework in on time, she'll be in detention for weeks."

"Then you best hurry," Roy said, standing to bid them farewell. "I wouldn't want to be on the wrong side of that lady."

"I'm so far on her wrong side she has to send a courier to give me my assignments," AJ griped as they left the detective's office.

The director of the Cayman Islands National Museum had not warmed to them by the time they entered her office at ten minutes to five. AJ handed over the bucket, newly replenished with soapy fresh water.

"You've attempted your own restoration, I see," Gladys said, staring at the artefact.

"You'd think us silly bringing you a lump of concretion and suggesting it might be something of historic value," AJ replied, having prepared a better argument this time. "We had to make a basic identification before troubling you. Hence the slight delay."

To AJ's annoyance, the director didn't appear to hear a word as she'd put on a pair of nitrile gloves and was studying the sword hilt.

"It's bronze," Gladys stated, more in narration than to the other two people in the room. "Marvellous engraving." She carefully inspected the pommel end. "Hmm."

AJ and Reg looked at each other and both shrugged their shoulders. Neither had any idea whatever it was the woman had spotted.

"See something interesting, Mrs Wright?" AJ asked.

The director looked up, seemingly startled that AJ and Reg were still there. "Oh, well, hmm," she mumbled, then held the pommel towards them. "I was just noting this is not the talwar the other fellow was asking about."

"Tal-whatty?" AJ asked.

Gladys gave her another disappointed look over her glasses. "A tal-wah, Miss Bailey. It's a design of sword from India. Perhaps you've heard of the Blade of Calcutta?"

17

THE RETURN

1703

The task of rebuilding felt overwhelming, but as usual, Mr Helms organised everyone and by the end of the first day, with the debris cleared from around the camp, it seemed achievable. Father helped pick up the mess around our hut and take down the ropes, but by noon he'd returned to his desk complaining about his gout. No one was sorry to see him go. Despite the brightening skies, Father's presence held a black cloud over the camp, and spirits raised when he went inside.

It also allowed Mother and me to visit the other camp to check on Marcus and his family. Their dwellings had fared a little better than ours, and they'd already cleared the area around their huts of debris. They were appreciative we'd come by to see them and immediately offered to help us in any way they could. Mother declined, knowing they had plenty still to do themselves, but Nathaniel, Marcus, and another man, who was Nathaniel's brother and Nelly's husband, insisted on returning with us.

Mr Helms welcomed the help. As the huts required much rebuilding, he'd decided to take the opportunity of raising them above the ground. This required the felling of lumber and the time-consuming process of forming planks for the floor. All the men would sleep in the raised hut while the work took place, so efforts were focused on repairs to Gordy and Duck's dwelling, as well as ours, for the rest of the day.

Mother sensibly made sure Mr Helms was not helping patch our roof, but Father still looked on in disapproval as the two Negro men weaved palm fronds into a thatch while Mother, Marcus and I gathered materials for them. Nathaniel and his brother worked faster than we could keep them in supplies, so they rehung the door which we'd found at the edge of camp, and rebuilt the window flaps while we scavenged fronds.

Shortly before sunset, a group of us walked to the beach to check on the rowboats. The tethers had held, but one of the boats had sustained damage from flying debris and would require repairs to be seaworthy again. White caps peppered the open ocean, but the waters closer to the island had already settled. Our coastline was littered with everything and anything the seas could deliver to the land. The odd patch of sand or ironshore was visible through the seaweed and sodden foliage, along with a few sections of wooden planking and a log we guessed had formerly been a mast.

Before we left the beach, I surveyed the horizon, considering the fate of the poor sailors whose ship had donated these pieces. As I scanned the deep blue water, I thought I could see a dark spot far out to sea, but I wasn't sure enough to say anything. Mother spoke a quick prayer for those who'd weathered the storm on the ocean, and we excitedly carried our prizes back to the camp.

The next morning brought clear blue skies and a gentle breeze. If it weren't for the labours awaiting us, it would have been easy to forget the storm had ever happened. The porous limestone had consumed the standing water and our clothes had finally dried out.

The lagoon level was higher than usual, and I wondered whether the onslaught of fresh water would affect the salt production. But the salt would have to wait. There was far too much left to be done.

Father complained about Gordy and Duck being utilised outside of his business needs, but fortunately his protests were confined to Mother and me. Neither of us responded, as the fight would have been pointless. I had no notion whether Mother had convinced him of her innocence with regard to Mr Helms, but neither of them broached the subject in my presence, so I assumed she had appeased him.

The men sawed the broken mast we'd retrieved from the beach into pieces, making nine pilings, three short of what we needed. We felled a sturdy tree from the woods to complete the shortfall. The new constructions would be slightly smaller than before, so four pilings per dwelling would provide enough support for the floor structure. Mr Helms wisely took council from Nathaniel and utilised many of the design features which had helped keep the Negroes' huts standing.

By the afternoon, with all hands on deck - except my father's of course - we had the floors ready on two of the rebuilds and the third close to being done. It was hot, sweaty work, but everyone was surprisingly cheerful and glad of the community help. Mr Helms instructed Marcus and me to return to the beach in search of more materials, and to scavenge along the whole western coast.

We walked through the narrow band of trees, past the rowboats, and stopped in our tracks when we reached the sand. The dot I thought I'd seen on the horizon hadn't been an apparition or figment of my imagination. It was a ship, which was now heading towards Salt Cay.

"Too soon for da merchant ship," Marcus said, reflecting my own thoughts.

I strained to make out the sail arrangement, but the vessel was still too far out to see clearly.

"Could be da *Royal Fortune*," Marcus said, once again mirroring my deduction... or simply my hope.

"We'll know by this evening," I replied, trying to keep my excitement in check.

"We should tell da udders," he said, ready to run back to camp.

"Not yet," I responded. "We have plenty of time before they reach us. We should do as Mr Helms asked first."

Marcus reluctantly agreed, and we began scouring the beach for more useful materials. We were both moving faster than the heat and our task warranted, and we chattered the whole time, speculating about the ship and its purpose.

"Dey could be Spanish," Marcus blurted, pausing his searching and shielding his eyes against the sun. "Dem wood swords ain't gonna do us no good if dey Spanish."

He was right. Mr Helms had diligently trained us, yet our skills were useless without a weapon to brandish. It was a subject we'd discussed but hadn't felt an urgency to resolve. Mr Helms and Mother intended to trade for cutlasses with one of the merchant ships, or pay them to bring swords next month. That vague plan felt desperately inadequate with a strange vessel approaching our shore.

Our necks were getting sore, hunting the shoreline one moment and staring out to sea the next, as though a sudden freak wind could have blown the ship to us. Steadily, it grew bigger as it neared, and I noted they were trimmed with only the mainsail and the foremast topsail unfurled. An odd configuration by my limited knowledge.

"I think it's the *Royal Fortune*," I shouted to Marcus, who was ahead of me.

He climbed up an ironshore outcrop for a better view.

"Why don't dey have all da sails up?"

I shook my head. "I don't know. Perhaps they're drying everything out after the storm."

It was a wild guess on my part, but Marcus seemed happy with the explanation and we quickly finished our scavenge to the southern tip of the island. On the way back, we gathered all the wood we had set aside until our arms were full. Most we'd found were dense, weathered branches which we knew would make good rafters or studs, but we did find a few more sections of planking.

Dead tired, we stumbled back into camp and dropped the wood near the newly reconstructed huts. The men had finished the third hut's floor structure and were working on repairing and adjusting the size of the walls which had survived.

"There's a ship approaching, sir," I told Mr Helms.

He paused from tying two poles together with twine and looked up. "Do you recognise the vessel?"

"It's da *Royal Fortune*, sir," Marcus blurted excitedly before I could reply.

Mother joined us. "The privateers have returned?"

"Perhaps," I quickly clarified. "It's hard to tell for certain at a distance, looking straight down the bow. They're also running light on sails."

"They would have been lucky to survive the storm in open water, Wil," Helms responded. "It was all a tempest could be short of a hurricane. They may well have damage and are seeking safe harbour for repairs."

Weathering the storm on land was terrifying enough. I couldn't imagine contending with wild seas to boot. The planks we found could well be from a ship which had succumbed to the wrath of the ocean.

"Will you stay wit us again, Miss?" Marcus asked, looking at Mother.

"I don't think it's necessary," she replied. "Everybody said they were pleasant enough."

"You're most welcome to stay wit us, Lady Crowe," Nathaniel said without stopping his work.

Mother looked at me and smiled, but I now questioned my assurances of the pirates' placidity. What if Mr Helms was right, and Badger and his shipmates saw a woman as a bounty worth taking?

"Davina, I must stress the need for caution in these circumstances," Mr Helms said. "Who knows what state of mind these men may arrive in?"

"I'm not even sure it's them," I added. "It could be Spaniards and we'll all need to hide."

"Then let us see as they approach closer," Mother replied, which I knew was her way of placating us with an eye for getting her way.

"We won't know until morning, Mother. They'll be at anchor after dark. It's best you stay with Bess tonight in case they try to come ashore before morning."

"I agree with Wil," Mr Helms said before Mother could protest. "I'll take a look before dark and be at the beach for first light. Once we know they're friend, not foe, Wil can come get you."

"Very well," Mother relented. "Then best we put our backs into this until dark, as you may be short-handed tomorrow."

"What if dey are Spanish?" Marcus asked. "We ain't all got cutlasses to fight dem."

"Cutlasses or not, young Marcus, we'll be heavily outnumbered. If they fly a Spanish flag, we shall conceal the women as best we can and throw ourselves upon the mercy of their captain."

"We ain't gonna try to defend da island?"

"The island is but sand and trees, my lad. There's plenty more like it. These fine people I see before me are not so easily replaceable, so yes, rather than face certain defeat, I suggest we present ourselves as peaceful labourers who bear no aggression to any nation." He turned to the other men, who were all now listening. "How say you?"

Gordy spoke up. "I'm not opposed to your approach, sir. I believe it has merit. But I shall hide my cutlass close by. If they choose hostility, I'd rather die with a blade in my hand than without."

"Aye," Duck grunted. "Might take one or two of them with us."

Helms held up a hand. "That's fair, gentlemen. But my sword will be in Wil's hand," he said, and my eyes widened. "As I'm likely to be the one greeting these rogues, I expect I'll fall first and be your cue for action. Hiding my blade will be a waste of steel."

My stomach twisted into knots, but I nodded to the man I respected far more than my own father.

18

THE BRAVEST CAPTAIN

Present Day

Gladys Wright moved some papers and looked under the numerous piles of books, files, and unopened letters on her desk. AJ had no doubt the woman was a stickler for procedures and rules when it came to historical items themselves, but her office looked more like a tornado had tossed everything around the room.

"He gave me a card," she mumbled, rummaging through a drawer. "Ahh, here it is."

She handed a business card across the desk to Reg, who frowned.

"Archaeological researcher," Reg groaned. "He's got some bloody nerve."

"I take it my visitor was the gentleman you mentioned?"

"It's him, all right," Reg confirmed.

AJ and Reg had told Gladys about Stone Pritchard and the rumours he'd been hunting for something on Little Cayman. The director had become more curious with the possibility a treasure hunter with a dubious past was searching in Cayman Islands waters. It took a murdering thief to do it, but for the first time, AJ didn't feel like the bad guy in Gladys's eyes.

"He gave me the sense he knew more than he was letting on," the director explained. "According to him, he's conducting research for a book about missing artefacts in the Caribbean."

"Did he ask about us or what we'd found the day before?" Reg asked.

"Not at all, no, and I didn't know anything about it until you two came by earlier."

"But he was asking about this Blade of Calcutta?" AJ asked.

"Yes, and I told him all I knew, which was very little. As I said, he gave me the impression he had more knowledge on the subject than I could recall. There's very little to go on, which is no doubt why it's never been found."

"What do we know about it, then?" Reg asked. "I thought I knew most of the rumoured treasures still out there, especially in the Cayman Islands, but I'd never heard of this blade business."

Gladys sat back in her chair. The ice had been broken, and now she seemed to AJ like an expert eager to discuss her chosen field she was passionate about.

"What we know comes from two sources," she began. "The first is in regard to the talwar itself. There are written records and accounts of the sword being crafted in Bengal, which is the region now known as Bangladesh and the eastern part of India, then presented to the English governor at Fort William. This was before the British ruled India, and in the early 18th century, the Bengal leaders gave control of three coastal villages to the English to encourage the East India Company to continue trading.

"The English built the fort, and the villages grew to become one. Originally called Kolkata, the English renamed the town Calcutta, and as I'm sure you know, the city reverted to its native name in modern times."

AJ found the history lesson fascinating, but her foot tapped on the floor in anticipation of Gladys getting to the part involving the Cayman Islands.

"The Bengal ruler had the talwar forged and decorated by his finest craftsmen, and presented it to Charles Eyre, the English governor. A talwar has a curved blade, not unlike a cutlass, and this one had a solid gold hilt and scabbard decoration, all ornately engraved. A ring of rubies was set into the pommel, capped off with a very large stone in the centre. I believe the blade was bronze, rather than steel. It was worth a tidy sum at the time, but with its provenance, it would be priceless today.

Eyre, wishing to ingratiate himself with Queen Anne, decided in turn to gift her the talwar, and sent it to England on the East India Company ship the *Brackley*. The unfortunate captain… whose name I don't recall…"

"How on earth can you remember all this other stuff?" AJ blurted. "I'm still working on saying talwar properly, leave alone the captain's name of some ship from the 1700s!"

Gladys smiled, an expression AJ wasn't sure the woman had possessed until that moment. "I admit, I read more details in my file after Mr Pritchard left."

"You have your own file about this?" Reg asked.

"Of course," Gladys replied. "So I suppose the correct statement was that I told him all I could recall at the time. Anyway, where was I? Oh, the *Brackley*, that's right. From the captain's report of his trip home, he was separated from the fleet during a storm and then attacked by a Spanish galleon in the Atlantic. The *Cielos de Oro* took their payload of spices, fabrics, and of course, the talwar sword destined for the Queen of England. Its captain then set them free.

"From there, the Spaniards sailed for Cuba but were themselves attacked by an English privateer ship, the name of which we don't know. A battle at dawn ensued, both ships taking heavy damage from cannon fire. The *Cielos de Oro* delivered a fatal blow to the privateers just as a second pirate ship arrived on the scene. The *Royal Fortune* was a smaller ship and would normally have been outgunned by the Spaniards, but the galleon was crippled. According to their report, the *Royal Fortune* was captained by a wily man who cleverly kept the English ship clear of the Spanish cannons, while using their own few weapons to great effect.

"The Spaniards surrendered, and the cargo from India was loaded into the hold of yet another ship. The English captain was a man named Crowe who we know very little about, and the fate of the *Royal Fortune* and its cargo became mostly a mystery from that moment on."

Gladys finally took a few breaths and AJ tried her best to absorb the story, still wondering what any of this had to do with the Cayman Islands.

"Mostly?" Reg questioned.

Gladys leaned forward in her chair. "This is the part which has stumped everyone who has ever searched for the Blade of Calcutta. A man by the name of William Crowe wrote a book in 1718 titled *The Bravest Captain*. This book supposedly tells his tale of his time as a teenage boy in the Caribbean."

"He's the son of the captain?" AJ asked.

"Correct," Gladys replied and then continued. "But all we have are a few references to the book's existence, but not one copy of the book itself. Charles Eyre, the English governor from Fort William, upon hearing of the *Brackley's* demise, wrote a letter to Queen Anne a year later, explaining the loss and expressing his apologies."

"Still trying to get credit for sending it, no doubt," Reg chuckled.

"Possibly," Gladys continued. "But in the letter, which survived and is part of a collection held in the British Library, he named the sword the Blade of Calcutta, which is the first reference we have to that moniker."

"Okay," AJ said, "but I'm still missing the link between all of this and what we found, or a connection to the Cayman Islands."

Gladys nodded. "There's a final piece to the puzzle. In 1921, an English explorer by the name of Christopher Michael Alpers, who'd retired from the British Navy after WWI, documented his search for the legendary talwar. He maintained diaries, in which he notes phrases and references from William Crowe's book."

"He had a copy?" Reg asked.

"It appears so," Gladys confirmed. "But Alpers, along with most of his diaries, his copy of the book, and two men he'd hired to help him, were lost at sea when they were caught in a storm returning by boat to Jamaica from Grand Cayman."

"Again, we have 'mostly'," Reg pointed out.

"Alpers's wife, Kate, had two of his early diaries at their home in England, which she kept private until a few years before her death in 1987. Those contained mainly personal thoughts and admirations for his wife, hence her reluctance to share them with the world, but also several of his initial entries in regards to the Blade of Calcutta and quotes from *The Bravest Captain*."

"Where are these diaries now?" AJ asked.

Gladys shuffled in her chair. "One is in the National Maritime Museum in Greenwich, London, where to my knowledge it is archived."

"Could you get access to it, or copies of the contents?" AJ asked. "Surely the pages are on the internet somewhere? Everything's on the internet."

Gladys shook her head. "None of the contents from the diaries are online, deliberately so at the request of Alpers's estate."

"And they're not on display?" AJ asked.

"No doubt one day they will be, but as I say, to my knowledge, they're currently archived and have been since 1987."

"Why all the secrecy if Kate Alpers made them available? I thought the idea behind a museum was to display historical artefacts and information?"

Gladys thought for a moment. "It was Kate's stipulation. They weren't to be displayed until the Blade of Calcutta was found."

"Kinda hard when she had the best clues to find it," AJ scoffed.

Gladys allowed her lips to curl into a brief smile.

"What is it you're not telling us?" Reg asked with a matching smirk. "You said the maritime museum has one of the diaries, but there's two still in existence, right?"

The director sighed and looked back and forth between AJ and

Reg. "I don't know why I'm going to share this with you, but something tells me it's time."

"Tell us what?" AJ blurted in anticipation. "You can trust us."

Gladys raised an eyebrow. "Perhaps."

"You have the second diary, don't you?" Reg said with a grin.

"Kate Alpers," Gladys began, "who was a frequent visitor to the Cayman Islands over the years, approached me a few years before her passing to discuss how best to preserve the diaries. I suggested the two locations for ultimate security against theft and natural disaster. She granted me permission to allow access to the pages, if and only when I felt a genuine effort and interest in recovering the Blade of Calcutta presented itself. Not for financial gain, but for the sake of history and preservation."

"Blimey," Reg muttered. "And you told Pritchard about all this?"

"When I said I'd told him all I could recall, I might have exaggerated, Mr Moore, but I still hadn't decided how much to share with the two of you."

AJ sat up straight in her chair. "I can speak for both of us, Mrs Wright, when I say how honoured we are to be entrusted with this information," she said proudly.

Gladys sighed. "That's lovely, Miss Bailey. But to be honest, I'm going to show you the diaries based purely on my concerns regarding this man, Stone Pritchard. I did a little digging after he left, and from what I can see from online articles, your assessment of his insincerity and ill intent for any artefacts recovered is accurate. I'm entrusting you with this information with the sole goal of keeping the Blade of Calcutta and anything else of historical value out of his hands."

"Oh," AJ said. "But you'll let us see what you have?"

"Reluctantly, and with your solemn oath you'll not repeat this information to anyone... yes."

19

NEW MAN

1703

The stars in the eastern sky disappeared when the first hint of morning tinted the horizon. It was still pitch black amongst the trees and as my eyes adjusted, I could make out the profile of a ship at anchor, barely silhouetted in the moonless night.

I'd hardly slept at all. Father had gone on another tirade when we told him Mother was to stay with Bess and Nathaniel. He'd even suggested she was using the ruse to spend the night with Mr Helms. Mother pointed out that Nathaniel and Marcus were waiting outside to escort her to the other camp, but he seemed convinced it was all part of a grand plan to deceive him.

Mother had finally left with his cruel words chasing her out the door, his cane waving in the air, and spittle flying from his mouth. Once she'd gone, he'd turned and glared at me. I'd quickly retired to my tiny corner of the hut and not another word was spoken that night.

Hearing a rustle behind me, I crouched low. "Declare yourself."

"It's me, Wil," came Mr Helms's whisper as his form appeared from the woods. "Any sign of movement?"

"No, sir," I replied, rising to my feet. "And still too dark to be sure whose ship it is."

"A few more minutes and we'll be able to see," Helms said, leaning against a palm. "They won't be able to see us here in the shadows until after sunrise."

Those few minutes seemed to take forever, but he was right. In the morning twilight, the ship became clear enough to identify, but we felt safe in the dark cover of the trees.

It was the *Royal Fortune*, and she looked battered. The masts were intact, but several of the yards appeared damaged and the rigging was a mess. It indeed appeared they'd limped to the island with the only working sails they had. I took a step forward, but his hand stopped me.

"Let them come to us, Wil. Who knows what their temperament might be after what I can only imagine was an arduous ordeal?"

To me, his caution felt unnecessary, but I wasn't about to argue with the man, so I relented.

"Go to the other camp and tell them it is the privateers who were here before," Helms instructed me. "We will send further word when it's safe."

"Yes, sir," I said, although I'd have much preferred to remain on the beach and greet Badger and the other men.

The only person who knew every trail, path, and shortcut anywhere on the island as well as I was Marcus. It didn't take me long to emerge from the woods, and I wasn't surprised to see most of the camp was already awake and busy. Nathaniel looked at me nervously and Marcus ran to greet me.

"It's the *Royal Fortune*," I announced. "No one has come ashore as yet, but Mr Helms asked us to stay hidden for now."

Nathaniel nodded, but still looked concerned. I figured everyone would share my excitement at seeing the pirates again, but it seemed I was alone in my relief. Marcus stood looking at me as though he was about to speak, yet no words were forthcoming.

"What's the matter with you?" I asked, slightly annoyed.

"It was her idea, Wil, I swear. We not havin' nuttin' to do wit dis."

The sun was clearing the horizon, ramping up the heat, and I was in no mood for guessing games.

"What are you babbling about?"

"Come see," Marcus said, and led me to the far side of his family's hut. My mother sat on a stool while Bess wielded a knife in her hands. Clumps of my mother's beautiful rich brown hair lay piled on the ground.

"What are you doing?" I asked both women.

Bess stepped back and looked as nervous as Nathaniel and Marcus had been.

"Bess is cutting my hair for me, Wil. Don't make a fuss."

"Make a fuss?" I said and laughed, although I wasn't seeing much humour in the situation. "The fuss will come when Father sees this."

"I expect you're right, so don't you scare Bess half to death. It took a lot of convincing to get her to do it."

"I am sorry, sir, but your mama insist," Bess said, holding the knife out of sight as though that would distance her from the event.

"But why, Mother?"

"If only men can be seen in camp, then only men they shall see, Wil."

I looked at her, sitting on the stool. "I think your dress might give you away."

She waved a hand at me. "Don't be silly. I have trousers and a man's shirt to put on."

I wasn't sure when she'd come up with this barmy idea, but apparently she'd put some thought into it.

"But Mother, you're obviously a woman," I said, talking myself into an embarrassing corner. "I mean… you have womanly parts…" I felt my cheeks flushing red. "And you're a beautiful lady. You'll never pass as a man."

Nathaniel and Marcus both turned away, even more uncomfortable than I. Mother just laughed.

"Good Lord, Wil. God didn't gift me with an ample bosom like Bess here. We can hide these," she replied, holding a hand to her chest. "And as for my looks, you'll be surprised what a little dirt and a hat will achieve. Now stand back while Bess finishes."

I stumbled rather than stepped back, lost for words. My mother was a determined woman when her mind was set, and it appeared her mind was firmly set. I dreaded the quarrel we faced when Father saw what she'd done. I sighed and turned away, walking with Marcus to the trees at the west edge of camp.

"I ain't never seen no lady do her best to look like a man before," Marcus said.

"How do you know that?" I replied, wondering if she could truly fool a stranger.

"'Cos I tellin' you, I ain't never seen it," Marcus reiterated.

"Unless someone successfully achieved the deception," I pointed out. "In which case you wouldn't know you'd seen a woman dressed as a man."

Marcus thought for a moment. "I accidentally seen my mama wit no clothes one time, and I see my papa when we wash. I sayin', dere ain't no way I mixing up da two."

I laughed. "Well, I believe Mother's plan is to remain fully clothed, so perhaps she can affect the duplicity."

Marcus looked at me and frowned.

"Trick everyone," I explained.

"Oh," he said. "Dis I gotta see."

I moved into the woods. "Come on. Let's see if the men have left the ship yet."

It didn't take us long to wind our way through the trees to the once sandy beach. We crouched behind the rowboats and watched the activity on the *Royal Fortune*. Men climbed all over the rigging and shouts rang out across the water as commands and directions were given. A cockboat rested in amongst the weed and detritus on the beach, tethered to the nearest palm.

"Someone's ashore," I said, and we moved east through the woods until we could see our camp.

Mr Helms was working on his hut with his men. Captain Rochefort stood nearby, talking with them, but he appeared to be the only one in the camp.

"He didn't row himself to da beach," Marcus commented, and I felt he had a point.

It was possible to row the cockboat alone, but it would be unwieldy, and unusual for a captain to undertake. It was likely at least one more of his men was with him somewhere. We sat and watched in silence for a while, waiting to know who else was around. If I went into camp, it meant Marcus had to leave and return to his, so I felt obligated to take my time.

Father's workers were out of sight, but I could hear their voices every once in a while and guessed they were at the lagoon. Their boss likely had them recovering whatever salt piles they could instead of aiding the rest of the community.

Father appeared at the steps of our hut and slipped away into the woods without the others noticing. He didn't even acknowledge them on his return from relieving himself.

I was about to tell Marcus to head home when another figure appeared from the far side of camp. It was one of the pirates, but I didn't recognise him. I thought they'd all been ashore during their last stay, but some only briefly, so it wasn't surprising the man didn't strike me as familiar.

"Dere's da udder rower," Marcus whispered. "You know dat one?"

"No," I replied as the new man approached Mr Helms and Rochefort.

He lifted his wide-brimmed black hat as though introducing himself. He was shorter than both men and leanly built, with a confident gait and a pistol tucked in one side of his belt and a dagger in the other.

"Stone the crows," I muttered, and stood up, still concealed by the shrubs.

"Maybe dat fellow not wit da ship last time dey here."

"That's a fact," I replied without taking my eyes from the group of men.

"You going into camp?" Marcus asked.

I nodded.

"What I tell your mama when I get back?"

I turned to my friend. "I don't think she's in your camp, Marcus," I said, tipping my head towards the new pirate. "That's my mother."

Marcus shuffled closer than I considered safe to the edge of the woods. "Dat ain't your mama."

"Stay hidden," I said firmly, and walked out into the open.

Everybody looked my way as I approached, then returned to their conversation. As I reached the group, Rochefort nodded. "Ah, Wil, how did you fare in the storm? Mr Helms and your father were just telling me about it. Looks like you've all whipped the place back into shape."

I felt all eyes were upon me. Captain Rochefort was expecting a conversational response, and the four others wondering how I'd react. Helms's men seemed baffled by the circumstances, and I couldn't look at Mother. It was simply too strange.

"Scary to be sure, sir, but everyone has pitched in and our camp will be better equipped if it happens again."

"Your father was telling me about the tethers you strung inside the hut to hold down the roof," Mr Helms said, as though we were having a normal conversation as we often did. "That was quick thinking, Wil. We'll have extra rope ready next time."

I managed a smile, but I felt my cheeks flush. Hopefully, they all thought it was the compliment, but only I knew I'd sneaked a glance at my mother. I was having trouble accepting how effectively she'd become a man.

20

PEBBLES

Present Day

AJ sat at a table and slowly read the page before her. It was dark outside, and they only had a few minutes more until Gladys was kicking her and Reg out for the night. The director had brought out her copies of the first diary, which was the one archived in England. The sheets were high resolution photographs of the pages, subsequently printed on archival A4 paper. Even so, Christopher Alpers's penmanship stood him in good stead to have been a doctor if he'd chosen such a path.

"This isn't as exciting as I'd hoped," AJ grumbled to Reg, who sat across from her at the small conference table, squeezed into a room intended to be a single office.

"This geezer rambled on a bit, didn't he?" Reg mumbled back.

"He's got more rabbit than Sainsbury's," AJ replied. "If I'm permitted to quote the classics."

"Permission granted, love," Reg chuckled. "We're in a museum facility, after all. No better place to quote the infamous Chas and Dave."

They sat in silence, both making occasional notes as they each read the diary, until Gladys entered the room.

"I'm afraid I must conclude today's reading. I'm leaving."

"Fair enough," Reg said, stifling a yawn and rolling his broad shoulders.

They both slid their notepads across the table to Gladys, who thumbed through each one in turn before returning them. She'd stipulated a list of rules before allowing the two to view Alpers's diaries. Gladys held their mobile phones. They could only make notations on a pad she provided, they couldn't copy any full sentence quotes, and she would review everything before they left.

AJ stood and stretched. "So, do you think the hilt and bone we found have something to do with the Blade of Calcutta?"

"It would appear doubtful," Gladys replied, gathering up the page copies. "But it's been the catalyst in revealing Mr Pritchard's research and he's taken an interest in what you found, so there's possibly a connection."

"But according to Alpers's diary entries, Crowe spoke in the book of them mooring in a shallow bay on the north-east coast of the northernmost island of Los Caymanas. That's Little Cayman," AJ said, following Gladys and Reg out of the tiny conference room.

"True, and I've seen no evidence to suggest he was mistaken," Gladys said, escorting them to the door. "Kate Alpers confirmed her husband was working on Little Cayman."

"Can we come back tomorrow afternoon?" AJ asked once outside.

"Guard those notes carefully, please," Gladys said in reply. "Tomorrow..." she added thoughtfully, "from 2:00pm until 5:00pm sharp will be fine. But I can't stay this late again."

With that, she closed and locked the door, leaving AJ and Reg on the outdoor walkway in the dim light from a single wall sconce over the stairs.

· · ·

Reg drove north through the waterfront downtown of George Town and AJ checked her watch. It was 8:15pm.

"Rackam's?" she asked, and Reg nodded.

He pulled into an almost empty car park belonging to one of the office buildings, locked the Land Rover, and they walked across North Church Street towards the restaurant on the water.

During the day, Rackam's bar and restaurant was full of tourists, especially when the cruise ships were in town, but in the evening, like many island businesses, it became a hang-out for locals and long-stay patrons. With mostly outdoor seating, the bar was lively and the restaurant tables extending on a deck over the water were usually packed. AJ found an open spot off to the side of the bar, where comfortable chairs and sofas surrounded coffee tables, creating a relaxed area to chill while waiting for a table.

Reg returned from the bar with a bottle of cold Strongbow for AJ, and a Seven Fathoms rum over ice for himself. They both took a sip of their drinks, then leaned forward and began talking quietly.

"Anything stand out to you?" AJ asked.

"Not really," Reg replied. "But most of what I read didn't talk about Crowe's book; he was talking about his missus, and planning their trip to the Caribbean."

"Yeah, I had some mentions of the book, but no quotes yet," AJ agreed.

They'd split up the pages between them, but neither had made it through their stack before Gladys had ordered them out.

"I have a feeling the second diary, the one she has, will have a lot more in it," Reg said, taking another sip from his glass.

"Hope so," AJ replied. "Otherwise Headmistress Wright has made a big fuss over nothing with this diary business."

"Worth a few hours out of our day all the same," Reg commented. "Might help your relationship with the director, if nothing else."

"*Our* relationship, mate. Don't forget she had you pegged as a troublemaker, too."

"Nah," Reg grunted. "She loves me. It's only you she's got the hump about."

The waitress arrived with two plates of food before AJ had time to say anything more, and they both ordered another drink. Reg had bought them both the chef's special, which happened to be lionfish tacos, which he knew AJ would love. They tucked into their food, and both thought in silence about all they'd learnt that day.

"One thing I meant to ask Gladys about and forgot," AJ said, wiping the corner of her mouth. "She said Alpers's boat went missing between Grand Cayman and Jamaica. So what was he doing going back to Grand from Little if his destination was Jamaica? Doesn't make much sense, does it?"

Reg thought about it for a few moments while he finished chewing. "Needed petrol, dropped someone off, buying supplies. Any number of reasons, right?"

"But it almost doubles the trip," AJ persisted. "Seems strange to me."

"Worth asking her ladyship tomorrow. I'll give you that," Reg replied, and they finished their dinner, lost in thought once again.

They both texted their partners as they walked from the restaurant back to the poorly lit car park, letting them know they were coming home. Drops of rain began falling, and AJ jogged to the passenger side of the Land Rover and tugged on the door handle. It opened.

"Hey, you didn't lock the car, you silly bugger."

"I did," Reg replied, arriving at the driver's side and opening the door.

They both peered inside. No interior light came on.

"Did you leave the headlights on?" AJ asked, rain now running down her face.

Reg reached in and checked the switch. "No... bugger," he groaned. "Where are the notebooks?"

AJ hopped in the Land Rover and looked in the front dashboard tray, the old vehicle's version of a glove box. "Bloody hell, Reg. They're gone."

"Are you sure you put them in there?" Reg urged.

"Yes, absolutely sure," AJ replied. "I tucked them in the box thing right there. And you're sure you locked the doors?"

Reg nodded, the rain beginning to soak his hair and shoulders. "Bloody Pritchard."

"Really?" AJ responded in surprise. "He'd break into your car? How would he know the notes were in here? And why's the battery dead?"

Reg walked around to the front and pulled the bonnet release. "It's not. The arsehole is just messing with me. He must have jimmied the lock, but the bonnet is latched out here." He lifted the bonnet, propping it up with its stay. "Oi, come and give me some light."

AJ opened the torch app on her mobile and stepped out into the tropical shower that was now dumping down. She held the light over the engine bay and Reg pointed to the battery in the left front corner. The cables hung limply by the side of the battery.

"At least the prick didn't cut them," Reg grunted, and went around to the back door and brought back a small tool roll.

"This bloke is English, right?" AJ asked, shivering despite the balmy temperature as the cool rain soaked her clothes.

"Yeah."

"Who the hell calls their kid Stone? Sounds like a name from an 80s American TV show," AJ said, then switched to a bad American accent. "Stone Pritchard, special agent."

Reg put the cables back on their posts and the interior light came on.

"I don't know if he changed his name to Stone, or if he was baptised that way," he said as he tightened the nuts. "But I always called him Pebbles. He loved that."

AJ laughed. "If I meet this plonker, I'll be sure to call him Pebbles. Right after I kick him in the how's your fathers."

Reg closed the bonnet. "Hopefully, you never have to deal with him."

They got inside the Land Rover, and Reg started the engine.

"You know who we will have to deal with?" AJ said, closing her door and putting her seat belt on.

Reg let out a sigh. "Best this be our little secret for now."

"I'm all for that," AJ replied. "If she finds out, she'll have our guts for garters. I guess it was good we hadn't come across anything particularly useful so far."

"True," Reg replied. "But that's not the problem."

AJ thought for a moment. "Oh, bugger."

"Exactly," Reg said, turning left out of the car park, heading back towards the museum office instead of home. "He knows Gladys has more than she showed him."

21

FLASH IN THE PAN

1703

Captain Rochefort was a friendly, educated, and eloquent man, so the idea that he was a pirate seemed impossible to my naïve mind. A privateer under a letter from the Queen sounded gallant and noble. This I could comprehend. He told us of their torturous time, barely surviving the storm. Waves crashing over the forecastle, yards and rigging ruined, and sadly losing four men. One of those crewmen had been Badger, the man who'd befriended me and given me my first lessons with a cutlass.

With no other choice, the captain had stowed all sails except the foremast main and surrendered to the mercy of the gale force winds. Which happened to blow them straight to our little island. Last night had been their first opportunity to take a reading from the stars, which Rochefort did himself as his navigator was one of the four lost.

I was consumed by his recounting of their ordeal, and for a time I completely forgot my mother stood by me pretending to be my father. When I glanced her way, I was shocked all over again. What if Father comes outside? What a scene that would be. My solace lay in the fact that Father rarely set foot outside our hut and usually kept as much distance from Mr Helms as he could manage.

Two of Rochefort's crew appeared from the woods to the east, each carrying a spade. They looked tired, filthy, and downhearted.

"We must return to the ship and bring Badger ashore," Rochefort said. "We lost the other three over the side, poor souls, but we'll pay our respects to them all when we lay Badger to rest. My hope is to pull anchor at first light tomorrow if we can make repairs in time."

He bade us farewell and walked towards the path through the trees to the shore.

My young life to date had been spared the sorrow of loss, and I wasn't sure why Badger's death affected me so as I'd hardly known the man, but for some reason it did. Perhaps because he'd treated me as an equal. It made little sense, but the lump in my throat wouldn't go away.

Lost in my thoughts, I was jolted back to our present circumstance when Mr Helms asked a question.

"Lady Crowe, may I ask why you've disguised yourself as a gentleman?"

My mother smiled, and the familiarity of her expression betrayed her masculine veil. "Did I fool you?"

Mr Helms looked at Gordy and Duck, who stared her way.

"Until you stood beside me, I believed you were one of Rochefort's men," Helms admitted.

"If the captain hadn't introduced himself as though you were a stranger, I'm not sure I'd have known, even with you standing right there," Duck commented.

"I dare say that's true," Helms added. "Although the voice was familiar, even with the lower tone you used."

"Then I'd call my ruse a success," Mother said, still smiling.

"But why?" Helms asked again. "For what purpose, Davina? If you'll forgive me saying, you're a beautiful woman. I believe most would agree you're a rose on this flowerless island."

"I thank you for the compliment, James, but I was tired of being hidden away when a strange ship arrives. If we must take up arms, I wish to do my share, and if conversations are to be had, I'd like to partake. As indeed I just did."

"How did you introduce yourself?" I asked.

Mother laughed. "I'm embarrassed to say I hadn't thought that part through, so I improvised in the moment. I told the captain I was Crowe. Your father."

"Oh," I mumbled, still conflicted over the lie I'd told.

"I suppose I do need a Christian name, don't I?"

"Are you planning on remaining in this guise, Davina?" Helms asked. "Or only while the ship is at anchor?"

"Just while strangers are amongst us," Mother replied, "although I may continue wearing trousers. They really are quite comfortable."

"Divi," I said. "Your friends back home call you Divi all the time."

"True, but it's still rather feminine, don't you think?"

"I knew a fellow named Vin many years ago," Mr Helms said. "Vin Crowe sounds like a fine name."

"It has a ring to it," Mother agreed. "I shall lose the disguise when the strangers leave, but I think it's best to call me Vin from now on, regardless. It may save us from error in the future."

"How did you get the pistol and knife?" I asked. "Weren't they in our hut?"

"Monty left to relieve himself shortly after I reached the camp," she explained. "I pulled the old cabinet from under the hut and was able to scramble through the window. Then I waited for him to come back before making my appearance."

I looked towards our hut and wondered if Father had looked outside since he'd returned.

"Yes," Mother said softly, seeing the look on my face. "We still have that bridge to cross."

"I'll come with you," I offered.

"No, stay out here and help Mr Helms. I need to deal with this alone."

I didn't move. "Mother…"

"Vin," she said, interrupting me and resting a hand on my shoulder. "Or Father." She smiled and winked at me. "Except when we're home."

"I don't…" I began, but she cut me off again.

"Stay out here, Wil. I'll be fine."

I watched her walk towards our hut. We both knew Father would find her disguise completely unacceptable and declare it a slight on the family name. It was what he would do about it that concerned me.

"Come on, Wil," Mr Helms said, guiding me away. "We need to gather more thin branches for wattle. There's a spot in the woods to the east I noticed had plenty strewn about after the storm."

We stayed busy for hours, and Mr Helms taught me how to weave the twigs and strips of thin wood into wattle. Once all the walls were in place, he said he would show me how to mix limestone dust, mud, sand, and straw to make the daub. It took my mind from whatever was going on with Mother and Father. Neither had appeared from our hut since Mother had gone home.

Captain Rochefort came back with a group of his men carrying the body of poor Badger wrapped in a sack. Mr Helms allowed me to join the mourners as they made their way to the island's grave-yard and the second hole to be dug there. I had never attended a funeral, so I didn't know what to expect. The captain spoke a few words, complimenting Badger on his service to the ship, honoured the other three lost, then read scripture from the Bible.

The men remained sombre until it was time to shovel the earth over their friend's corpse. As they scooped the sandy dirt into the hole, one by one they began telling stories about their shipmate. It was a good thing the captain had closed his Bible, as most of the tales weren't fit for a church congregation, but the crew laughed, joked, and shared their memories. I liked the way they celebrated his life. It seemed fitting for the spirit of the man.

When the work was done, they hammered a cross into the dirt with 'Badger' scratched into the wood. If the man had a full name, it appeared no one knew it or cared to use it. Mr Helms's words about taking life had more meaning to me for the first time as I stood back and observed the funeral. This was a man I'd barely known and yet I felt his loss. I couldn't imagine the pain of losing someone I cared for, like Mother. Or Marcus.

Captain Rochefort quietly left, but the crew broke out a bottle of something they called rumbullion, and their stories turned even more risqué. A man named Hinchcliffe, who seemed in charge with the captain absent, stayed quiet but carefully watched and listened. His sun-darkened face furrowed with lines, his stare seemed to bore right through me. He sat on a tree stump with one hand resting on the hilt of his cutlass, as though he might draw it at any time.

After a while, Hinchcliffe rose and cajoled the group into leaving as, according to him, they had much work to do on the ship. I received a slap on the back from most of the men and was told Badger would have appreciated me being there. I hoped that was true.

I remained at the grave site for reasons I didn't know. Mr Helms still needed help, and I was desperately concerned about Mother, yet I found it hard to leave. I could visit his grave any time I chose, but somehow, walking away the first time felt like the end. Of what I didn't know.

It was late afternoon, and I could feel the sun's intensity waning. There were still several hours of daylight left to make progress on the reconstruction, so with a final goodbye to Badger, I strolled through the woods to camp.

Mr Helms was hard at work on the second hut, its walls almost complete. I glanced at my family's hut and wondered if Mother had calmed Father down yet. She had probably long ago resorted to silence until he wore himself out of anger. I jogged over and loudly ran up the steps, the door open to allow in the breeze. The hut was empty. I checked beyond the bedroom partition, but found no one. Strewn across my parents' bed were the clothes she had been wearing. Men's trousers and blouse borrowed from Nathaniel.

Returning to the doorway, I shouted across the camp. "Mr Helms, did you see where Mother and Father went, sir?"

Helms nodded as he stretched his back. I jumped down the steps and ran to his side.

"Left not long before you came out of the woods," he told me. "Surprised you didn't cross paths."

I looked to the east where the graveyard sat on the slightly higher land beyond the section of woods which stretched from the lagoon to the north coast. *How could I have missed them?* My mind had been wandering as I'd made my way along the narrow path we'd cleared. I certainly didn't pass them on the way.

"In truth, I assumed they were coming to see you," Mr Helms added.

"Was Mother all right?" I asked.

Mr Helms wiped the sweat from his forehead. "I couldn't say for sure, Wil. I only noticed them once they were near the trees," he said, pointing to the woods. "But they took the trail closer to the lagoon, so perhaps they were going to see his men. He ordered them back to work on the salt a while earlier."

My stomach was twisted in knots. It had been an eventful day with Mother's disguise, Badger's funeral, and now my parents leaving the hut... together. It was awful to think of them being together as an anomaly, but that was a truth. He never went anywhere with us. He'd leave the hut to check on the salt production and answer the call of nature; otherwise he sat at his desk or slept.

Without another word, I returned to our hut and looked below where Mr Helms had stashed his cutlass for me. It was still there, the bronze hilt barely visible under a sack. To avoid revealing what I was up to, I crawled underneath the house, then reached back from the shadows and retrieved the blade. Mr Helms had returned to work and wasn't paying attention to me.

I wriggled across and crawled out from the far side of the hut, then ran into the woods where I could traverse unseen to the pathway my parents had taken. I had no idea what I was planning to do with the cutlass, but my knotted insides were screaming danger. Reaching the trail, I ran at full speed, little branches whipping my arms as I slalomed between the trees.

When I burst from cover on the other side, Mother and Father stood in the clearing before me. I gasped for breath.

"There you are," Mother said. "We were trying to find you."

Father looked at the weapon in my hand, and a frown creased his brow. From the belt around his waist, he pulled his pistol, which had been hidden below his billowy shirt. The one Mother had carried earlier in the day. "Actually, I really wasn't looking for the damned boy, but he seems to have ruined things once again."

Mother took a step back. "What are you doing, Monty?"

As she turned back and forth, I noticed the red welt on her cheek.

"Enough is enough, Davina," Father growled, his eyes wide and manic like a wild animal.

"You told me we were coming out here to talk to Wil! To settle things so we could all be happier."

"And settle things I shall," he said, his attention on my cutlass.

"You were going to execute me!" Mother groaned as the realisation hit her. "And what of Wil? What plans did you have for him in your madness?"

"He would have had a choice," Father spat back. "But it appears he's made that decision already."

The pistol in Father's hand was a flintlock, the latest of its kind at the time we left England. Ornately decorated, more reliable than older pistols, and accurate in close range. But it fired one ball before the barrel had to be unscrewed to reload. I held his biggest threat in my hand, and he could only shoot one of us. If he shot me, Mother would at least have a fighting chance.

"Wil, no!" she yelled, reading my mind as I ran towards them.

Father brought the pistol to bear, but I was staring past the barrel, seeing his cold, unloving eyes preparing to murder his own flesh and blood. I was two paces away when I watched the cock release, striking the flint down the face of the frizzen. My world slowed as I registered the flash of the igniting pan charge.

The bright white light obscured my view of the callous look on my father's face, and I lunged forward, praying the ball wouldn't halt my charge as I sacrificed myself. A sharp pain punched into my chest, and the idea of seeing my friend Badger so soon crossed my mind, just before the blade of the cutlass met a firm resistance.

Throughout my training and practice, I had never considered what it would feel like to plunge the sword into the flesh of a man. It required more force than I'd imagined, but my momentum provided all that was needed. The hilt twisted and bucked in my hand as the steel glanced off rib bones on its way into my father's body.

"Wil!" Mother screamed from beside me as I came to an abrupt stop, inches from my father's face. I let go of the hilt and he dropped to the ground, where his lifeless eyes stared into the sky and a patch of red stained his white shirt around the steel blade. Looking down at myself, I expected the pain to hit me at any moment. I touched my chest, but could see or feel no wound.

Mother threw her hands around me, and we embraced. Her breaths were deep, as though she was gulping for air. After a few moments, we both stepped back and looked at the man lying dead on the ground.

"I can't believe he missed me," I mumbled.

"He didn't," Mother said, picking up the pistol. "It was a flash in the pan."

The one time my father had attempted to use his new pistol, and it didn't ignite the main charge. I'd simply run into the barrel.

"You know he hasn't touched that pistol since he loaded it in England," Mother said. "He never knew how to take care of anything himself."

Neither of us shed a tear. I desperately wanted to feel more sorrow, but the emotion wasn't there. Numb and disconnected somehow, I even felt relieved. I sensed my fear and anger had drowned out the regret which might hit me later when the enormity of the event would wrap itself around me like a dark cloak. I'd taken my first life.

"What do we do now?" I asked, looking around the clearing and seeing the freshly planted cross on Badger's grave.

Mother followed my gaze. She tucked the pistol in her waistband and reached down, taking a firm grip on the hilt of the cutlass. With a foot on her husband's chest, she withdrew the sword from his body.

"Regardless of what we say, in the eyes of English law, we killed a lord, and for that, we'll hang," she said solemnly.

"I killed him, Mother; you'll not hang for this."

"His death is my responsibility, Wil. I drove him to madness with my independence and stubbornness."

I put my hand on her arm. "If England will see us hang, then we shall never return."

She let out a long sigh. "Then we cannot remain here. The salt ship will be by in a week or less, and I cannot ask Mr Helms to lie on our behalf."

I nodded and walked towards the trail. "Then we'd best leave."

22

PEGGING THE FUN-METER

Present Day

Reg parked on Goring, one street over from the museum office, dug a torch out of the back of the Land Rover, and grabbed the wheel brace.

"Think we'll need that?" AJ asked, surprised to see her friend arming himself.

"Doubt it," he replied, making sure he locked all the doors. "But it won't be much good in the back of the Landy if we do."

They walked towards the office, using the dimly lit car park behind the harbour-front buildings, and stopped short of the dark walkway. The shower had passed through and now every surface steamed a hazy vapour. No lights were on inside the office above them, so they walked between the buildings to the little courtyard. Looking up, the wall sconce lit the first-floor walkway, but no other lights were visible. They waited, looking for signs of a torch moving behind the windows, but all appeared to be quiet.

"I'll check the door, but it looks like he's either been and gone, or didn't come here at all," Reg whispered.

"I was thinking," AJ said, and Reg paused. "Our notes didn't say anything about the museum or Gladys. How would he know we'd been here?"

"How did he know we were at Rackam's?" Reg countered. "He followed us, that's how. Which means he knew where we'd come from."

"Ooh, that feels creepy," AJ mumbled. "I don't like the idea someone's been spying on us. Now I'm wondering if I picked my teeth or scratched my bum. You hope no one sees you do that sort of stuff."

Reg frowned at her. "That's what springs to mind when you find out a ruthless prick has been following us? You're a right pillock sometimes, my girl."

"The following and stealing stuff freaks me out, too," AJ hissed back. "I'm just saying... bloody hell, Reg, it doesn't matter. I'm sodding wet, so get on with it, will you?"

Reg grunted and went up the stairs as softly as a man of his size could manage. The wood creaked in protest and AJ winced with each step he took.

"Quiet as a church mouse riding a bloody elephant," she muttered to herself.

Reg tried the door and AJ could see it opened. He leaned over the rail and nodded towards the entry, then signalled for her to keep an eye out from where she was. Spending much of their time using hand signals underwater had its benefits. He disappeared inside and she waited below, shivering and wondering what she was supposed to do if this Pritchard bloke showed up.

Muffled voices and laughter wafted from the harbour restaurants, but otherwise the business district, where hundreds of the world's financial institutions had a physical address no matter how small, was silent. It had only been a few minutes, but AJ was already getting worried. She hadn't heard anything from upstairs to suggest Reg had a problem, but on the other hand, he hadn't reappeared to tell her all was clear.

She seriously doubted Mrs Wright would forget to lock the

door, so someone had been inside since they'd all left over an hour before. AJ considered going up the steps and seeing what was taking Reg so long, but she knew he'd bark at her for not doing what she was told. A police siren began howling from not far away, making AJ jump.

The sound grew closer, and she wondered if they were coming to the office. AJ groaned. How were they going to explain all this to the police, and even worse, to Gladys Wright? Listening carefully, she thought the noisy siren was starting to move away, but it must have been shielded by buildings or turned a corner, as it became louder once more.

Above her, the wood creaked, and she turned and looked up. "About bloody time, Reg," she whispered urgently. "The bloody rozzers are coming. Did you set off an alarm?"

There was no reply, and a figure moved nimbly down the steps to the shadows in the courtyard. AJ instantly knew it wasn't Reg. The big man had about as much nimble in him as a pig on roller skates.

"Stop there!" she called out. "The police are here. There's no way out."

The man stepped from the cover and AJ briefly saw the face of a man in his fifties with dark hair and clothing. The only other detail she noted was the smile on his face right before he ploughed his forearm into her chest, knocking her backwards against a wall. He didn't stop, but darted down the dark walkway, silhouetted by the streetlights on Shedden Road until he turned left and disappeared from view.

AJ pushed away from the wall and chased after the man, not really knowing what she planned to do, but angry enough to try something. She reached the street and looked to the left, where she'd seen him go. The road was empty. The police siren wailed, and she turned to see them make the corner and stop beside her, blinding her with a combination of headlights and flashing blue and red.

"He went that way," she yelled, shielding her eyes, but the two policemen slowly got out of the car and one of them came towards her.

"If you hurry, you might still catch him," she urged.

"AJ?" the policeman asked.

She squinted, still unable to see much with the ridiculously bright lights shining and flashing at her. "Maybe," she said stubbornly.

The policeman laughed. "It's Jacob. Nora's partner. What you doin' running around downtown all soakin' wet, now?"

"Hey lads," Reg said from the alleyway. "Someone broke into the museum office. I called for you lot."

"You called the police?" AJ blurted. "What did you do that for?"

"'Cos that's what you do when you discover a break-in, love," Reg replied.

"How about you stop the bugger who broke in?" she barked.

"I would have if he was still there," Reg said impatiently.

"He was, you big donkey!"

"No, he wasn't. I checked every room."

"I'm telling you he was!" AJ groaned. "Believe me, I didn't throw myself against the wall back there. He came out after you'd been in there a few minutes."

"He did?"

"Yes!" she said, throwing her hands in the air.

"Did he have anything with him?"

AJ turned to Jacob, who had asked his partner for the night to turn the lights off. "Can you believe this bloke? Not a 'How are you, love?' or a 'Hope he didn't hurt you'. I get 'Did he have anything with him?'"

Reg let out a big sigh. "I'm sorry. Are you okay?"

AJ shrugged her shoulders. "Course I'm okay, takes more than some wanker running into me, yer know?"

Now Reg threw his hands in the air, and Jacob laughed again.

"How 'bout we go inside and see what happened 'ere?"

An old Volvo pulled up, stopping abruptly behind the police car. The driver's door flung open and Gladys Wright stepped out.

"You'd better duck, Jacob," AJ said.

"What's dat, miss?"

"The shit is about to hit the fan in the biggest possible way."

It was midnight by the time Reg finally drove AJ back to West Bay. Gladys had thoroughly searched the premises and couldn't find anything missing. The copies of the diary were in a safe which hadn't been touched, and they kept all original artefacts and documents at the museum itself, which had a security system, unlike the office. It appeared Reg had disturbed the intruder before he'd found the safe or attempted to open it.

After an initial verbal assault, which Jacob had curtailed by suggesting Mrs Wright check the office, Gladys had calmed and seemed to accept that whoever was running amok was the bad guy, rather than AJ and Reg.

Positively identifying the perpetrator was a different matter. Reg, who hadn't seen the man, was convinced it was Stone Pritchard. AJ, whom he'd bowled over, couldn't confirm it was Pritchard after seeing a handful of pictures from the internet. Gladys looked at the same reference photographs and had similar doubts regarding the man who had visited her.

In the pictures, Pritchard had military-style buzzed hair and a greying beard. The man AJ and Gladys had seen was clean shaven with a full head of dark hair. Both easy changes that could drastically alter his appearance, but until the immigration department opened in the morning, the police couldn't retrieve his passport and entry photos.

With nothing missing, the Royal Cayman Islands Police Service didn't have the resources to bring a SOCO over to search for prints, so in all likelihood, the case would officially go no farther.

"I'll call Whittaker in the morning and let him know what happened," Reg said as he pulled up outside the resplendent house on Seven Mile Beach where AJ and Jackson lived in a small guest cottage. "He won't be able to do much more, but at least Pritchard will be on his radar."

"We need to get the site guarded at Anchor Point," AJ said, getting out of the Land Rover.

"They don't have the manpower for that," Reg replied. "Best they can do is send a Joint Marine Unit boat to wander by every once in a while. Best chance we have is to be out there ourselves."

"I have customers in the morning. I can't get away until lunchtime."

"Pebbles can't accomplish much without a boat and mailboxes," Reg commented, referring to the big tubes treasure hunters used to redirect their propeller blasts to the sea floor, moving the sand to see what's below. "We were stupid lucky to find that poor geezer's thigh bone. It was only because it happened to be under a lump of steel pipe."

AJ nodded. "Night, Reg," she said and closed the door.

She was damp, tired, and not sure what to do next except shower and sleep. There were far too many pieces missing to the puzzle and still no real leads tying William Crowe's story of the Blade of Calcutta to Grand Cayman.

AJ opened the gate in the wooden fence and plodded across the lawn to her cottage. The door opened and she let Jackson wrap his arms around her and kiss the top of her head.

"Rough day?" he whispered.

AJ groaned into his chest. "Found a dead guy. Reg's Landy got broken into, then I ran into a murdering thief. I think I pegged my fun-meter."

23

THE LETTER

1703

It felt like we were hiding from everyone. Mother from the pirates, and us both from the men in the camp as we were returning without Father. Although it was likely to take days, his body could be discovered at any time, and the threat lingered over us like an unbearable load. In hindsight, good sense would have been to hide the body or bury him somewhere, but we left in haste, with our thoughts turned to the problems which lay ahead.

We returned along the same path I'd taken, staying under cover until we reached our hut. Going through the door meant revealing ourselves to Mr Helms, so we quietly dragged the old cabinet from under the house and climbed through the back window opening. Lying on the floor inside was Father's cane, dropped after he'd used it to strike his wife across the face.

She told me he'd fallen silent afterwards, and she'd planned to run to Mr Helms if he'd picked up the cane again. He didn't, and when he'd spoken he had appeared calm and suggested they find me. It was time to bring our family together and stop our disagreements, he'd suggested. It was even sadder knowing Father had planned to murder his wife. A fit of rage would have been terrible, but imagining him making a decision and then calmly acting out the lie without second guessing himself was simply awful.

"Pack everything you want to use or see again, Wil," Mother instructed me as she busied herself.

I had very little worth taking. I rolled up two more pairs of lightweight trousers and three shirts. The only shoes worthy of the Caribbean were the pair I wore every day. I possessed no hat which would remain on my head in a strong ocean wind, so I left both I owned behind. The linen from my bed and the knife Mother had carried earlier were the only other items of value I bound together with the clothes.

Mother took powder and balls for the pistol, kept Mr Helms's cutlass, and changed back into her clothes borrowed from Nathaniel. She took another pair of trousers and two shirts of Father's, and her own bed linen. Her hat was not ideal for a ship, but an important part of her disguise, so she kept it, along with several scarves.

We hadn't discussed our plan, but it didn't require conversation. If we were to leave the island, we needed a ship, and unless we waited and took our chances with one of the merchant vessels collecting salt, the *Royal Fortune* was our only option.

"I must say goodbye to Marcus," I said, realising I was unlikely to ever see my friend again. "I can't just leave without a word."

Mother moved across the room and placed her hand on my shoulder. "Wil, that's exactly what you have to do. We cannot risk telling anyone. I'm writing a note for Mr Helms. Why don't you do the same for Marcus?"

Mother was right, of course. Any talk of what happened required explanation and invited questions. None of which favoured us. Our friends on the island may well believe we acted in self-defence, but a court in England would side with Lord Crowe. Involving anyone here would simply make life complicated and unfair to them.

I sat down at the desk and dipped Father's quill in the ink. The nib then hung over the blank piece of paper while the right words escaped me. We had become brothers. A deep friendship which never could have happened in England, or most places on the planet, including this island, if my father had had his way.

Finally, I dropped quill to parchment and began to write.

Dearest Marcus,

It is with great sadness we must leave Salt Cay, and I offer my sincere apologies for the abruptness of our departure. Sometimes life takes a turn you neither expect nor crave, and while I have no foretelling what the future holds, turn we must.

I hold our friendship dear and hope God graces us with the opportunity to meet again one day under finer circumstances than today. Wherever I reside, my door will always be open to you.

My life will be lessened without you, but I will never forget our bond.

Yours truly,

William Crowe

"We must leave, Wil," Mother said gently. "Before it's dark."

I folded the parchment and wrote Marcus's name on the front, placing it beside Mother's note for Mr Helms.

"Did you tell Mr Helms he could have our hut and furniture, Mother?"

"I did," she replied, herding me towards the back window. "And, Wil, you cannot call me Mother until this ordeal is through, understand me? A small slip could be the end for us. Men are deathly superstitious about women working on ships. If I'm discovered, I dread to think of the consequences."

I climbed through the window opening and dropped to the cabinet below and then the ground. It seemed a simple task to use another name, but habits die hard, and my heart skipped at the notion I'd slip up.

"What name should I use?"

Mother dropped beside me and listened for sounds of anyone else close by.

"Father, Vin, or Crowe," she whispered.

We moved to the trees between camp and the lagoon, then made our way west.

"Father is too strange," I said, batting branches aside. "I'm very worried about this, Moth... See, I'm going to mess this up."

"Vin, use Vin," Mother said. "Once you get used to it, it'll become second nature."

"But who calls their parents by their Christian name?"

Mother paused as we neared the beach. "Some adults use their parents' Christian names," she said and sighed. "And I'm afraid you're being forced into growing up too quickly. Let's try Vin. You'll figure it out."

"I hope so," I mumbled in response, lacking the confidence she had in me.

A cockboat was at the water's edge and Captain Rochefort stood beside it, waiting. I was expecting to row ourselves out to the *Royal Fortune* in our one good rowboat, which we'd then need to return.

"What if they'll not have us?" I whispered.

"You heard the captain, Wil. They lost four men, including his navigator. It was fortuitous you chose that role for me."

"Fortuitous for us," I corrected.

"True. God rest his soul," Mother agreed, crossing herself. "How do I look?" she asked.

"Like Vin Crowe," I replied.

She grinned and walked out of the trees and on to the beach towards the captain. I took a deep breath and followed the person I now knew as Vin.

"Mr Crowe and young Wil," Rochefort greeted us. "I hope you don't mind. My men are collecting a few dozen coconuts before we leave. We're not completely finished with repairs, but good enough to set sail."

"You're welcome to all you can carry," Vin replied, and I wondered if she'd be able to keep up the deeper tone full time.

"You mentioned you'd lost your navigator along with several other hands, Captain," Vin continued. "My boy and I were talking. There's nothing keeping us here, so I'd like to apply for the vacant position."

Rochefort squinted against the sun, now low across the water. "Have you sailed on a privateer ship in the past?" he asked in a careful tone. "We're not a merchant vessel, Mr Crowe."

Vin laughed. "Do you use the same wind as the rest of us, sir?"

The captain smiled. "That we do. But our business is to disrupt the enemies of our Queen," he said, then paused and lifted a foot to rest it on the gunwale of the cockboat. "It's dangerous work. You'll be asked to use that cutlass and pistol."

Vin nodded. "I don't carry them for decoration, sir."

Rochefort looked at me. "What of Wil, here? He's a well raised, educated lad. Are you sure you want him amongst the rogues and thieves I call a crew?"

"Wil's a hard worker, and he knows his way around a ship, sir," Vin responded. "He's trained with a cutlass and will fight if we're boarded, but I'd prefer we give him time to grow before he joins an offensive."

The captain scratched his chin as he considered, looking us both over. "We work from shares. Whatever we haul is split. Captain takes two shares; the crew takes a share apiece. Navigator usually takes a share and a half. Not sure what will be acceptable to the men in this situation."

"Does a navigator have a berth, sir?"

"He does. Small, but private."

Until Vin had asked the question, I'd not even considered the obvious problems of my mother sharing quarters with a bunch of men. If she breathed a sigh of relief, she gave no hint of it.

"Then the boy can berth with me, and we'll take a share and a half for us both. You get an extra hand for the price of feeding him."

Rustling came from the trees, and I prayed it wasn't Mr Helms or the other men from the camp. A raucous laugh told me it was Rochefort's men. First one to appear was the man they called Dutch.

"We sail at daybreak, heading north of Hispaniola. I'll navigate alongside you. If you're worthy of the job, you'll have it. If you're not, you'll be dropped somewhere near the next land we see. Is that clear?"

"As I would expect, Captain," Vin replied confidently.

I wasn't sure if Mother was truly feeling that sure of herself, or if the bravado came with the disguise and improvised personality, but she was convincing. I, on the other hand, was terrified.

The captain extended his hand, and Vin shook. "Welcome aboard the *Royal Fortune*."

"Thank you, Captain, and may fortune indeed shine upon us."

Rochefort winked at me. "You'd better help your shipmates row us home, young Wil. Show these men how you'll earn your dinner."

"Aye, sir," I replied, and began loading coconuts into the boat.

"Coming with us?" Dutch asked as he handed me their cache.

"Yes, sir," I replied with a smile.

"Then you best watch out for yerself," he whispered as we pushed the wooden boat into the shallow water. "Not all the crew is friendly, like Badger. Captain's right, you better earn your share. Else you're stealing money from our pockets, lad."

I decided I'd been merely nervous before, because now I was truly terrified.

24

A DOUBLE AGENT THINGY

Present Day

AJ operated on caffeine and autopilot for the morning, guiding the shallow second dive on the *Ore Verde* wreck. The ship had been reduced to metal rubble scattered across the sand by numerous storms, but made for a great dive exploring under all the twisted hull sections and parts. Reg was ready and waiting when she docked *Hazel's Odyssey*, so she bade farewell to her customers and left Thomas, who was happy to prep for the following day before taking the afternoon off.

"Am I bringing dive gear, or we going to the museum?" AJ asked Reg.

"Bring your gear, but we'll start with Gladys."

She ran back to the boat and grabbed her BCD and fins, her computer, mask, and torch still hanging from D-rings on her rig.

"If you're diving Anchor Point again, Boss," Thomas shouted after her. "You be careful widout me to keep an eye on you."

AJ gave him an okay sign and a grin before she flung her gear into a plastic tub in the back of Reg's Land Rover. His gear was already on board, and he'd strapped four tanks against the bench seat on one side.

"More coffee," AJ groaned, as Reg pulled out of their little car park and turned right.

"Foster's will have to do," Reg replied. "I need lunch too, but we can't wait on them making sandwiches. Just grab something off the shelf and we'll eat as we drive into town."

AJ could tell Reg had a plan rolling, which he would undoubtedly share with her once they were heading for George Town. In the market, she found a cold, coffee-flavoured energy drink, which she'd become partial to in the afternoons, and grabbed two French baguettes from the bakery, along with a package of Swiss cheese slices and a bag of salt and vinegar crisps.

As they left the market, she tore the baguettes down the middle and shoved slices of cheese between the bread still warm from the oven, added a handful of crisps, then handed one of her master-pieces to Reg. He raised an eyebrow, then bit into the hastily made sandwich. AJ took a few bites of her own and a long drink from the can before Reg began talking.

"We need to get the rest of the information from the diaries," he began. "Alpers's notes are our only real lead, and more impor-tantly, it's information Pritchard doesn't have."

"Except for the first diary, he has our notes from that," AJ pointed out.

"Right, but there was bugger-all worth worrying about in that one."

"Fair enough," she agreed. "And if he did have any of the diary info, he wouldn't be following us and breaking in everywhere, right?"

"Exactly," Reg agreed. "Whittaker issued a BOLO for Pritchard earlier after finding out he'd checked out of the Sunshine Suites yesterday morning. He has one of his plods checking the other hotels."

"Did immigration come up with anything?" AJ asked.

Reg tossed her his mobile, which he had wedged in a tray in the sparse dashboard. "There's a text from Roy with a picture."

AJ found the text string and looked at the picture. It was the digital photograph taken at the airport's immigration entry desk, from which they used facial recognition software to match the image to the one on record from the passport. The man had dark, curly hair and a clean-shaven face. The hair, which she guessed was dyed, made him look a lot younger, but the wrinkles around his tanned face belied his age.

"That's him," AJ confirmed.

"Figured as much," Reg grunted. "Reply to Whittaker and tell him so. If he starts sending that picture around the island, it'll make it much harder for Pebbles to move about."

AJ talked as she typed a response. "Bet he's buzzed his hair already, or taken the wig off. He really looks different with more hair."

"Roy'll send out both pictures, I'm sure," Reg replied in between bites of his sandwich. "And I'm hoping they get the hurry up going on the hilt and the leg bone, so the site becomes an official archaeological project. Right now, if we caught anyone out there diving the Reef Balls, there's nothing we can do about it."

Reg found a rarely available spot to park on Harbour Drive, where it would take a foolish person to break into the Land Rover in front of the people milling about the waterfront. He made sure all three doors were locked, although they both knew the simple locks wouldn't delay anyone for very long.

"I thought I said 2:00pm?" Gladys greeted them frostily.

"Figured after last night, best we get straight to it," Reg replied, putting on his best customer service tone.

Unless someone knew him as well as AJ did, they probably couldn't tell any difference, but she appreciated his effort.

"I was about to leave for my lunch," the director said. "But I suppose I can get you set up before I go."

"That would be much appreciated," Reg said, and smiled behind his thick beard.

Gladys muttered something to herself and beetled off to get the diary copies. AJ and Reg made themselves comfortable in the conference room, but AJ instinctively sat up straighter when Gladys came in and handed them each a new notepad.

"Apparently my directive to keep these safe went unheeded yesterday. Perhaps you can do better today."

"Yes, Mrs Wright," AJ responded. "Thank you."

Reg just shook his head and frowned at AJ.

Gladys left a stack of paper on the table, mumbled under her breath some more, then left for lunch. AJ slouched in her chair.

"Don't say it," she grumbled, and Reg chuckled, sorting through the pages to find where he'd got up to.

"We're not starting over, are we?" he asked.

"Sod that," AJ replied, taking sheets for herself. "I think I can remember the little I'd noted yesterday, so I planned to jot it down first." She paused and looked up at Reg. "But you know what? We could get a bit devious with your mate, Pebbles."

"What do you mean?"

She grinned. "What's the chances of this bloke trying to nick our notes again?"

"Almost a guarantee, I'd say," Reg replied. "Clearly he's stuck, else he'd be digging in Little Cayman instead of being a pain in our arse."

"That's what I was thinking too," AJ agreed, tapping the table with her finger. "I reckon we should accidentally leave our notes somewhere he might look for them."

Reg stopped trying to remember what he'd written the day before and furrowed his brow, looking across the table. "What are you cackling on about?"

AJ leaned a little closer. "We feed him a bit of false info, you big dummy. Like a double agent thingy in the spy films."

"Of all the hare-brained schemes you come up with," Reg started, then paused a moment and thought it over. "This one might actually be worth a shit."

"Bloody right," AJ chuckled. "I don't watch all them James Bond movies for nothing, you know."

Setting her idea aside for now, AJ focused on reading through the diary pages and gleaning as many notes as possible. Their assumption had been correct. The second diary held more nuggets and a few direct quotes. Gladys returned from lunch and checked in on them before leaving them be for the afternoon. Nearing 4:00pm, AJ sat back, stretched, yawned, and declared she was done.

"Suppose we should compare what we've come up with," Reg said, standing and stretching himself.

They were both used to being outside all day, so being stuck in an office studying was far more tiring to them than the manual labour of their jobs.

"I'll see if Gladys wants to join us," Reg suggested. "I'm sure she'd like to hear what we've come up with, even though she's read it all."

"Critique our work, more likely," AJ grumbled, but she knew it was the right thing to do.

Once the three of them were seated around the table, AJ led off with her summation. "I had the early pages of both diaries, and not much happened in the first one. Alpers just talks about the book and mentions how it reads like a swashbuckling adventure tale. He does say this William Crowe fellow was only twelve when his father was sent to Salt Cay to set up an English supply from there."

"I got the impression Mr Crowe didn't think too highly of his father," Gladys added.

"Alpers seemed to think he was much closer to his mother," AJ agreed.

"What were those lines you were rattling on about earlier?" Reg asked.

AJ shuffled through the copies of the diary pages. "These were written off to the side," she said, finding the right sheet. "I don't know if he was working on a poem, or what. He wrote 'the treasure of the priceless sword' then 'William Crowe's lost treasure', 'an island's buried secret', and 'a forgotten treasure'."

"None of that rhymes," Reg pointed out.

"Poems don't always have to rhyme," AJ responded.

"Those are titles for the book Alpers intended to write," Gladys intervened. "Kate Alpers told me as much. To her knowledge, he never settled on his favourite."

A thought came to AJ. "Did Kate recall any of the details from the later diaries? Surely she could remember at least some of what was written or what Christopher told her?"

"Kate never saw the later diaries," Gladys explained. "She went as far as Jamaica with him, then stayed there when he left for the Cayman Islands. The only reason she had the first two diaries was because he'd left them with her. She told me he already had a third complete and was working on a fourth when he left. These newer two he took, and Kate told me her husband usually filled one of the little notebooks every week to two weeks."

"So we don't know how many diaries were actually lost, or if indeed more than four ever existed," Reg said.

"He was gone from Jamaica for over four weeks before the storm," Gladys replied. "Kate was sure there would have been several more diaries, but of course it doesn't matter. We know all was lost."

"How do we know they went down in the storm?" AJ asked. "If he was gone for four weeks, maybe he sank ten miles from port the day he left."

"Kate became concerned after the storm and flew to the closest place she could get to Little Cayman, which of course, was Grand by seaplane. It was there she found out he'd been by George Town for provisions and left for Jamaica a day before the storm came from the south."

"What a horrible feeling that must have been for her," AJ said quietly, and they sat in silence for a few moments. It was easy to forget the trauma and personal loss when talking about events which happened a century past. Or three centuries. Perhaps because the people would be dead by now even if they'd led long lives, she thought. But Kate Alpers must have felt devastated and wondered for ages if her husband might show up one day with a long story of being marooned somewhere.

"What did this fellow Crowe do?" Reg asked. "I didn't see anything in what I had about where he lived, worked, died – nothing."

"I had a bit about him," AJ said, thumbing through her notepad. "Here it is. When he returned to England, he lived in Portchester, near Portsmouth, with his mother's family. Apparently, he eventually inherited their large estate, named Seafarer. It was still in the family when Alpers visited and found records dating back to the 1600s. I did an internet search and unfortunately the estate was levelled during WWII from stray bombs aimed at the docks, so all those papers and, no doubt, copies of Crowe's book were lost."

AJ paused and turned a page in her notes. "William Crowe not only worked for the family, he also started a business with his uncle in 1718. They owned several ships which they hired out as escorts to merchantmen travelling to the Caribbean. They both captained their own ships for many years. Crowe inherited the estate in 1742 after his uncle died, then Crowe himself passed away in 1757 at age 67. They are both buried in the family cemetery on the grounds of the estate."

"The uncle must not have had children," Reg pointed out.

"Or boys," Gladys corrected. "This was mid 1700s. It may have passed to the first male in line."

"The estate was then handed on to William's son, who he named Vin." AJ said and looked up again, smiling at the other two. "That's fitting, isn't it?" she added.

"We know from court records of the time that William's father, Lord Montgomery Crowe, died under suspicious circumstances on Salt Cay," Gladys added. "So although no one appeared to be aware at the time, certainly not the Spanish captain who complimented his attackers, it was William's mother, Davina Crowe, who may well have been the 'Bravest Captain' of whom he wrote."

"That would be some accomplishment for that era," AJ said.

Gladys nodded. "Quite so. And I don't believe you mentioned the third partner who continued their business?"

AJ returned to her scribbled notes. "Oh right. William and his uncle had another partner who outlived them both. His name was Marcus. Marcus Smith."

25

BLOOD IN THE WATER

1703

Mother soon proved her worth as navigator. We sailed within sight of Hispaniola and Captain Rochefort declared we were now part of the crew. Before we'd pulled anchor at Salt Cay, the captain had held a meeting on deck with all hands. He'd told the crew of his arrangement with us and asked if anyone objected. There had been mumblings and groans, but no hands were raised. Hardly a glowing vote of confidence, but our passage from Salt Cay was secure.

With Rochefort's seal of approval, we didn't have to worry about swimming to shore, but our worth had still to be proven to some members of the crew. Most treated me well, or at least without hostility, but a few, led by Dutch, seemed reluctant to accept us. The boatswain, Hinchcliffe, was amongst them.

Unfortunately, he ran the ship, so I often found myself on the short end of the chores. I was getting good at scrubbing and varnishing, as well as the filthy job of applying pitch to leaky seams in the hull. When he first sent me up into the rigging, I was excited, followed by abject fear as the ship swayed in the peaks and troughs of the open water swells. From up high, it felt as though the *Royal Fortune* was capsizing with every dip and roll.

After a time, I became used to the motion and the noise of the crashing waves mixed with the bellows of the sails in the wind. It was strenuous work, and I was glad my salt production labours had strengthened me or I'd have never managed. As it was, I worked from sunrise to sunset before eating every scrap they'd allow me and then collapsing onto the tiny cot I shared with Vin. It was still strange, but I was coming to terms with the name.

Boatswain rotated the crew for night duty, which took the same manpower as sailing during the day, but all other chores were saved for daylight. I found myself on duty in the dark more than most. It was cooler, quieter, and often Mother… I mean Vin, was at the helm.

Our first real taste of excitement came as we continued through the Windward Passage. Heading south-west, our lookout could see the western tip of Hispaniola on the horizon off our port side, and spotted a mast to the north. Hoping for a trade ship coming from Cuba, the captain had us turn across the wind and current. It was amazing how well the *Royal Fortune* made speed with wind to our flank.

The build-up over the next few hours was far more exhilarating than the capture. It was a relatively small ketch with two masts, the second evident as we drew closer. The sailors made one course change to avoid our approach, then quickly dropped their sails when it was clear we would easily outrun them. Tied alongside, six swarthy men stood on deck without a weapon in sight.

"Boatswain, put those men under guard and inspect the hold," Rochefort ordered.

"Aye, sir," Hinchcliffe growled and chose ten of his men to board the Spanish vessel.

I spotted Dutch and Lefty amongst those he chose, putting

Dutch in charge of the six Spaniards, who looked resolute but scared. One of them began speaking to Dutch until the pirate bashed the man across the cheek with the hilt of his cutlass.

Vin stepped closer to the captain. "Sir, if I may offer my services, I speak some Spanish. That man was asking that his crew be spared. He offered himself."

"Did he now?" Rochefort replied. "How noble."

Hinchcliffe appeared from below deck. "Sugar cane. Nothing but sugar cane."

Captain Rochefort sighed. "That's disappointing, boatswain."

Two more of the pirates came up the steps from the hold, except they carried two bottles in each hand.

"But they also have six crates of rumbullion," Hinchcliffe shouted, and the men burst into cheers of jubilation.

Rochefort sighed again and turned to his navigator. "This will cost us two days of useful activity, damn it."

"Best we find safe harbour, sir," Vin replied. "If the men aren't fit to sail, I'd hate to be caught in open water."

I heard Mother mention *men* and held my breath, but the captain didn't blink an eye and I realised the statement was only striking to me as I knew our hidden truth.

"Safe harbour is Jamaica, and that's two days from here, three to Kingston itself," Rochefort replied. "Nearest anchorage is Hispaniola to the south."

The men began hauling the crates of liquor aboard and corks were being pulled as they did.

"Hispaniola is Spanish controlled, is it not, sir?" Vin asked.

The captain swept a hand across the horizon. "All these waters are Spanish controlled, Mr Crowe. We've run from a ship of the line or two in our time through the Windward Passage. England holds Jamaica, and until we moor up there, you best consider yourself in hostile seas."

"What about them, Captain?" Hinchcliffe shouted from the ketch, pointing towards the merchant sailors.

"Tie 'em to the mast and blow a hole in the bilge!" Dutch yelled and the crew cheered in agreement.

Dutch began dragging the first man towards the mast. Rochefort looked at Hinchcliffe and shook his head.

"Hold up!" the boatswain shouted to be heard over the crew's encouragement.

Dutch stopped and shoved the Spaniard to his knees. The men quietened, and all eyes turned to the captain.

"Gentlemen," Rochefort began. "We make our living from Spanish merchantmen, such as this one," he said, pointing to the ketch. "These men and this ship can be no use to us at the bottom of the Caribbean Sea. I'd be happy to take their rumbullion again, next time we meet!"

The crew cheered again at the prospect of more grog. When they settled again, Hinchcliffe spoke up.

"What message do we send if we leave these men alive, Captain?"

"Mr Hinchcliffe, we send no message at all if the ship and crew are never seen again."

The boatswain ran his tongue around his teeth as he thought for a moment, hands on hips. The other men waited eagerly to see if he would challenge the captain any further.

"Captain makes a fair point," Hinchcliffe said boldly. "I propose we allow three of them to sail on and let the Spanish bastards know the *Royal Fortune* is a ship to fear. We take the other three and show them why!"

Once again, the crew screamed and cheered, eager for blood.

"I don't think the Spanish navy will fear us, sir," Vin said quietly, and I stepped a little closer to hear clearly above the raucous men. "But they may well send warships looking for us."

Rochefort nodded. "Indeed, they may. It's a fine line between building a reputation and inviting unwanted attention. The merchants will put more effort into evading us if they think we'll slaughter them. These men dropped sail, as it was a better option than facing our cannons. If they know we'll cut their throats, next time they'll risk our aim and keep sailing."

"Then you'll set them all free, sir?"

Rochefort looked at my mother. "You'll soon learn, leading a group of rogues is a balancing act between good sense and appeasing the crew. These two goals are often in conflict."

The captain turned back to Hinchcliffe and nodded. The cheers grew louder still.

"Let me speak with them first, Captain," Vin said quickly, as we watched Dutch drag his man back to the group.

"For what purpose, Crowe?"

"Perhaps we can save a family from losing their father."

Rochefort frowned at Vin, but his face quickly softened as he thought it over.

"Boatswain," he shouted. "Let Crowe speak with these men a moment. They may have knowledge of other ships."

Hinchcliffe held up a hand to Dutch, who already had a knife at a man's throat.

"You speak their gibberish?" the boatswain asked as Vin hopped to the ketch.

"Some," she replied and strode over to the men.

"¿Quién es el capitán?" Vin asked, and the man who'd spoken earlier stepped forward.

He appeared older than the other men, and although short in stature and small in girth, he stood upright and looked Vin in the eyes. They continued in conversation, none of which I, nor anyone else on our crew to my knowledge, understood. Several times I could tell Vin didn't understand the answer, and the Spaniard repeated himself. There was a lot of looking back and forth amongst the six captives.

"Let's get on with this," Dutch finally shouted, and the English crew whooped their approval.

Vin spoke a few more words to the captain and the six men began animatedly talking amongst themselves. One man dropped to his knees and two more crossed themselves. Vin put a hand on three men in turn, including the Spanish captain.

"These three sail on," she said firmly and walked away.

Dutch looked at the boatswain, whose eyes narrowed as Vin strode his way. Hinchcliffe reached out and took Vin by the arm. He asked her something quietly, and Vin answered. I couldn't hear the exchange, but Hinchcliffe appeared satisfied and called to Dutch.

"Leave the three Crowe picked out."

Dutch had held his knife to the throat of one of the men Vin had selected. He shoved the man away and grabbed one of the fated three. In one callous and brutal motion, he swiped his blade across the man's throat and dragged him to the gunwale, throwing him over the side. The Spaniard barely had time to clutch his neck before he hit the water, which quickly turned red all around him as he splashed about.

The pirate crew went crazy, running across the deck to the forecastle for a better view. Three of our crew, already on the ketch, helped Dutch drag the other two victims to the gunwale where they held them. The Spaniards pleaded and fought, but the pirates held them firmly as everyone watched the life ebb from the man in the water. He was still and lifeless by the time the first triangular grey fin circled.

The dead Spaniard's body shuddered and bobbed underwater as more sharks appeared, ripping flesh from the easy meal. My legs felt weak as the noise of the crew's joy and excitement rang through my ears and I watched Dutch slice into the next man's thigh before tossing him over the side. Below the *Royal Fortune*, the waters broiled with a frenzy of sharks fighting over the bodies of the poor men.

Vin grabbed my arm and led me away, stumbling as I tried to will my limbs into holding me upright.

"You don't want to see this," she said, steering me down the steps to our tiny berth in the stern.

I could still hear the screams of dying men mixed with the

elation of the bloodthirsty pirates as Vin slammed the door closed and dropped to the floor in tears.

My whole body was shaking, and I collapsed on the narrow cot. The words Mr Helms had spoken to me came flooding back. For the first time, I truly understood why he'd been insistent on not trusting the privateers. I desperately imagined Badger not allowing the vicious slaughter to take place, but it was easy to conjure that thought… as Badger wasn't here to prove me wrong.

26

PLUS OR MINUS TWENTY-FIVE YEARS

Present Day

Reg and AJ climbed into the Land Rover and quickly wound down the windows to release the hot, humid air inside. The rundown of notes and subsequent conversation had taken another forty-five minutes, but the diaries ended far too soon to yield the critical details they needed. They now knew the name of the privateer ship, and Davina Crowe's ambition to return to England with her son, but not much else.

Either William, or subsequently Christopher Alpers, had glossed over the reason for the two leaving the islands with pirates rather than waiting for another form of transport. Alpers also appeared to be suspicious of the accidental death of Lord Crowe but offered no tangible reasons. Gladys had said William had been cleared of any wrongdoing back in England, so whatever happened to Lord Crowe remained a mystery.

"Turn the air conditioner on," AJ urged, and Reg started the engine but didn't drive away. More hot air dumped out of the air vents and AJ quickly switched the fan off.

"Where now?" Reg thought aloud.

"Too late to dive," AJ replied. "It'd be sunset by the time we reached East End. I don't care where you drive, but drive somewhere and get some air moving."

Reg pulled around to Harbour Drive, where the traffic was bumper to bumper.

"Nice work," AJ grumbled.

"I forgot it was rush hour," Reg said defensively. "At least we might see Pebbles if he tries following us again."

AJ fanned herself with one of the notepads. "If he's smart, he'll follow us on foot. He could sit in Sharkeez and enjoy a beer while watching us inch by," she replied, waving a hand towards the bar overlooking the road and the harbour.

Reg grunted.

"What?" AJ asked, sensing he'd thought of something else.

"What if he is sitting comfortably somewhere tracking us?"

"I don't follow," AJ replied.

"I thought you were all James bloody Bond?" he said, grinning. "What if he's *put* a tracker on the Landy?"

"Blimey, that would be a bit flash, wouldn't it?"

Reg shrugged his shoulders. "Not really. You can buy 'em on Amazon for cheap and follow along on your mobile. I have them on each of my boats, hard-wired in, but this would be the battery style which last three or four days before needing a charge."

"That's right," AJ responded. "I forgot you put them on your boats. I don't really need one, as I'm usually where the boat is all but one day a week."

Reg inched out into the traffic, which shuffled ahead a hundred feet and stopped again. He tooted his horn and thanked the driver who'd politely let him in. AJ opened her door and got out.

"Shout before you move, please," she announced, and scooted under the Land Rover.

Cars from 1970 weren't made out of plastic like today, so every surface she could see was steel where a magnet could attach. Everything looked like an option except for the axles, which spun. Or the oil pan and lower half of the engine and engine bay, which had a mucky coating of oil from a leak somewhere. And the gearbox which appeared also to have a leak, or had benefitted from the engine gunk blowing backwards.

"Moving!" Reg shouted from above and AJ slid out from underneath and walked alongside.

"You've got a pretty good oil leak from somewhere," she informed him through the open window.

"That's my rust prevention system," he replied. "The salt air is a bugger on old cars."

He stopped again, and she dived back underneath, the hot asphalt burning any bare flesh it contacted. AJ looked along the box section chassis rails on each side, carefully avoiding the exhaust pipe. She couldn't see anything that didn't look like it belonged under the old Landy.

"Moving!" Reg shouted again, and she wriggled out and walked alongside once more.

"See anything?" he asked.

"Nothing you can't do without," she replied, dusting herself off as they moved forward to the traffic lights at Fort Street, where Harbour Drive became North Church Street for no apparent reason. The light turned red just as they got there.

"Rear bumper," Reg said. "Look there."

AJ ran around to the back and waved to the woman in the Trisha's Roses delivery van behind them. The lady stared back as though AJ were mad, but managed a tentative wave in return.

AJ lay on her back and wriggled under the Land Rover, feeling around the backside of the steel bumper, avoiding the big silencer hanging below the chassis. Her fingers felt the dirty residue from decades of road grime and oil leaks, then a smooth section right before she touched a small object. She couldn't see what it was, so she wiggled it, hoping she wasn't dislodging a key piece of wiring, or the flux capacitor.

She chuckled to herself and gave the little box a good tug. It moved around on the back of the bumper, but it didn't come free, so she gave it a solid pull. This time, she overcame the magnet, and it popped from the metal, sending the back of her hand into the hot silencer.

AJ yelped and scurried out, looking at the little black object in her hand. She held it up to the Trisha's Roses lady as though seeing the unidentifiable piece of plastic would help it all make sense. The lady looked like she tried to smile, but it came out more like a mixture of confusion and concern.

"Moving!" Reg yelled. "Get in!"

The traffic eased once they were past the traffic lights, and AJ showed Reg the little plastic box she held in her filthy hands.

"That'll be it," Reg confirmed, and AJ found a rag under her seat to wipe the tracker clean, along with her hands.

"I think we're ready for Operation Scorpionfish!" AJ declared.

"I'll call Whittaker," Reg said, picking up his mobile as they rolled slowly along in the line of traffic.

Without the wind noise drowning out the call, Reg dialled the number on speaker, and they waited for their friend to answer. He didn't, and it went to voicemail. Reg ended the call, and a few seconds later, a text popped up. He handed his mobile to AJ.

"He's in a meeting for another hour or more," she read aloud. "He's asking if it's urgent?"

"I think it is, but he might not agree," Reg replied.

AJ grabbed her own phone and dialled a number, putting hers on speaker as it rang.

"*Hei,*" came her friend Nora's Scandinavian voice.

"Are you off work?" AJ asked.

"*Ja.*"

"Doing anything special?"

"Having a drink on my deck with Edvard."

"How would you feel about helping Reg and me with something?"

"Is it fun?"

AJ thought for a moment. Her young Norwegian friend didn't follow tradition schools of thought about pretty much anything, so her idea of fun wasn't always easy to guess. But AJ knew her well.

"We're setting up a sting operation to grab a treasure thief, and Whittaker's in a meeting. He has a BOLO out for this bloke. We just need a copper there when we snag the wanker."

"Do you think he'll resist arrest?" Nora asked.

"No question about it," Reg chimed in.

"Okay," Nora said flatly. "Where?"

After giving Nora the details, AJ ended the call and thought their plan over for a minute.

"I was originally thinking we'd give Pebbles the made-up notes, so he goes traipsing off looking in the wrong place," she began. "But now we're arresting him on charges that aren't likely to stick."

"Whittaker can detain him for a few days, maybe longer after you ID him," Reg replied. "That keeps him out of our hair, and we'll know exactly where the bugger is."

"S'pose," AJ said, mulling it over. "Though I kinda liked the idea of duping him into running off somewhere."

"I'd rather he spent some time behind bars," Reg commented. "And while he's there, maybe they can figure out a hundred other offences to charge him with."

"You're right," AJ mumbled.

"What was that, love?" Reg asked.

"You heard, you old goat."

Reg laughed. "Yeah, but it doesn't hurt to hear again."

The cars were moving along steadily once they passed the cemetery and traffic lights where North Church became West Bay Road… for no determinable reason.

"Nora have a boyfriend now?" Reg asked.

"Not that I know of."

"Who's Edward, then?"

"Oh, Edvard," she replied, emphasising the 'v'. "He's a blue iguana who hangs out at the shack."

Reg looked at AJ and furrowed his brow. "She couldn't have a dog or a bloody cat like everyone else, could she?"

"I think you'd have to ask Edvard about it," AJ chuckled. "From what she told me, the iguana befriended her, not the other way around."

Reg shook his head as AJ's mobile rang. According to the caller ID, it was the George Town police station calling. "Hello, Roy," AJ answered.

"Actually, it's Rasha," the scene of crime officer said. "Hope that's not disappointing?"

AJ laughed. "More like an upgrade."

"I won't tell Roy you said that," Rasha joked. "Am I on speaker?"

"Yeah, but it's just me and Reg in his car."

"Okay," Rasha continued. "It's preliminary, but after initial inspection and a C-14 radiocarbon dating test, which I managed to fast track, I know enough to say the bone is from a human who died around 1700, plus or minus twenty-five years. It must have been buried in the sand to have survived this long without decomposing completely."

AJ and Reg both looked at each other.

"That's right around the time Watler and Bodden settled on the island, isn't it?" AJ asked.

"It's believed so," Rasha replied. "Isaac Bodden was the grandson born on Grand Cayman around the turn of the century, and it's thought the families were permanently living here from about that time forward."

"On the west and south, correct?" Reg asked.

"Yes," Rasha confirmed.

"So, not much chance a settler would have died or been buried near Anchor Point," he added.

"Not impossible, but more likely this person arrived by boat," Rasha said, choosing her words carefully.

"You used 'person'," AJ noted. "No determination whether it's male or female?"

Rasha paused for a moment before replying. "No. I can't be sure of that yet, nor the age, although I can say for certain the bone belonged to an adult."

They thanked Rasha and ended the call, continuing north behind Seven Mile Beach.

"We've still got nothing tying Crowe's story or the *Royal Fortune* to Grand Cayman," AJ pointed out.

"True," Reg agreed. "But the circumstantial evidence keeps building."

AJ didn't reply, but she slowly nodded, chewing the details over in her mind.

27

WHAT MUST BE DONE

1703

When I woke, I was alone in the cabin, and the *Royal Fortune* was under sail. From the sunlight streaming in through the window, I knew it was still daytime. A wave of nausea rushed over me as I recalled the events of earlier. I moved to the window and the fresh air helped the moment pass. In the distance, I noticed the mast of a ship. I prayed the three men who'd been spared would live long and happy lives, but I imagined their friends' deaths would plague their minds. As they would mine.

Up until that moment, I thought of Marcus every day and wished he could be with me, experiencing the adventure by my side. Now, all I wanted was to be off this ship, never to see any one of the crew again. But I knew that wasn't possible, not until we made Jamaica. Reluctantly, I left the cabin and before I'd climbed the steps to the main deck could hear the men were in high spirits.

I turned and looked above me to the quarterdeck. Vin was at the helm with Captain Rochefort alongside. I climbed the steps to view over the forecastle and saw land ahead.

"Hispaniola," Vin said.

Rochefort barked orders to Hinchcliffe, who appeared to be sober. He in turn yelled directions to the men, who pulled on ropes to trim the sails. The main sail was already furled as we slowed our approach, and the captain picked out a spot to anchor. He chose a large bay which hid us from ships passing to the north and south. A seaman shouted out depths every few minutes as he dropped a lead line and hauled it back in.

"Let go the anchor!" the captain called, and I heard a big splash.

The rest of the sails were furled, and the *Royal Fortune* continued its momentum towards the coastline until the anchor bit in the sandy sea floor and the ship swung around to a stop.

"Anchor secure," a man yelled from the bow.

"We sail at daybreak, day after tomorrow, boatswain," the captain said. "Make sure every man is ready by then."

"Aye, sir," Hinchcliffe replied. "I'll bring a bottle to your cabin, sir," he added, and eyed Vin with a look of disdain. "The rest of you can join us for yer share."

"The men can have mine, with my compliments," Rochefort said, then he nodded to Vin and left the quarterdeck.

Hinchcliffe stared at Vin for a few moments. "Drinking man?" he asked.

"Occasionally," she replied.

"Then this should be one of those occasions," he said without a smile, and left.

Our cabin was stifling hot now the ship wasn't moving, but it was away from the crew whom we could hear on deck, singing loudly accompanied by drunken laughter.

Vin sniffed the bottle she'd been handed on our way down and turned up her nose at the smell.

"This stuff would strip the varnish off the deck," she said, blinking the fumes from her eyes.

She poured three quarters of the bottle out the window into the sea and topped it back off with water from a jug.

"Are you going out there?" I asked.

She nodded. "I must. If we're to keep up appearances until we reach Kingston, I must fit in with the crew."

"How could you stand to be near these men?" I asked in astonishment. "They're barbarians."

Vin turned to me, and I tried to read the expression on her face. *Anger?* Determination, I decided.

"I'm doing what must be done to survive, Wil. You saw how Hinchcliffe challenged the captain and stared me down. That man thinks he should be navigator, and I wouldn't be surprised if he has ambitions to be captain. The men listen to him. We can't afford to be in his bad graces."

"I'm already there," I scoffed. "He finds all the worst jobs for me to do."

"I'm so sorry, Wil, but this won't be for long. We'll jump ship in Kingston and find passage home."

"It scared me when the boatswain grabbed you on the Spanish ship," I admitted. "He's an evil man."

Vin nodded. "That he is, Wil. But that's why I need to do all I can to stay in his good graces."

Her words made sense, but the thought of her amongst those savage men who'd all be drunk was terrifying. "Why did he stop you?" I asked, thinking back to that moment on the deck of the merchantman.

"He wanted to know why I'd chosen the men I had."

"Did you tell him?"

"I lied," she said quietly. "I told him I'd chosen the youngest, strongest men to be executed, as they were more likely to take arms against the English in the future."

I looked at the wooden deck beneath our shoes, worn and stained from years of tired feet dragging their way to and fro. We'd been aboard for no more than a month, but every sliver of excitement had now vanished from the adventure in one slash of a pirate's blade. A moment I couldn't unsee, and I wished we'd stayed on Salt Cay to face our fortunes there.

"What *did* you say to them?" I asked.

"Say to whom?"

"The Spanish men," I whispered, struggling to speak the words as the events replayed in my mind.

Vin sighed as though the breath was forced from her body. "I asked who of them had families."

I looked up at her. "Why?"

She closed her eyes. "Because I chose the men with families to be spared."

I could see her teeth were gritted, and she was forcing back tears. I stepped forward and embraced my mother. Even hugging her felt different now, her whole body firm. Gone was the soft feel of her chest against me, the warm, safe cradle I'd known my whole life. But her arms enveloped me tightly in the loving way they always had, and once again I believed everything would be alright.

"Be careful," I said softly, and she squeezed me one more time before letting me go and leaving the cabin with the bottle in hand.

"Happy new year," Vin said, as I woke. It had been several weeks since the incident with the Spanish vessel and we had hunted the area between Hispaniola and Cuba without further success. Which I had mixed feelings about. The sooner we filled our hold, the sooner we'd sail for Jamaica and begin our journey home. But any ship we captured would likely suffer the same fate as the ketch, a sight I hoped to never witness again.

"A better one, I hope," I responded, rolling off the bed and looking outside where the early morning light streamed in through the open window.

"This year, 1704, will see us home," Vin replied, already dressed and ready. "Chin up, son. I was thinking we'd live with my family in Sussex when we return. What do you think about that?"

My grandparents on my mother's side were wealthy aristocrats with a large estate which they operated with the minimum of servants. Neither had personal valets, choosing to dress and groom themselves or take assistance from one of the housemaids as needed. Their butler and his wife had worked for the family for over forty years, and while a distinct line remained between employer and servants, I'd never heard a request given without the word 'please' attached. A far cry from my father's treatment of staff.

I realised my uncle, who was five years younger than my mother, had been more like an older brother and then a father figure to me as we'd grown up. I felt closer to him than I'd ever felt to the man we'd left on the ground in a pool of blood on Salt Cay.

I smiled for what felt like the first time in forever. "I'd like it very much."

An unintelligible voice yelled from above, and the message was shouted from man to man until we could hear what was being said.

"Ship ahoy!"

Vin opened the door and paused for a moment. "Wil, come below if we capture the ship. Don't stay on deck."

I nodded, and she ran up the steps. As I pulled on my breeches, I steeled myself for what may lie ahead, reminding myself I was now the man of the family, despite my mother's disguise, and it was time I acted as such. The days of hiding behind her like a child were a luxury we could no longer afford. I finished dressing and ran up top, where the captain called me to his side.

"Take a look through the glass, lad. Tell me what you see."

I took the brass spyglass from him and trained it on the horizon to the south off our starboard bow as he directed. I found the ship and tried my best to keep it in sight as we rolled through the swells.

"Two masts, sir," I said, once I was sure. I watched a wave break over the bow, confirming the ship's direction of travel. "A brig, sir. The aft mast is taller than the fore, and I see a trysail on the bow."

"A flag?" Rochefort asked.

"Too far away for me to tell, sir," I replied.

"Heading?"

I took the spyglass from my eye and blinked a few times to clear my vision. The captain held his compass in front of me and I studied the rose once the needle had settled on north. Taking my time, I took one more look at the brig before replying.

"North-west, sir. They're beam reaching."

"Aye," he agreed. "That's what I made of it. Puts them on a line from Port-au-Prince to Santiago de Cuba. It's a Spanish ship, all right."

I handed him the spyglass. "And we're upwind."

"Precisely. Trick here is not to make our approach too soon."

I caught Vin's eye, and she smiled from the helm. Her ease gave me confidence to ask a question.

"Can't we get in position to intercept, then reduce sail as we close, sir?"

"Ask yourself this, lad," he replied, resting a hand on my shoulder. "What would you do if you were captain of that brig, and a ship such as this changed course to meet you?"

I thought for a moment. "That would depend on my purpose, sir."

"Aye. If you're a merchantman with thirty hands and no cannon, what then?"

"I'd daresay I'd be keen to avoid a conflict, sir."

"Precisely, lad. So if we go galloping towards an intercept point, what does that tell you as captain of that brig full of cargo?"

"I should take evasive action, sir."

"Correct. And what would that be?"

We were sailing on roughly a parallel but opposite course to the brig, and I wondered why the captain was wasting time giving me lessons instead of starting his run, and then it dawned on me.

"If you turn to starboard, you'll reveal your intent, so I'd turn north and sail close hauled, taking position upwind of you. It would make it almost impossible for you to get position on me."

He nodded and smiled. "Now, what if you're a Spanish ship of the line with sixty men and two dozen cannon?"

"And you cut south-west to intercept?"

"Indeed. Same scenario."

"I'd make the same move to take the advantageous position, but then I'd attack, sir."

"Exactly."

"So," I surmised, "we remain upwind and continue parallel as though we're happy to pass by, then once we get a better look and we're past the point they could manoeuvre to our port side, we'll make our move."

"Or keep on sailing if it's a man-o-war."

"Of course, sir."

"Stay close by, Wil. Your eyes are younger and keener than mine," he said, and took another look for himself. "We'll close our angle slightly, but not so much as we give them the idea we're interested."

Rochefort barked orders to the boatswain, who in turn yelled the instructions to the men. The ship was abuzz with energy and excitement, and I found myself caught up in the thrill of the chase. I was eager for the challenge of outsmarting the other ship with nothing more than our wits against the other captain's skills. The wind was a fickle beast who chose no sides and was reliable only in its inconsistencies. The victor of this contest would be the one who used that beast to their best advantage. At least as far as positioning was concerned.

"Thank you, Captain," Vin said, steering to the adjusted heading. "For giving Wil the lesson."

Rochefort grinned. "This is the part I love; the chase." He lowered his voice as he continued. "If we catch the buggers, I'd happily move on and leave them be, but no crew will sail with me without a prize at the end of the day."

I felt better knowing the man wasn't interested in the blood sport, but his words were a jarring reminder that we indeed faced a consequence if we captured the Spanish ship.

28

THE STING

Present Day

Reg turned left on the small, divided lane between Seven Mile Beach Resort and the Hampton Inn, then right into the Hampton's car park, where he found an open spot.

"He'll think we're in the hotel, won't he?" AJ said as they got out of the Land Rover.

Reg looked around them. "We live here. Why would he think we're staying in a hotel?"

"Because we're parked in a hotel car park, you plonker."

Reg waved her off. "Nah, he knows if there's a bar nearby I'm likely to be in it."

"Hmm," AJ grumbled as they walked towards the lobby of the hotel.

AJ waited outside while Reg went in and spoke to a young woman at the front desk. When he returned, they continued around the building to Ms Piper's, the detached bar and restaurant by the pool. "He better not think we're… you know…" she said, pointing her thumb at the hotel.

Reg laughed. "Nah, he knows I have good taste, too."

AJ slapped him on the arm. "You ought to be so lucky, mister."

"Okay," he countered, "that's enough of that talk."

"Yeah, I'm getting weirded out now."

They found an open table in the courtyard and ordered drinks when the waitress came by. AJ asked for water, but Reg ordered a Seven Fathoms over ice.

"We're on the job here," AJ pointed out.

"Don't mean I can't enjoy a beverage," Reg argued.

AJ opened the notepad and began talking about William Crowe and Christopher Alpers, leaning closer to Reg as she did.

"You know we'll have to keep this up for a while, right?" Reg pointed out.

"I suppose," AJ agreed. "He has to see the Landy stopped somewhere, then decide it's worth investigating."

"Unless he happens to be staying at the Hampton," Reg joked.

"He'll have a hard time finding anywhere on the island who takes cash," AJ said thoughtfully, "and he's probably trying to avoid using a credit card."

Reg shook his head. "I bet he has three different cards under three different names. It's too easy these days. No one anywhere checks signatures or IDs anymore."

AJ looked around the outdoor bar and tables arranged on a patio area lined by palm trees and tropical shrubs. A few kids played in the swimming pool while their parents soaked up the last rays of the day, although most of the area was already shaded by the five-storey South Bay Beach Club set between the Hampton and the beach.

Most of the bar stools were filled with couples or small groups huddled around a few seated friends. On the far end sat a tall, slender blonde wearing black leggings, a Metallica T-shirt, purple trainers, and dark sunglasses. She sipped on what appeared to be an alcohol-infused fruity Caribbean drink with a slice of pineapple speared by the obligatory umbrella. She was alone, but a bronzed guy in board shorts and no shirt was edging towards her. AJ grinned. Two hours a day in the gym was not going to help Mr Muscles get anywhere with Nora.

Their drinks arrived, and the waiter asked if they'd care for anything else.

"Bugger it," AJ mumbled. "I'll have a bottle of Strongbow and the veggie nachos, please."

"I don't tink we have da Strongbow, ma'am," he replied, sliding the menu towards her. "We have a nice selection of cocktails."

"Same as him then, please," she said, shrugging her shoulders.

"I'll have one more of these when you bring the grub, mate," Reg said, holding up the glass of rum he'd just received. "And get me one of them cones of chips."

"Yes, sir. Nachos, chips, and two rums over ice."

Reg raised an eyebrow. "Not just any old rum."

"No sir," the waiter smiled. "Seven Fathoms, sir."

"Good lad," Reg said with a wink.

AJ and Reg sat and chatted, turning pages in the fake notepad, but talking more about the real notes they'd made than the half-truths AJ had written on the third pad. Mostly they hashed over the same few details they'd gleaned. They kept coming back to the need for a copy of Crowe's original book, as Alpers's important notes had long since rotted away on the sea floor.

Most of the open ocean between Grand Cayman and Jamaica covered the Cayman Trench, a deep channel running alongside the Cayman Ridge, the underwater mountain range which barely peaked above the water, forming the three islands. The unfortunate Christopher Alpers, along with his helpers and their boat, could be as deep as 25,000 feet down.

"It's hard to imagine there's not a copy of *The Bravest Captain* somewhere in the world," AJ said, between bites of her nachos.

"Who knows?" Reg replied, setting his second glass of rum down. "Printing was a different game back then. *The Daily Courant* was the first British daily newspaper, and it only came out in seven-teen oh... something. Books were laborious to make, so it's possible only a few of Crowe's were ever printed."

AJ sipped her rum, enjoying the smooth taste for a few moments. "Pebbles has to have searched for one," she said, thinking it through. "And until he nicked our notes, he probably didn't know Alpers's diaries existed even if he knew the man searched for the Blade of Calcutta."

"All true, I'd say."

"So when we catch Pebbles, how do we get him to tell us all he knows?"

"Gimme half an hour alone with him," Reg replied.

"We're already going to be on thin ice with Whittaker. We can't hand Pebbles over with bits missing."

Reg grunted. "Didn't say anything about handing him over. He could simply disappear and save everyone the trouble."

AJ frowned at the big man and was about to tell him off when her mobile buzzed.

"Nora says we're a go," she whispered.

"I didn't see him, did you?" Reg whispered back.

They both leaned in again and avoided looking up.

"No, but I was distracted by you threatening to off people."

Reg picked up his mobile and sent a quick text while AJ tried to relax after feeling a surge of adrenaline. Reg's phone buzzed and he glanced at the screen.

"On her way. Two minutes," he said as AJ downed the rest of her drink.

She pushed the plate with a few nachos left to one side as though she were done and attempted small talk in a quiet tone. Two minutes went by slowly, and it took all of her willpower not to survey the patio and pick out their man.

"Hello there," came a familiar voice from across the courtyard, and they both rose and walked over to greet Pearl.

Reg kissed her and AJ gave her a hug, both taking plenty of time.

"What now?" Pearl whispered.

"See anything happen behind us?" Reg asked.

"No, but you're in the way, so I can't see much of anything," she replied.

AJ turned and looked at their table. "Bloody hell. It's gone," she blurted and looked towards the bar. Nora was nowhere in sight.

A man wailed loudly from beyond the hotel somewhere and AJ took off running. Behind her, Reg told Pearl to wait at their table and lumbered after her. He was faster than his size suggested when suitably motivated, but AJ ran the beach three or four times a week and found the cause of the ruckus before Reg had even turned the corner to the car park.

Nora had a man on the ground with her knee in his back and one arm twisted behind him. The notepad lay on the ground next to them. AJ ran up and looked down at the man whose face was pinned against the asphalt. He was snorting and fighting for breath in between swearing.

"Well, that's not him," AJ said, staring at the twenty-something dark-skinned man squirming on the ground.

"You didn't think he'd come himself, did you?" Nora said in her matter-of-fact tone.

Reg arrived huffing and puffing, and leaned over to look at the man. "That ain't him."

"He's the guy who scoped you both out and pinched your book as soon as you weren't looking," Nora responded, keeping the prisoner pinned. "Maybe you should ask him where to find the guy you're looking for."

"Let him up then," AJ said.

Nora looked up at her. "He's more likely to tell you something right now," she said and put more pressure on the man's arm.

He yelped. "I don't know nuttin', man. Some dude says to grab dat book, and he pays me. He says it his book and you take it from him."

"Where did you meet him?" Reg growled. "Where's he staying?"

"He found me, man. I playing dominoes under da shade tree over by West Bay dock and he walks up." He paused and gulped a few breaths. "You really hurtin' my arm, lady," he groaned. "Dis illegal what you doin' ere."

"I'm an off-duty police officer who witnessed a theft in progress and intervened," Nora said nonchalantly, although holding the man in place had to take considerable effort. "Want to chat about it some more?"

"No, no, I talk, just let me up!"

"Hey," AJ said, nodding towards the hotel where several people had gathered.

One of the tourists was filming the disturbance with her camera phone. Nora kept hold of the man's wrist but stepped to one side, letting her knee off his back.

"Give me your other wrist," she ordered, and the man complied, finally breathing easier. She produced a large zip tie like a magician pulling a rabbit from a hat and secured it around the man's wrists. Then Reg helped her pick him up to his feet.

"You always carry restraints off duty?" the man asked, giving her lean figure a look over, no doubt wondering where she concealed anything more than a toothpick.

"*Ja*," she replied.

"Where are you supposed to meet to hand it over?" Reg asked.

"He say to drop it at da front desk at da Marriott. Dey den s'posed to give me an envelope wit da rest of da money."

"Cut him loose," Reg said, and Nora hesitated.

"Better call Whittaker," she said firmly. "This was fun, but taking someone down at the Marriott front desk will cost me my job."

"Told you dis wasn't legal," the man muttered.

"What's your name, mate?" Reg asked.

"Virgil."

"Tell you what, Virgil," Reg said. "You play along and help us out, and we'll make sure you don't get nicked for the theft you're on the hook for."

Virgil looked at Nora, then back at Reg. "You a copper too?"

"No, but the detective I'm about to call is a good mate of mine."

"She gonna roll wit dis plan?" Virgil asked, looking at Nora again.

"Depends if you call me 'she' when I'm standing right here. Perp."

"Damn, you tough, girl. I tink I hear about you in town."

"We have a deal?" Reg persisted.

"She... I mean da lady here, agree?" Virgil asked.

Nora nodded.

"Den we got a deal, man."

"Now that's sorted, let's get out of sight," AJ suggested, as the crowd had grown bigger.

Nora produced a knife from somewhere else unknown and cut the zip tie. "Run, and I won't go easy on you again."

"Dat were easy on me?" Virgil scoffed.

AJ looked at him and nodded. Virgil's eyes got wider.

"Come on, I didn't finish my nachos."

"I'm starvin', man. Dis mean I get fed now?"

"Don't push your luck," Reg growled. "I'll meet you there," he said to AJ and Nora. "I'll call Roy."

29

KINGSTON

1704

I chewed my lip and struggled to hold the spyglass steady.

"Well, lad?" Rochefort asked, his voice beginning to sound impatient. "Are there muzzles are not?"

"I don't see any, sir," I said, praying I was right.

"Gun ports? Do you see gun ports?"

"No, sir," I said, handing him the spyglass.

"We're trusting the word of the ship's boy?" Hinchcliffe growled from close by. "Send your glass to the crow's nest. Sir."

He took his time adding the respectful address and glared at me.

"The crow's nest is too unstable in these seas, boatswain. The lad has keen eyes," the captain sharply retorted. "Now bring us to starboard, and run windward."

"Aye, sir," Hinchcliffe replied, and barked the orders out to the crew, who frantically pulled on ropes and adjusted sails.

Vin spun the wheel, steering the ship to starboard, putting the Spanish vessel off our port bow. Our carrack heeled over before squaring up as the wind filled the sails and we sped towards our prey.

The Spanish captain made the only sensible move left available to him and turned downwind in an effort to outrun us. Perhaps he was optimistically keeping his destination in mind, but he ran slightly west of perfectly windward, and with his laden cargo and our running start, we gained quickly.

We were short on quantity of cannon, but what we had were five-inch-long guns mounted on the main deck. This allowed our firing crews to aim in wider angles if needed. As we closed within 200 yards, Rochefort ordered a slight shift to starboard, giving the port side cannon a difficult but achievable shot.

"Fire," he called, and the blast was deafening.

My whole body shuddered from the power in the explosion as smoke billowed from the muzzle. I watched the Spanish ship's topsail begin to flap and realised the aim was high. The cannonball went through the sail and landed well beyond the brig.

Rochefort's warning shot did the trick. A sailor waved a white piece of cloth from their poop deck, and the brig's sails began to drop. Our crew cheered loudly and Rochfort issued a series of orders to bring us alongside. Once Hinchcliffe had relayed the commands, the captain beckoned him over.

"Boatswain, there'll be twenty to thirty hands manning this ship. We can take their payload without blood, or engage in a fight we'll likely win, but with losses. We're already shy on men. I'd prefer to keep the ones we have."

Hinchcliffe looked from the captain to the brig we were approaching. His head bobbed as he appeared to be counting, a talent not all the crew possessed.

Finally, he turned back. "Aye, Captain. I'll pass the word."

I breathed a sigh of relief but still wondered if the blood-thirsty pirates would adhere to the plan. They certainly wouldn't if the Spaniards threw the first punch.

It took thirty minutes to line up the two ships and lash them together.

"With me," Rochefort said to Vin, and she followed him to the gunwale.

I tagged along at a distance, looking at our crew standing at the ready with cutlasses and pistols in hand, but not pointed at our adversaries. The pirates looked terrifyingly threatening. Perhaps more so by the fact I knew what they were capable of.

"I am Capitán José García Guerra," an older, well-dressed man said in accented English.

He stood no more than ten feet from me. It was the closest I'd ever been to a people I'd been told were my enemy.

"Captain Rochefort, sailing under the flag of the Queen of England. Pleased to meet you, sir."

The Spaniard raised his eyebrows and surveyed the eager pirates lining the gunwale. His own crew appeared unarmed and nervous.

"You'll forgive me, sir, if I don't feel the same way."

Rochefort smiled. "I understand, Captain. May I ask what you carry below?"

"Cacao seed and coffee," Guerra replied.

Vin looked at me and winked. I took it to mean our next stop would now be Kingston, Jamaica.

"Perhaps you'd care to join me while my men relieve you of your cargo, Captain?" Rochefort offered, and the Spaniard nodded but didn't move.

"Captain Rochefort, *¿habla usted español?*"

"*No, pero yo sí,*" Vin replied, then turned to Rochefort. "He wanted to know if you spoke Spanish, sir."

"*Ordenaré a mis hombres que depongan las armas si me prometen paso libre,*" the Spaniard continued.

Rochefort looked at Vin in confusion.

Vin whispered the translation, which neither I nor any of the crew could hear, which I assumed was the point.

"*Sí,*" Rochefort said directly to Guerra, and the Spanish captain turned and addressed his crew.

"Proceed, boatswain. Peacefully," Rochefort said, "I've given my word."

"Aye, sir," Hinchcliffe replied, without giving much effort to hiding his disappointment.

Guerra stepped aboard the *Royal Fortune*, and the pirates descended on the merchant vessel, but at least they'd sheathed their cutlasses. I prayed no one decided to be stupid or brave.

Our hold and part of the crew's berth were packed tight with sacks by the time we sailed west. Everyone kept their promise and to my relief, no blood was shed. I felt a ray of hope that this ordeal would soon be over. I'd learnt much about the inner workings of sailing a ship of this size, for which I was grateful, but I couldn't put behind me the ruthlessness of my shipmates.

The crew were in great spirits, with a payday approaching and a few days in Kingston. Many of the older men spoke of the wild days and nights in Port Royal before an earthquake and subsequent tidal wave destroyed the town in 1692. Renowned for its reputation as a pirates' lair, the town was being rebuilt until a fire razed it all to the ground except for the defensive castle. Under pressure from England, and concerned the place was cursed, the Governor of Jamaica chose not to rebuild Port Royal again, and instead developed the smaller town of Kingston on the north shore of the natural harbour. The seasoned men far preferred the old town packed with bars and brothels, but they seemed confident Kingston could still provide the entertainment they sought.

With the wind to our stern, we made rapid progress and within two days, the call came down from the crow's nest that land had been sighted. As we turned the south-west corner of the large island, we began to see more ships coming and going.

We sailed into a huge bay shielded by a spit of land, and Lefty pointed out Port Royal to me. Once the largest town in the Caribbean, it now lay mostly in ruin at the tip of the slender ribbon of land protecting the bay. Local fishing boats moored to its docks, where I imagined the majestic ships used to be.

Those ships were now moored outside the busy port of Kingston, half of which appeared to be under construction. Several were alongside the dock being loaded or offloaded and we dropped anchor amongst a group awaiting their turn. Vin joined the captain, who had one of the cockboats lowered and asked for two men to row them ashore. I quickly volunteered, eager to go ashore and find a vessel home.

Hinchcliffe and several of the men laughed at me, but none of them were keen for the extra work. Until the captain returned with the crew's shares, they had little incentive to step ashore and watch other sailors enjoying themselves. Thankfully, Lefty raised his hand and said he'd go, and the boatswain told us to get on with it.

The dock was a hive of activity, and if it weren't for the stifling heat and humidity, I may have thought we were in Portsmouth. Another difference was the throngs of Negroes in shackles being herded through the docks and marched out of town to the sugar plantations. I thought of Marcus and wondered if relatives of his were amongst the poor souls being treated like animals.

Slavery wasn't technically legal in England, but it certainly seemed like plenty of Englishmen and their ships were engaged in the slave trade. The contradiction between my own experience with Negroes and what I now saw on the docks was so far apart, I found it hard to fathom. Man's cruelty towards his own kind was a trait that seemed to have no bounds.

Rochefort and Vin left us to officially transfer our 'forced trade' - as our stolen goods were laughingly called - to the *Royal Fortune* by the Admiralty court. After that, they intended to go in search of buyers. Traders often bid against each other for the pirates' prizes, accumulating goods to be resold and shipped by merchantmen to the New World or England. With instructions not to wander too far and regularly check back at the cockboat in case the captain returned, my shipmate and I were left to our own devices.

If he hadn't been as keen as the others for blood sport with the

Spaniards, I would have really liked Lefty. He treated me like an equal. A few of the others did too, but most looked down on me as the ship's boy, and some thinly veiled their outright hostility. According to Lefty, the hateful ones disliked anyone who could read or write and spoke the Queen's English, and there was nothing I could do about it, so I shouldn't bother worrying over them. That was easy for him to say. He didn't have a dozen angry pirates giving him threatening stares every day.

Regardless, it didn't matter as I would be leaving port on a different ship and would never have to see those men again. We didn't have to go far to find pubs. It seemed like every other business behind the docks was full of drunk or soon to be drunk sailors. We walked the street, which I noticed was very straight, and all the other streets leading from it were wide and equally unwavering. The town had been laid out in a symmetrical grid pattern, most unlike England, where cities and towns grew from villages which were built around natural obstacles in no particular pattern.

Most of the men I saw had the same look as the crew of the *Royal Fortune*. A few soldiers mingled, and the only women wore clothes of the like I'd never seen. The custom in Jamaica was to reveal plenty of bosom and leg, and I recalled my father speaking of strumpets in reference to such women. I found myself staring at them, but Lefty did the same, so I presumed it was acceptable behaviour.

We walked, and I peeked inside the doors and windows as we went, looking for gentlemen who might know of passage home. Of course, I couldn't let Lefty know my intentions, but perhaps I could slip away if the opportunity arose. We came across an English newspaper, the *Daily Courant*, which described a great storm which had ravaged England in December, the news just reaching Kingston. I read the details to Lefty, shocked at the loss of life and property from the freak cyclone.

"Best head back, lad," Lefty said when we reached the end of the street.

We returned along the other side of the broad street, and I

continued my search without any luck. As we reached the last pub before our turn to the dock front, I heard a familiar voice. At first, I was about to call out to the man, then realised my error and stepped beyond the window.

Inside, at a table by the opening, my father's two workers sat drinking ale and talking loudly over the other lively voices in the pub.

"What's up with you, then?" Lefty asked as I hid from view.

I shushed him and pulled him against the brick building.

"Bloody hell, lad," he grumbled.

I listened intently, trying to pick their voices out of the raucous laughter and chatter around them. One of them was talking about the English authorities, and then my heart stopped. Gordy babbled about rewards and made guesses at various amounts before telling Duck they needed to be the first ones to spot the *Royal Fortune* docking.

"We'll hand her and the kid in," Duck said, slamming his tankard on the table. "Get something for working for that bloody bastard!"

"Shame about her ladyship, mind you," Gordy added. "She's a looker, and she was always good to us. Hate to see a rope hung around that pretty neck."

"Pretty or ugly, pays the same, mate," Duck replied. "Can't be getting soft about it."

30

PURPLE PEOPLE EATER

Present Day

It was dark when Detective Roy Whittaker arrived at Ms Piper's, where AJ, Reg, Pearl, Nora, and Virgil waited. When Pearl and Nora had ordered food, they'd succumbed and bought Virgil a burger, but turned down his request for a beer. Whittaker and Reg walked away from the table so Reg could bring the detective up to speed, and while they were away, AJ's mobile rang.

"It's Buck Reilly," she grinned, looking at Nora. "I spoke with him earlier. He says he's in a relationship."

Nora smirked and took the phone from AJ, hitting the accept button, then put the call on speaker. "Hello, Buck, this is Nora. Are you coming to see us?"

She winked at AJ, who stifled a laugh.

"Nora? Oh hi. I thought I'd called AJ's phone."

"You did, but I saw it was you and wanted to hear your voice."

The line went silent for a few moments. "Damn it…" Buck muttered. "Wait. You're messing with me, aren't you?"

"Hi, Buck," AJ stepped in, starting to feel sorry for the poor man.

Why, she wasn't sure as he'd recently hit a treasure hunting jackpot and was back to being 'King Buck' after a few tough years, the title resurrected from the first time he'd hit it big. More importantly, according to him, he was now in a committed relationship.

"AJ, okay," he said, gathering up his wits once again. "I hear people in the background. You'd better take me off speaker for this."

AJ took her mobile back from Nora and clicked it off speaker as she stood and walked away from the now busy bar.

"I'm alone. What's up?"

"Ever heard of the Blade of Calcutta?" he asked.

A million thoughts raced through AJ's mind, not least of which was how and why Buck was bringing this up now. She hadn't known about it and therefore couldn't have mentioned the lost sword two days prior when they'd spoken.

"I hadn't until yesterday," AJ replied. "I'm sure we didn't find the hilt from the Blade of Calcutta."

"You didn't," Buck agreed, "but your find had me thinking. Do you know there's a diary by a guy named..."

"Christopher Alpers," AJ interrupted. "How do you know about them?"

Buck laughed quietly on the other end. "Let's just say I have an influential friend who helped me gain access to the National Maritime Museum in the UK."

AJ remembered back to when they'd spent time together hunting down items from the famous Baker Street bank robbery. Buck had a contact who seemed to have access to anything, anywhere, especially in England.

"But you said them in reference to the diaries," Buck continued. "As in plural."

Now AJ felt like she was in a pickle. She'd accidentally given away what was supposed to be a trusted secret.

"Did I?" she replied, buying time while she thought of an escape.

Buck laughed again. "Yup, and it wasn't the ones lost with Alpers, so I'm guessing his widow had more than just the one in London."

AJ sighed. "Perhaps, but I couldn't say, Buck. Really, I couldn't." The line was quiet.

"But, if there *were* a second diary," AJ continued in a whisper. "I doubt it would reveal much more about Crowe's book. So a copy of *The Bravest Captain* is still what's needed to move forward."

"Okay, that's fair," Buck responded. "It was actually the book I was calling you about."

"You have a copy?" AJ asked excitedly.

"Cool your jets," he said in amusement. "If I had a copy of the book, believe me, I'd have already landed in the islands."

"Well, I don't have one, if that's what you were wondering," AJ replied, feeling like she was getting nowhere in this conversation.

"You don't, and neither does Pritchard," Buck said. "And yes, of course I know who he is, and what he's capable of. I also know he was on Little Cayman until news of your discovery leaked out."

"Hopefully, the wanker is about to spend a few nights in jail," AJ said. "We just caught a guy he paid to nick our notes. We're setting up a sting operation to take the bugger down in a few minutes."

"Really?" Buck replied, sounding impressed. "I hope you're successful, and if there's an opportunity to kick him in the balls, tell him it's from me."

AJ laughed. "I'll do my best, but if the opportunity presents itself, I think Reg will take care of Pritchard for everyone. He's made friends far and wide, has our Pebbles."

"That's the truth," Buck agreed. "And most would like to see him resting peacefully at the bottom of the ocean."

"I'd hate to inflict him on the fish," AJ joked.

"Okay, so let me give you a quick synopsis of what I know," Buck began. "The *Royal Fortune* was never seen again after attacking the *Cielos de Oro,* and the only references to its movements come from Alpers's notes where he quotes Crowe mentioning a shallow bay on the north-east coast of the northernmost island of Los Caymanas. That would be Little Cayman."

"Yup, I'm with you so far," AJ said, while Buck took a breath.

"No doubt Crowe went into more detail, but it must have been in Alpers's later diaries which are long gone. We know William Crowe ended up back in England, so either he remained on Little Cayman and took a passing ship home, or the *Royal Fortune* made another stop where they parted ways. If the pirate ship did reach port somewhere else, there's no known record of it, and the other mystery, of course, is the fate of his mother, as she didn't return with him."

"Why is it believed that the Blade of Calcutta stayed on Little Cayman with Crowe?" AJ asked. "Seems far more likely it suffered whatever fate befell the *Royal Fortune.*"

"We don't know for sure," Buck explained. "But did you see Alpers's notations about titling his own book, which he planned to write?"

"Kate Alpers told the museum director here that her husband intended to write a book," AJ said, recalling the text which had initially confused her.

"From a mixture of those potential titles, we surmised Alpers knew the Blade of Calcutta remained on Little Cayman after Crowe left."

"Why would he have made notes in an earlier diary about something he'd learnt farther into the book?" AJ asked. "It's out of sequence."

"I figured he read *The Bravest Captain* at least once before he decided to try to find the Blade of Calcutta. My guess is it happened to be that point he'd reached in the diary when he thought about his own book."

"Makes sense," she replied, then thought for a moment. "Hang on, Bucky Boy. So how would Pritchard know about that? If he was searching on Little Cayman, he has to have seen the diaries too!"

"Only the first one," Buck replied sheepishly.

"How did he get access to that?"

Buck was quiet for a moment. "Because I showed copies of the pages to him."

"Why the bloody hell would you do that?" AJ seethed.

"Go easy on me, Purple People Eater. As much as it pains me to say, we were partners on the project for a short time."

"Purple People Eater?" AJ asked, running her fingers through her purple-streaked hair. "What the hell is that?"

"You know, the defensive line of the Minnesota Vikings," Buck started. "Back in…"

"Forget it, doesn't matter," AJ groaned, mistakenly assuming she was being insulted. "So you're calling to warn me the arsehole we're trying to arrest is operating on the information you gave him?"

"Not exactly," Buck replied. "I was calling to discuss *The Bravest Captain.*"

AJ looked through the palms and saw Reg and Whittaker rejoining the table. "So, get to the point, Buck. Looks like we're ready for phase two of Operation Scorpionfish. I have to go."

If Buck wondered exactly what Operation Scorpionfish was, he must have sensed the urgency, and ignored the reference. "Okay, okay, I'm just trying to help. I chased down this rabbit hole a few years back and came across the same roadblock as everyone else, which is no copy of the book seems to still exist. I had to move on to a higher percentage project, but the last lead I dug up might have some legs. If you're interested?"

AJ had been half listening as she saw everyone get to their feet from the table, but she heard Buck's last sentence. "Of course, yes. What was the lead?"

"You know William Crowe returned home and formed a shipping company with his mother's brother, right?"

"Yep, and another bloke, Marcus Smith."

"Correct," Buck explained. "And everyone who searched has concentrated on the Crowe family line, which ends in WWII when

Seafarer was bombed and everything was lost. If anyone outside the estate possessed a copy, they've never said a word about it, and I tracked down several descendants who knew their family history."

"So what *did* you find?" AJ asked with a mixture of impatience and anticipation.

"The Smith family," Buck replied. "I followed the family tree until WWII, where I hit a brick wall. Marcus Smith's direct descendants down through the male lineage appeared to finish after eight generations, when both sons of Albert Smith were killed in France. Neither had children."

"That's quite a story, but I'm not sure what I can do with it from there, Buck? I'd say you're right, it's a brick wall."

She heard Buck laugh a little. "A year after I'd moved on and was consumed with my own troubles, I received a letter from a lady in England claiming to be the granddaughter of Albert's sister. She told me one of the sons, Marleigh, survived the war. He was a POW until after V-E Day and then stayed in Europe instead of returning to England."

"Marley? Like Bob?"

"Pronounced the same, but spelt differently," Buck replied. "I'll text it to you."

"Is he still alive?" AJ asked. "He'd be ancient by now."

"I've no idea," Buck replied. "But the lady told me her father had mentioned Marleigh a few times when she was growing up, and after Albert died in the 80s, he came to England for the funeral. Afterwards, he shipped everything he wanted to keep of his father's to his home."

"In Europe?"

"No," Buck replied. "Grand Cayman."

31

LEFTY

1704

I hurried back towards the cockboat, praying the captain and Vin had already returned. It felt like every pair of eyes was upon me and each man we passed knew our secret.

"Oi, lad," Lefty grunted from two steps behind me. "What's the bloody rush all of a sudden?"

"We shouldn't keep the captain waiting," I replied without breaking stride.

"Nah," he said suspiciously, starting to huff and puff from the brisk walk. "What did you see in that pub?"

Lies were not a talent I'd been raised to perfect and, riddled with paranoia, I wasn't prepared with a plausible reply.

"More talk of the storm," I bumbled out. "I hope my family back home is all right."

Lefty was wheezing and trying to catch his breath behind me. I suspected the older man could carry a barrel of ale on his shoulder, but would die if asked to run the length of the ship. I had a few minutes to come up with a better story before we stopped, and he had time to recover enough to keep grilling me.

We reached the cockboat and, to my disappointment, found no one there. Lefty caught up and sat on the sea wall, catching his breath. He squinted at me and shrugged his shoulders as if to ask me why all the sudden madness. I'd heard someone once say that the best tales are based in truth, and without further contemplation, I blurted out a story I hoped wouldn't be the death of me.

"I killed a man. Back on Salt Cay. That's why my m… father and I left with the *Royal Fortune*."

I cringed at how close I'd come to really screwing up. I was taking a tremendous risk trusting Lefty, but I was only willing to reveal so much.

"Blimey, you did?" he spluttered.

I nodded. "My uncle. He was not a good man, and he threatened us. It was self-defence."

Lefty laughed. "I had you pegged as the squeamish type. I thought you were gonna spew your guts out when we offed them Spaniards."

"That was different," I retorted angrily. "They were seamen, not soldiers or navy sailors."

"Bloody Spaniards, lad," he said, rising to his feet. "They'll not show you any mercy, believe me. They're all the bloody same to me."

I took a deep breath. This certainly wasn't the time to get into a debate over the morality of executing our enemy's civilians.

"I saw two men who worked for my uncle," I said, changing the subject back to something I wanted to talk about only slightly less than slaughtering Spanish seamen. "I didn't want them to see me."

Lefty grinned. "Wanted man, eh?"

"As I said, my uncle wasn't a good man, so I doubt anyone will mourn his passing," I replied, now stretching the truth.

I felt a knot in my stomach. *What had I done?* It was stupid to trust this cutthroat. Surely, if he got wind of a reward, he'd hand me in without a second thought, and probably enjoy watching Vin and me hang.

"You're in good company now, lad," Lefty said, still smiling.

My mind was still reeling from my own stupidity, and I wasn't sure what he meant.

"Every man on the *Royal Fortune* is wanted for something, somewhere, lad," Lefty continued with amusement. "We call ourselves privateers, hiding behind a letter of marque from the Governor on behalf of the Queen. He's just using us to attack Spaniards and keep them out of Jamaica, but everyone knows we're nothing more than thieves and villains." He slapped me on the shoulder. "Most of us are glad to leave our real names behind," he added. "There's a noose waiting for those scallywags. No one's looking for ol' Lefty though," he said, letting out a belly laugh. "This'll set you right with the crew, lad. You're one of us after all."

I wanted to heave a sigh of relief, but there were still two men who would happily turn us in, given the chance, and standing around at the docks wasn't the best place to be. It felt like forever but was probably less than an hour when Rochefort and Vin showed up. They seemed in good spirits. Lefty took the hint when I quickly began dragging the cockboat into the water and wasted no time helping.

Once we were knee deep, we held the rowing boat steady while our passengers climbed aboard, followed by Lefty. I stayed in the water and shoved until the water was over my waist, then hauled myself over the gunwale. As I sat my oar in the rowlock, I glanced to shore and quickly spotted my father's two men walking to the dock. I dipped my head and began to row, causing Lefty to grumble as he wasn't ready.

It took a few moments to straighten us out, but pretty soon we were on our way and the two men were lost in the throngs of people on the docks. I hoped they were too merry after drinking ale all afternoon to notice the new arrival at anchor in the bay, or think to ask the dockmaster.

The captain talked with Vin most of the way out to the *Royal*

Fortune, and once I was sure Gordy and Duck hadn't spotted us, I relaxed enough to listen. From their conversation, I gleaned we'd be dockside midday tomorrow, when we'd spend the afternoon unloading our cargo, which Rochefort already had buyers for. Then the seamen would be paid and set free in town to squander their earnings. A skeleton crew would help manoeuvre the ship back out to a mooring, and the plan would be to weigh anchor the following morning. According to the captain, the men would be out of money, hired on another ship, or dead by then. He would leave with whoever made it back in time to sail.

There was no way our ship, or Vin and I, would remain unnoticed for two whole days. It also gave Father's men time to rally the authorities. If they posted signs, the whole town would hunt us looking for an easy payday.

With my mind whirring, Lefty and I tied the cockboat alongside while the captain and Vin scaled the boarding net up the side of the ship.

"I could make your problem go away, yer know," Lefty said to me when we were done.

"What do you mean?" I asked naively.

"Those two blokes you're all churned up over. I can make them disappear," he said and grinned. "For a small fee, of course."

"Kill them?" I blurted.

Lefty rolled his eyes. "No, have 'em over for a brew. Bloody hell, lad. You have yourself a problem, and what I'm saying is, I can make that problem go away. Sounds like that's what you're needing."

"I don't want them dead, Lefty. I worked with them for months."

We both began climbing the boarding net, which was easier for me having all my fingers.

"Don't sound like they have a problem seeing you hang, lad," he pointed out.

"That's because my fa... my uncle, he treated them poorly," I replied, almost slipping up again. "They were pleasant to me, and I don't believe they'd wish me harm under better circumstances."

We clambered over the gunwale and stood on the deck.

"These are the circumstances you have, though, ain't they?" Lefty said, breathing heavily once more. "No skin off my nose either way, mate, but I'd prefer you didn't swing." He gave me a shove. "I mean, who's gonna do all the lousy jobs if you're gone, eh?"

I managed a smile. "I do appreciate your offer, Lefty, but let's hope it doesn't come to that."

"Fair enough, lad," he said, shrugged his shoulders, and went in search of dinner.

It was dark before Vin made it to our cabin and I could finally tell her what had happened. We both sat on the edge of the cot and stared out at the blackness beyond the stern window.

"We're not safe in town, and we're not safe on the ship," I said, voicing my fear.

She put a hand on my knee but said nothing, deep in thought.

"Lefty offered to make them go away," I joked, and she quickly turned to me.

"We'll not have any of that. I imagine these men left Salt Cay unpaid. We can't blame them for seeking compensation."

"I told Lefty as much," I assured her.

"Hmm," she grunted. "Perhaps we can use Lefty's help, though, if he's willing."

"You just said we're not killing the men," I said, confused.

"We're not, and neither is Lefty. We only need them silenced for two days, not a lifetime."

I smiled, starting to understand her plan. "He was willing to help for a fee."

She shook her head and scoffed. "Better than being handed over for a reward."

"I hope they all feel that way," I said, wondering if Lefty had already passed the word around.

"Whatever we do, it best be done in the morning before we dock, and before the Governor puts a price on our heads."

"So what's the plan?" I asked, feeling buoyed by the fact my mother was once again going to make things all right.

"Quietly now, fetch Lefty," she told me. "I'll speak with the captain and meet you back here shortly. Let's see what price Lefty has in mind to help us out."

32

OPERATION SCORPIONFISH PART II

Present Day

Whittaker took Nora to one side and although it was hard to tell from her unwaveringly stern expression, AJ presumed she was being told all the reasons why she shouldn't have participated in Operation Scorpionfish Part I. When they returned to the waiting group at the table, Whittaker handed out his instructions.

"Everyone except Nora, Virgil, and myself will stay here," he began. "I have patrol cars stationed in both directions on West Bay Road, and I've spoken to the hotel manager, so he is expecting Virgil and he tells me a man indeed left an envelope at the desk."

"Did he see who dropped the envelope?" Reg asked.

"He's having the lobby video reviewed, but they just had a shift change, so no one currently at the desk saw the person. It appears it was left prior to 5:00pm."

"Bet it wasn't Pritchard who dropped the envelope," Reg added. "Nor him who'll pick up the notebook."

"I dare say you're correct, Reg," Whittaker responded. "But he may be nearby, or whoever he sends should be able to tell us the next meeting place. He can't continue using stand-ins. At some point Pritchard has to get his hands on the notebook."

"How about we move to the patio bar at the Marriott by the beach?" AJ suggested. "We can't be seen from the lobby, but we'll see if Pebbles is out there or arrives from that direction."

"I'm presuming 'Pebbles' is Mr Stone Pritchard," Whittaker replied, "and he'll recognise you two if indeed he's been following you. I think it's too risky."

"What if Pearl takes the Landy home?" AJ said. "You know, with the tracker. Pebbles will think Reg and I left."

The detective pondered the idea for a moment.

"We're short on people, sir," Nora offered. "This would cover one of the exits."

"Okay, but approach from the beach and stay out of view," Whittaker relented. "If you spot Pritchard, text or call me."

"Will do," AJ said, and Reg handed his wife the keys to the Land Rover, giving her a kiss.

"I'll walk you out, love," he said. "We can pick up the real note-books from the front desk on the way."

"Dat one not what da man lookin' for?" Virgil asked.

AJ grinned and shook her head.

"Damn, he woulda been mad at me. Don't feel so bad helpin' you now."

"Operation Scorpionfish, mate," AJ said, holding up her fingers like a gun in the James Bond pose. "Pebbles is getting stung!"

Reg shook his head. Whittaker let out a long sigh, and Nora looked confused.

"English is my second language, but I don't think sting in this context has a past tense."

Pearl patted AJ on the arm. "I thought that was very secret agent-like, love; don't listen to them."

Most people had left the adjacent pool after sunset, so the crowd was concentrated around the Marriott's patio bar, where all the stools were occupied. AJ and Reg waited in the shadows by the sea wall until they were sure Pebbles wasn't lurking on the patio somewhere. They then walked up the steps and swiftly moved to the far side of the bar under the large circular canopy.

The lobby was on the street side of the building, which was a square built around a central courtyard where paths and streams wound around casual seating areas. It was impossible to see the lobby from the patio.

"Bet he's waiting in the courtyard," AJ whispered.

Reg nodded. "Probably."

"Maybe we should take a peek?"

"Maybe we should do what Roy said and stay out here," Reg countered.

AJ grunted her displeasure.

"I'm getting a drink," Reg declared. "Want one?"

"Not very professional when we're on a special assignment."

Reg scoffed and waved to the bartender.

AJ scoured the patio area, carefully watching anyone who came and went, while Reg sipped his rum over ice and made sure his observations were far less obvious.

"Will you relax?" he whispered, which sounded more like a throaty growl. "Virgil has probably only just made the exchange. He said he wasn't told to make any contact or signal when he'd done it, which means Pebbles either plans to stop by later, or he's watching."

"Do you think he was watching Virgil at Ms Piper's?" AJ asked as the thought occurred to her.

Reg shrugged his shoulders. "Possibly, but let's hope not, or this'll be a long wait for nothing."

AJ grew more and more antsy as time wore slowly on. Reg had ordered another rum and complained to AJ about the Marriott's prices, but didn't ask if she wanted anything this time. Instead, he informed her she would be driving them home.

"In what?" AJ rebutted. "Pearl took your Landy."

"Pearl and Nora got here in something, didn't they?"

AJ grunted again. "I saw Nora's Jeep at the Hampton." She checked her watch. They'd been outside for over an hour. "Just a little peek," she said, and started to walk away.

"Oi, stay here, girl," Reg hissed, but she kept walking.

Reg swigged the last of his drink and plonked the glass on a table as he hustled after her, finally catching up by the walkway into the courtyard. AJ paused behind the cover of one of the palm trees liberally spread throughout the open-top area.

"Do you see him?" AJ asked.

"No, it's all mood lighting in here. I can't see a bloody thing," he snapped. "But he's probably seen us by now."

"It would be helpful if you weren't the size of a lorry, wouldn't it?"

"Don't make this my fault. I can't help being this big."

"True, but you could've stayed out there and let me look around all secret agent-like."

"Hush a minute," Reg hissed. "I think I see him."

"You do? Where?" AJ blurted, looking all around the courtyard.

"Will you stop sticking your noggin out there like a bloody meerkat? Follow me," he said and moved along one of the pathways down the right side, walking nonchalantly.

AJ scurried after him. "I still don't see him."

"Over there, in the chair in the far corner behind those palms and that little hedgerow thing," Reg said, nodding in the direction but stopping short of pointing.

"Blimey, that is him, isn't it?"

"AJ Bailey?" a man's voice greeted them, and they both came to an abrupt stop.

A small, skinny man with glasses stood before them.

"Carlson, keep your bloody voice down," AJ groaned at the reporter. "What are you doing here?"

Sean Carlson laughed. "I was meeting a friend for a drink outside. Would you like to join us?"

"That's a lie right there," Reg grumbled. "No chance you have any friends."

"Ouch, Mr Moore. That's not very cordial," Carlson replied, but didn't look in the least bit offended. "What's the latest on your artefact?" he continued, undeterred, looking at AJ.

"You picked the absolutely worst time to run into us," AJ whispered, pulling the young man behind a pair of palm trees.

"He's gone!" Reg growled, and AJ released Carlson, jumping back to the path.

"Bollocks!" she gasped. "Take the patio, Reg. I'll go inside!"

"What's going on?" Carlson asked, but he was talking to himself as AJ and Reg ran in opposite directions.

AJ reached the doors at the back of the courtyard, which automatically slid apart just as she arrived. She ran smack into a young woman exiting the lobby and the two of them went crashing to the ground in a heap.

"Bugger!" AJ squealed, and the woman let out a gush of air as the wind knocked out of her.

AJ sat up and looked around the lobby where every face was staring her way. She couldn't see Pritchard, but Nora came running by in a full sprint, followed by Whittaker, who moved at a brisk walk.

"Sorry," AJ said to the woman dressed in jeans and a T-shirt who was slowly recovering.

Picking herself up, AJ extended a hand, and it was then she noticed the notebook lying on the tiled floor. "You're kidding me? You're the pickup?" She pulled the woman to her feet, then grabbed her arm before she could bolt. "Where were you taking the notebook?"

"Into the bloody courtyard where he was waiting until you cocked it all up," Reg said between gasps of breath.

Nora arrived as well, followed by Detective Whittaker, who reached down and picked up the notebook full of fake notes.

He handed it to AJ. "I believe the plan was for you two to stay outside."

"That's how I remember it," Reg grumbled.

AJ's face turned beet red.

"Hey guys," came a voice, and they all instinctively turned around in time for the flash from Sean Carlson's mobile camera to blind them.

"Not another word, Reg. Not another bloody word," AJ grumbled.

33

THE TRAP

1704

We were behind the oars again. The sun was slowly emerging over the eastern end of the island, casting a beautiful orange glow across the still waters of the bay. As anxious as I felt, I was content taking our time and rowing at Lefty's pace as we headed for the shore.

Vin sat on the stern thwart, occasionally giving us directions as our backs were to the docks. Across her shoulder hung a satchel with everything she said we needed, and in her waistband was Mr Helms's cutlass and Father's pistol. She had cleaned and test fired the pistol several times since we'd left the island.

Our first problem was finding Gordy and Duck. Most of the pubs and taverns offered rooms or bunks, depending on your budget, but there was no guarantee they were staying at the pub I'd seen them in. The salt ship had dropped them, along with a portion of their cargo, and sailed on the day before we arrived, so it was doubtful they had joined the crew of another ship yet. Vin had discovered a galleon was sailing for England in three days, which would likely be their vessel home if they chose to leave.

It would also be our method of returning to England if we could navigate the treacherous waters of our current predicament. We had lain awake discussing our options until late into the night, and much depended on how quickly word spread. Once the captain of the galleon was aware of two fugitives named Crowe, simply lying about our names may not get us past their gangplank. If Father's men had spoken with Mr Helms or the other workers, they may also know of Vin's disguise.

We dragged the cockboat ashore above the high tide line and gazed around the docks. Seamen and dock workers were starting their day, but the town was much quieter than our prior visit. I guessed most men were sleeping off a hefty hangover before they began drinking again as soon as the taverns opened. Walking towards the pub from the day before, we saw several men who hadn't made it to a bunk anywhere, curled up in the dirt by the buildings. Coughs, snores, and pungent smells emanated from all of them.

A large woman wiped down the bar in the pub when we stepped inside.

"We're closed," she grunted.

Vin tipped her hat. "Madam, we are seeking two friends of ours who were seen here yesterday afternoon. Perhaps you could help us."

"Doubt it," the woman said without looking up.

Vin ignored her resistance and gave her a description of the men, making sure to detail Duck's distinctive scar.

"We had about a hundred blokes through here matching what you just said, love."

"The scar is quite distinctive," Vin reiterated.

The woman stopped wiping and laughed. "You know most all of 'em have something missing, broken, or scarred, love. They all look the bloody same," she said, then raised her eyebrows when Lefty held up his hand. "Yeah. See."

Vin slapped a coin on the bar and slid it towards the women. "A scar, right here," she said again, wiping her finger across her own forehead and down her cheek, demonstrating the location.

The woman pocketed the coin. "Friends, you say?"

"I did."

"You're well armed for visiting friends," she said, eyeing the weapons.

"Our friends may have enemies," Vin quipped in return.

The woman wagged a finger at Vin. "Don't you make any trouble. I don't need a reputation for grassing on blokes dossing here. You understand? Bad for business."

"Quiet as a church mouse, I promise," Vin replied.

The woman shook her head. "I doubt that. Out back. Got a pen I was raising a pig in, but we butchered him last week. They barely had a penny each after their bar tab, so best I could offer."

Vin tipped her hat once again, and we walked through the pub and out the back door to the yard behind.

The space was not large, backing up to another business fronting the next street over with a similar backyard. A fence made of scrap timber divided the two. On our left was the straw-lined pigpen the woman had spoken of, where snores broke the silence of the morning.

"How're we getting 'em out of here, then?" Lefty whispered.

Our options were thin. There was no way to leave from the yard, so our only choice was back through the pub. Vin shooed us back inside the building.

"Wil, wake them up and tell them you heard they were in town. Then offer to take them to me," she said with a wink. "We'll wait by the boat. Tell them I'm on the *Royal Fortune*."

I nodded. "What if they try to take me in?"

"They won't," Vin assured me. "They'll be too keen to get us both."

She squeezed my shoulder before she and Lefty retreated through the pub. I heard her tell the woman thank you as they left. I walked over to the pen and looked down at the two men I'd worked alongside for months. After our bumpy start, they'd been nothing but friendly towards me. I couldn't imagine they would see us hang over wages we had nothing to do with.

"Hello gentlemen," I said loudly and reached down, prodding the closest of them.

Gordy stirred and squinted up at me. "Wil Crowe?"

"Yes, sir. I was told I'd find you here."

"Oi," he said, nudging his partner awake. "Look who's here."

Duck groaned and sat up, rubbing his head where his scar marked his brow. "Bloody hell. Wil?"

"Hello. It's good to see you both."

The men stood and dusted themselves off. They both looked exactly as you'd imagine two seamen who'd collapsed drunk and slept in a pigpen would.

"My mother will be glad to see a friendly face," I said. "I could take you to her if you'd like?"

They looked at each other, neither hiding their surprise nor eagerness.

"Too right," Duck answered.

They clambered out of the pen and slapped me on the back.

"Growing like a weed, you are," Gordy said. "Look about a foot taller than when you left the island."

"I've been working hard on the ship," I said, glad of being able to tell the truth about something.

"Come on, then," Duck urged me. "Let's go see her ladyship."

I led them through the pub and noticed Duck carried a cutlass and Gordy a long dagger tucked in a sheath hanging from his belt. Neither had a pistol. The woman watched us cautiously as we walked out, but didn't say a word.

"We've been on the *Royal Fortune* since we left," I said. "I'll take you out there."

"Wait a minute," Gordy said, grabbing my arm. "We're not going out to no pirate ship."

"Privateers," I corrected.

"Privateers, pirates, no matter what you call 'em, we ain't stepping foot on that ship. We might not get to leave. That's how they recruit their crews half the time. She needs to come ashore."

The only part of the plan I knew was getting them to the rowboat, and I figured it didn't matter how.

"I'm sure that will be fine," I said jovially as I started walking again. "Give me a shove off the beach and I'll bring her back then."

The two men followed me, and once I had the rowboat in sight, I noticed Lefty was the only one there. The boat had been dragged into the shallows already. I hoped Vin had something arranged to stop Gordy and Duck asking about my mother, or Lefty would soon know our secret. I wasn't sure he'd be so keen regarding this second deception.

"That's my friend, Lefty," I said as we approached. "He rowed across with me."

The footsteps halted behind me.

"Not a word," I heard a low voice growl.

I turned and Vin had a pistol in the small of Duck's back and a blade to Gordy's neck.

"Wil, take these," Vin said, handing me two rags and pieces of twine. "Move," she said, shoving the two men towards the rowboat.

"No need f…" Duck started, but Vin cuffed him across the ear with the stock of the pistol. Duck groaned and clutched the side of his head.

"I said, not a word," Vin reiterated.

They reached the cockboat and Lefty helped me put the gags in the men's mouths, then tie them in place with the twine. Vin pulled two hoods from her waistband and placed them over their heads.

"Let's get going," she growled, and I steered them one by one to Lefty, who instructed them to step into the boat and sit down on the bow thwart. I held the boat while Lefty and Vin tied the prisoners' hands behind their backs, then the three of us pulled the cockboat clear of the sand and rocks.

We rowed in silence to the *Royal Fortune*, the odd groan or grunt coming from under the hoods. I was terrified Gordy or Duck would escape their gags and blurt something about Mother, leaving us explaining ourselves to Lefty. Reaching the ship, we tied the cockboat in at the base of the boarding net, and Vin sent Lefty up first. Once he was out of earshot, she moved closer to the two prisoners.

"There are two ways this can go for you," she whispered. "If you stay silent and don't reveal me to the crew, I'll set you free when we weigh anchor. Option two is you give me grief, and I cut your throats. Understand?"

Both hoods frantically nodded.

"Did you report us to the authorities in Kingston?" she asked, and both men sat rigidly still.

"I'll not punish you for doing so, but I need to know," she urged. "I can tip one of you over the side if you need persuasion to answer." Vin reached forward and grabbed one arm of both men.

Thinking each was the one going in the water, they both nodded so hard I thought they might shake off their hoods.

"I thought as much," Vin hissed. "We were nothing but kind to you, yet you'd see us hang?" she spat. "I ought to throw you both to the sharks."

The men grunted their defence unintelligibly behind the rags in their mouths.

"Stop snivelling you fools. Wil, free their hands," she ordered, and I cut the twine.

Vin took Duck by the arm and hauled him to his feet on the rocking boat and he swung a hand in the air, trying to steady himself.

"Use the net. Reach to your right," she barked.

Duck found the netting and began blindly fumbling his way up. I helped Gordy to his feet, as he snorted and grunted in near panic. We steered him to the netting, and he began to climb, leaving the two of us below in the rowboat.

"If they've reported us, how can we go ashore and find a ship to England?" I asked as we prepared to scale the nets.

Vin reached over and squeezed my shoulder. "We can't, Wil. It's not safe. Even if we're not caught in town, they'll have notified the captain of the galleon to be on the lookout."

"Won't they search the *Royal Fortune* when we dock?" I asked, feeling my own panic rising.

"They won't board the ship."

"How can you be sure?"

"Because I told Rochefort we needed to stop them from coming aboard."

"But won't they ask about a woman and a boy? The captain will know… you know…"

"He won't because I'll be greeting the officials at the dock."

"How will you stop them from coming aboard?"

"I'll pay them not to."

"What if they can't be bribed?"

Vin laughed. "This is Kingston, Jamaica, Wil. Everyone can be bribed."

34

A SURPRISE EACH MORNING

Present Day

AJ sat on the bar stool with her chin on her folded arms, staring at the condensation rolling down the side of her rum glass. She turned her head to look at Nora seated next to her.

"You haven't said anything yet. Don't you want to have your pound of flesh?"

Nora's hand paused with a scoop of ice cream from her sundae dribbling over the edges of the spoon. "What is the term the Americans say? Beating a horse?"

"A dead horse," AJ corrected. "That's the point, see. You won't get anywhere beating a horse who's already dead."

Nora ate the spoonful of ice cream before it all melted. "Yes. Dead horse." She said after swallowing. "You know you screwed up, so no point telling you over and over again."

"Yeah. Thank you."

"It won't make any difference," Nora added.

"Exactly. Let the past be the past and look ahead instead of behind."

"That's not what I meant."

AJ picked her head up and scooped up her glass. "You said it correctly."

"I know. But I didn't mean what you think I meant."

"What did you mean, then?"

"I meant you'd do it again, so it doesn't matter what I say."

AJ's head dropped to her arms once again and her glass clonked on the bar top. Reg laughed until she thought he might hurt himself.

"And you lot are my best friends," AJ complained. She lifted one eye to see Nora. "Ever heard of the pot calling the kettle black?"

"I don't think I've seen a black kettle," Nora replied. "They're metal coloured."

"Metal isn't a colour, love," Reg pointed out. "We'd say it's silver."

"In Norway, we don't make kettles from silver," Nora replied. "That seems like an expensive kettle. The one I bought here is metal."

"No, love. Silver coloured, not silver, the precious metal."

"Stone the crows, you two," AJ blurted. "It's from hundreds of years ago when kettles and pots were made of cast iron. They were blackened by the fire," AJ explained with little enthusiasm.

"I know that," Reg chimed in.

"I know you know, but she doesn't."

"So what did the pot say to the kettle in this old story?" Nora asked.

AJ groaned. "Forget it, Viking."

Nora went back to eating her ice cream sundae.

"What now then, Johnny English?" Reg asked. "Seeing as this was a total cock-up. Suppose we can go back and muck about in the sand at Anchor Point, see if there's anything else kicking about from 300 years ago."

AJ shrugged her shoulders. "Suppose."

"We need to get over to Little Cayman and start looking there,"

Reg continued. "But I can't get away for more than a day, and it'll take months to search, starting from ground zero."

"Your mate Pebbles has already been trying, right?" AJ said, tilting her head Reg's way. "He hasn't found anything or he wouldn't have come running over here."

"True enough. But we also need to make sure Pebbles doesn't mess with Anchor Point," Reg continued. "He'll blow the sea floor apart looking for stuff. Our finds might have nothing to do with the Blade of Calcutta, but it seems like they're still of archaeological interest. We should go have another look before *your* mate, Mrs Wright, shuts the site down."

AJ picked up her mobile to see the time, as it was easier than unwrapping her arms to see her Rolex. "Bloody hell!"

"How late is it?" Reg asked, suddenly worried he'd lost a few hours.

"That doesn't matter," AJ exclaimed, sitting up in her chair. "I forgot about Buck!"

"Buck Reilly?" Reg asked.

"Yes! He gave me a name to track down."

"Who?" Nora asked, sliding her empty sundae bowl away.

AJ looked at the unread text from Buck. "Marleigh Smith."

"Marley, like Bob?" Reg asked.

"Yes, but spelt differently."

"Smith?" Nora questioned. "Isn't that the most common name?"

"Yes, Marleigh Smith, and yes."

"Who is Marleigh Smith, then?" Reg asked.

"He's a descendent of Marcus Smith, William Crowe's partner."

"He has more of these diary books?" Nora asked.

"No, they're all at the bottom of the sea," AJ replied.

"But he might have a copy of *The Bravest Captain*?" Reg asked.

"Bingo," AJ replied. "If he's alive."

"Wait, so we're looking for some geezer who might not even be alive?"

"Well, he'll be getting on a bit by now."

Reg sighed. "Is this another wild bloody goose chase?"

"Maybe," AJ replied. "But have you got a better lead?"

Reg chuckled and sipped his rum. "No, suppose not. So where is this bloke? Assuming for the moment he's not six feet under."

"That's the great part," AJ said excitedly. "Last known, he was here on the island."

"Strewth. So even if he is brown bread, he might have family here."

"Maybe," AJ agreed, and they both turned to Nora.

"What?" she replied, with one eyebrow slightly raised. "You want me to find him, don't you?"

"You're the one with access to a police computer full of names, love," Reg said.

"Which are not for personal use. It's against the rules." Nora pointed out.

"Pretty please," AJ said with a big smile. "Besides, when has a little thing like rules ever stood in your way?"

Nora shrugged her shoulders. "Fine. I'll look in the morning before anyone gets to the station."

"Ha!" AJ exclaimed. "See, you're a black kettle!"

Nora looked at her blankly. "Pay for my sundae if you want a ride. I'm leaving before you get me into more trouble."

Thomas stood on the dock looking worried as AJ nestled *Hazel's Odyssey* alongside. He tied the Newton into the cleats and waited until AJ shut the diesels down.

"What I forget, Boss?" he asked.

AJ came down the ladder with coffee in hand. "Nothing," she replied. "I woke up early and had too much on my mind to go back to sleep."

Thomas's face brightened a little, relieved he hadn't screwed up. Not that AJ would haul him over the coals if he had. The young Caymanian was diligent, eager, and had bailed her out more times than she could remember. She wished he wouldn't call her 'Boss', as they operated more like co-workers than owner and employee, but for him it was a sign of respect, so she'd given up telling him to stop.

"Jackson is getting ice as soon as Foster's opens. Me and Reg are heading to Anchor Point, so I asked him to cover for me. That okay?"

"Of course," Thomas replied, hopping aboard and beginning the daily preparations. "Still seven people today?"

The two discussed the details of the morning trip as they brought rental BCDs and regulators up from the bow cabin. The boat gently rocking and the fenders squeaking against the dock were the only other sound besides the water lapping on the hull.

Soon, the sunrise overpowered the streetlight by West Bay dock, and the tranquillity of the little jetty gave way to a hive of activity as Reg's crew arrived to bring his boats in. Jackson parked the van, then brought the ice and fresh snacks to the boat, and no matter how many times AJ checked her mobile, it didn't ring.

Reg, who was usually the first one there with Thomas, parked his Land Rover by the top of the jetty and loaded eight tanks into the back.

"What did you do with the tracker?" AJ asked him.

Reg grinned. "Pearl has it at the house. She's meeting Jen in a bit."

Their friend Jen used to own and run Greenhouse Cafe in George Town but now had a gourmet food delivery business she'd started while the island had been shut down. Once she prepared the meals to fulfil her orders, she spent the rest of the morning delivering them all over half the island.

AJ grinned back at him. "She's going to take it with her?"

Reg nodded. "Ought to keep Pebbles busy for a while figuring that one out."

AJ loaded her dive gear into the Landy. "Whittaker will be turning up the heat on the search for him today, so hopefully he'll have a hard time moving around the island without being seen."

"Hopefully," Reg replied as he carefully laid the magnetometer in the back on top of their gear. "But the bugger's used to having people after him. He's good at staying off the radar."

Customers began to arrive, and AJ's mobile remained silent. Not even a text. She greeted the people, who were all returning customers, and helped load their gear aboard. For most of her clientele, part of the fun and appeal was diving with AJ herself, so she felt guilty not being on the boat for the morning trip and made a point of chatting with them all before she left.

Once *Hazel's Odyssey* was ready to leave, AJ stepped to the dock and wished everyone a good morning.

"Come on then," Reg said, after making sure his own boats were all set. "It'll take us a bit with morning traffic."

They made one stop at Cafe Del Sol for coffee and breakfast pastries, then trundled along in the morning rush hour through George Town. With the windows down, they were moving just fast enough to keep a steady breeze knocking the edge off the heat, and once they passed the airport, eastbound traffic lightened.

Beyond Grand Harbour, heading for Spotts, AJ's mind had turned to the diving that lay ahead. Needle in a haystack didn't come close to describing the challenge. She knew too well that just because they'd found two items in the same vicinity, it didn't mean anything else of interest was close by.

In the past three centuries, the sea floor would have been churned over countless times, sands shifted, and the coastline reshaped by erosion and changing sea levels. The reef was a living entity formed and shaped by new coral polyps growing over the limestone formed by their dead brethren. The whole environment was constantly changing and evolving.

AJ jumped when her mobile vibrated and rang in her hand. She manically waved at Reg to pull over, then pressed accept and put the call on speaker for them both to hear.

"What have you found?" she asked without preamble.

"I think I have your guy," Nora replied. "How old were you thinking he'd be?"

"He fought in WWII, so he has to be ancient."

"So ninety-nine later this year sounds right?" Nora replied.

"Blimey, yeah, I suppose that would be."

"Is he alive?" Reg asked as he brought the Land Rover to a stop by the side of the road.

"I think so," Nora replied.

"What do you mean, you think so?" AJ countered.

"I mean, I don't see a record of him dying, but he's nearly ninety-nine years old. He's probably surprised when he opens his eyes each new morning."

"Where is he?" Reg asked.

"Last known address is in West Bay," Nora replied. "Same house he's owned for over fifty years."

35

DEVIL IN HIS HEART

1704

The crew members who noticed us moving two hooded prisoners below deck barely batted an eye. Perhaps Gordy was right... they did replenish their crews by abduction. We hid them in our tiny berth, their hands retied and their feet bound. The hoods and gags stayed on except for when I gave them water. Without Vin there, the two men tried persuading me to release them on the guarantee they wouldn't say a word to anyone about us. All three of us knew that was a lie.

The crew used the kedging method to haul the ship closer to shore, dropping a smaller anchor from the cockboat ahead of the ship, then hauling the *Royal Fortune* forward by pulling on the line. Once close, a similar method called warping was used to drag the ship alongside the dock, running a long line around a bollard on the wharf instead of using the anchor. Once there, Vin took up station on the dock and I watched anxiously from the forecastle.

Hinchcliffe barked orders at the men as they carried sack after sack of our 'forced trade' up the wharf where a man was directing them. He appeared to be having them neatly stack the goods in preparation for loading onto another vessel. I noticed the boatswain was also keeping a suspicious eye on Vin, presumably wondering why she was loitering on the docks.

From town, I spotted a well-dressed man striding towards our ship, scattering seamen from his path by waving a cane at them. Two hefty-looking men followed him, both with cutlasses sheathed on their belts and pistols tucked in their waistbands. Vin quickly moved towards them and halted the gentleman. They were out of my earshot, but it was clear by his arm waving the man was keen to move past and continue to the *Royal Fortune*.

Vin stepped in his way again and placed a hand on his arm. The two thugs quickly came forward and grabbed her. She didn't struggle and whatever she said next made the gentleman pause. He called his hired muscle off and they released Vin. She leaned in and spoke to the man. This time, he listened intently.

Movement caught my eye on the wharf, and I saw Hinchcliffe in full stride. He was no more than ten paces away from Vin and about to stick his nose where we certainly didn't want it. I looked around me, frantically searching for some way to cause a distraction. Vin was oblivious to the approaching boatswain, deep in conversation with the gentleman. Seeing nothing useful around me, I was about to scream.

"Boatswain!" came a booming voice from midships.

Everyone in the immediate vicinity turned to look at the captain, including Vin, the gentleman, and Hinchcliffe. Rochefort waved, calling the boatswain back to the ship. Hinchcliffe looked at Vin, who stared back, seeing how close he'd come to interrupting her. Finally, the boatswain stomped up the wharf towards the *Royal Fortune*. I looked at the captain and he winked at me.

I let out a long sigh, realising I hadn't taken a breath in ages. Vin handed something to the gentleman, who tipped his hat and retreated, his two henchmen in tow. It felt like we were living on the ridgeline of a mountain with sheer drops into the abyss on either side. I could see the galleon bound for England at anchor not more than half a mile from us. Our passage home was right there, yet it might as well have been sitting at the port in London for all the use it was.

A sense of dread consumed me, churning in my stomach and causing my throat to turn dry. Kingston was the hub of English shipping traffic in the Caribbean. If we couldn't gain passage here, what would we do? I glanced down at the dock where Vin was strolling back to the ship. She looked up and smiled at me. My gut slowly unclenched and my tension eased, slipping away, just as the Governor's man had done. Vin would have a plan for what came next. She always found a way to figure everything out.

A few of us moved the ship off the dock before sundown after Rochefort stood on the wharf, dividing out the takings. The crew bolted for town the moment the notes and coins hit their palms. The cockboat made a final run ashore with those who'd help anchor the ship, leaving Captain Rochefort, Vin, me, and our hidden prisoners the only ones aboard.

It was a beautiful evening with a bright moon, a million stars, and a soft, cooling breeze rustling through the rigging. The captain invited us to join him on deck, where we sat on small barrels and he and Vin drank brandy from a bottle he'd kept hidden in his cabin. They gave me a small glass of the stuff which burned my throat as though I'd swallowed fire.

Conversation fell into tales from England and both the captain and Vin expressed their desire to return at some point in time. Rochefort was on his fourth glass of brandy, with his speech beginning to lose its crispness, when he admitted he was tired of the life of a privateer.

"There's a galleon sailing for England," Vin said, pointing across the dark harbour. "Right over there somewhere."

"It is tempting," he responded, rubbing his brow. "But I officially took ownership of the *Royal Fortune* today. She's too valuable to abandon."

"Can't you sell her here, in Kingston?" Vin asked.

Rochefort nodded slowly. "I dare say I could, but the crew would lynch me for doing so. Back in the days of Port Royal, they could walk down the waterfront and find another ship to crew, but nowadays the privateers are fewer, and the military presence keeps the true pirates away. They'll hang the ones who're not sailing under a letter of marque." He raised his eyes to look at Vin. "Hinchcliffe has a piece of the devil in his heart. Remember that. He'd run me through and sail the men from this harbour if he even heard this conversation."

I shuddered as though my feet were in the snow of a London winter night.

"He's not a man I'd turn my back to," Vin said.

"You best keep that in mind as we sail on," Rochefort added, downing the last of the brandy in his glass. "He has the ear of more than a few of the men to boot."

On the next day, as the captain had predicted, most of the crew had run out of money and the ability to stay conscious by the evening. Many were back aboard, some were sleeping it off where they last fell down in town, and a few who'd paced themselves were preparing for a second night of fun.

By first light the following morning enough crew were sober, although unenthused having been rudely woken by the boatswain, to sail the ship. It was slack tide, which made weighing anchor an easier task, and the captain ordered the foremast main unfurled to let the north-east breeze take us out of the harbour. Rochefort kept Hinchcliffe and his deviously inquisitive nose busy while we marched the two prisoners up on deck.

The crew looked on in mild curiosity dampened by hangovers as Vin cut the twine on Gordy and Duck's hands and feet. Before pulling the hoods from their heads, she reminded them to keep their mouths shut, pressing the knife blade against their necks to reinforce the order.

"Eyes forward," Vin commanded as I cut them free of the gags.

"I don't swim," Duck said, looking down at the bay as we approached the point of the headland where what remained of Port Royal stood.

"I'd say this would be a good time to learn," Vin responded without sympathy.

"You can't feed us to the damn sharks," Gordy begged, searching the water for fins.

"Even the sharks have better taste than to lower themselves to feed on the likes of you two," Vin growled. "Now jump, or I'll wait until we're in the open ocean before I throw you over."

The two men looked nervously at each other.

"Eyes front!" Vin reminded them with a shove in the back.

Duck crossed himself. "You gotta help me, Gordy. I don't swim. I don't even like the bloody water."

Gordy threw his legs over the gunwale and sat on the side, guiding his friend to do the same.

"Come on, Duck, else we'll be out of the harbour."

Duck sat on the edge of the ship, shaking like a leaf, and Gordy grabbed his shirt. "We shouldn't have crossed you like we did, Lady Crowe," Gordy whispered. "But your husband did us wrong."

"He did us all wrong," Vin replied softly, then shoved the two men into the water.

The crew of the *Royal Fortune* let out a half-hearted cheer and some of them ran to the gunwale to see the two strangers splashing in the bay.

"You should've bled 'em first," Hinchcliffe said from behind us, surprising me. "Sharks'll find 'em in no time."

Vin turned and looked the boatswain in the eye. "I would have," she said calmly, "if they weren't friends of mine."

Hinchcliffe clenched his teeth and glared at Vin. Slowly, his lips drew back and he burst into laughter, then walked away.

I turned back to the bay where our two prisoners were attempting to make their way to the shore. He hadn't lied; Duck didn't appear to be able to swim. Gordy was doing his best to keep him calm, but the man was thrashing wildly. The crew were making bets on who would reach dry land and who wouldn't, with Lefty keeping track of the wagers, as none of the sailors currently had any money left to bet with.

"I hope they make it," I said as I watched Gordy desperately try to calm Duck down.

"I do too, Wil," Vin replied, then turned me away from the gunwale and made her way to the quarterdeck.

"Heading, sir?" she asked the captain, who stood at the helm.

"What's your fancy, Mr Crowe?" he said in reply.

Vin thought for a moment. "West, along the south coast of Jamaica, then north to catch the Spanish shipping running below Cuba, sir."

Rochefort nodded. "That was my thinking, but don't take us farther north than Los Caymanas," he said, stepping away from the wheel. "We might find us a merchantman heading that way."

Vin took the wheel.

"Maybe we'll re-provision there ourselves in a week or two," he added before stepping to the front of the quarterdeck, ready to give out sail plan orders.

A mixture of groans and cheers erupted from the main deck and Lefty looked up at us.

"Pay up, lads, pay up," he yelled. "Only three of you fools had them both making it."

I grinned at Vin, who kept her eyes on the horizon, but I caught a hint of a smile on her face too.

Captain Rochefort spoke to the boatswain, who yelled at the men, who in turn unfurled sails, and the *Royal Fortune* rapidly picked up speed with the wind filling the broad linen sails. It was a wonderful feeling, being on the ocean with the sun on my face and the wind propelling us towards a new adventure. I felt alive and confident that, although our plans had changed once more, everything would be all right. Mother had made it so.

Fate had put another twist in our journey, but dealt us a fair hand again.

36

ALIENS HAVE LANDED?

Present Day

AJ and Reg sat by the side of Shamrock Road in Spotts, unsure of what to do next.

"I think we should turn around and go see Marleigh Smith," AJ said. "We've been saying we're lost without a copy of *The Bravest Captain*, and he's our best hope of finding one."

"You understand that's the long shot of all long shots, right?" Reg replied. "Even if this ol' boy is compos mentis, which is unlikely at his age, what are the chances of him having a copy of a book from three centuries ago?"

"About the same as us finding anything else at Anchor Point, which we know won't be the Blade of Calcutta, 'cos it's in Little Cayman."

"According to what?" Reg challenged. "The theory that this sword is on Little is solely based on Alpers jotting down ideas for a title to a book he never wrote. It's far more likely the sword was lost with the *Royal Fortune*, and nobody knows where she sank. Not even Crowe, as best we know."

AJ groaned. "So what do you want to do? Sitting here cooking without the air conditioning running isn't an option. I'm sweating like a glassblower's arse. Are we going diving or to see Marleigh Smith?"

Reg started the engine and put the Land Rover in gear just as AJ's mobile buzzed with a text. She looked at the screen.

"Stop," she told Reg, who swore, then turned the Landy off again.

"It's from Thomas."

"Boat trouble?" Reg asked.

"Worse," AJ mumbled, clicking a link to a web page. She held the screen up for Reg to see. "That little wanker Carlson posted a picture of us from last night."

"Treasure hunting divers botch police operation," Reg read from the screen. "He'd better make every breath he takes count, 'cos when I get hold of him, he'll be huffing his last," Reg seethed.

"He's not getting off that easy," AJ added. "He deserves a slow, painful exit from this world."

"I'm not sure I'll be able to restrain myself long enough to torture the skinny bastard," Reg muttered, restarting the Land Rover.

"I'm thinking a couple of days in a brightly lit room with Christmas music playing non-stop," AJ said as Reg turned around and started heading for town. "Not the good stuff, just three or four of the really annoying ones that make you want to stick a pin in your ear. Played over and over, nice and loud."

"You're a cruel woman, Annabelle Jayne, a cruel woman," Reg chuckled.

AJ's mobile rang again, and Reg's shoulders slumped as he slowed once more.

"I'm scared to answer this one," AJ said, staring at the screen.

"Who is it?"

AJ hit accept, and winced in anticipation as she put the phone to her ear. "Hello Roy."

"You'll need a press agent if you continue to dominate the local news, young lady."

"I'm so sorry, Roy. I really goofed up last night," AJ said, her voice deflated.

"Water under the bridge, AJ," Whittaker replied. "I was only calling to let you know we've officially handed the human bone you found over to the museum as an archaeological investigation. Rasha tells me she's confident the bone is well over 100 years old, which puts it beyond our interest, as any perpetrator of wrongdoing, if indeed there was a crime committed, would be long since dead."

"Okay, thanks for letting us know," AJ replied. "Do you know what that means for the site at Anchor Point?"

"That'll be up to Gladys," he replied. "The Joint Marine Unit and DoE will support her as best they can if she officially closes the location to the public pending further searches, but you know how thinly stretched everyone is."

"Any sign of Pritchard this morning?"

"I was about to ask you the same question," Whittaker replied. "So no, nothing yet, but the day is young. We've distributed his picture to all the hotels. Maybe we'll get lucky with that. The man has to have slept somewhere last night."

They said goodbye, ended the call, and Reg pulled away yet again.

"Did Nora give you an address?" he asked.

"Yeah. It's not far from Cobalt Coast off King Road."

"Great," Reg groaned. "Now we get the traffic going the other bloody way."

By the time they reached Hurley's market at Grand Harbour, they were edging along with all the local workers, making their way west from the eastern towns where they could still afford to live. Barely.

. . .

Ten miles and fifty-two minutes later, Reg drove slowly down a marl road to a small cottage on the north-west-facing coastline of West Bay. The old home was battered and beaten but sat on a sizeable ocean view lot worth well into seven figures. AJ loved seeing the local holdouts with their traditional, sturdy block homes on what had become prime property over the decades since overseas developers and buyers had replaced their neighbouring cottages with mansions, condos, and now high-rises. It took a strong will to turn away the constant offers for a piece of land like Marleigh Smith still owned.

They parked and walked up to the front door. Paint peeled from window frames, and the concrete steps were cracked and tilted from storm erosion, but the front yard was tidy, albeit a little over-grown with weeds.

Reg knocked on the door and they waited for a while, not hearing any movement inside. He knocked again, and AJ resisted the urge to peer through one of the windows. Last thing she wanted to do was scare the poor old man to death when he saw a strange face pressed to the glass.

The front door creaked open and startled them both. Neither of them had heard a single step from inside. An ancient-looking man, no taller than AJ and probably weighing the same as she did, stared into Reg's barrel chest, then slowly raised his gaze upwards until he met his face. Reg smiled, but it was mostly obscured by his scraggy beard.

"Ain't selling," the man said fiercely. "Now leave and don't come back."

His accent was English but heavily tinted by the local lilt and his light brown skin as weathered as his home, but he seemed remarkably spry for a man of his age.

"We don't want your house, Mr Smith," Reg quickly responded. "We were hoping to chat with you about your family."

He seemed to notice AJ for the first time and looked at her tattooed arms. "Don't need insurance, if that's what you sellin'," he said with slightly less animosity.

"We're not selling anything, sir," Reg forged on. "We've been researching your family history and our trail has led us from…" Reg paused and looked at AJ.

"Marcus Smith," she filled in for him.

"Right, Marcus Smith. All the way to you. Could you spare a few minutes to talk with us, sir?"

"We'd be happy to chat outside, Mr Smith," AJ said. "If you'd prefer we don't come inside your home."

The old man looked back and forth between them a few times, sizing them up with a mind that likely had slowed given its age, but still appeared to be operating well enough.

"I can talk a little," he said. "Outside on the deck, like you say."

"No problem, sir," AJ responded with a smile. "We'll walk around."

Reg turned to walk down the steps and around the house, but the old man opened the door wider.

"Come through here," he said. "Less bother than going round."

AJ stifled a laugh and walked inside the home, entering the kitchen and dining area. It was clean and tidy, but didn't look like a single appliance or piece of furniture had been replaced since the 70s. Reg followed and looked like an ogre as he passed by the frail little man.

"Through here?" AJ asked, pointing to an opening into what she guessed to be a living room.

"Yessum," he said, closing the front door.

Every window in the home was open, and net curtains fluttered in the breeze. It was hot and sticky from the humidity, but cooler than outside, and ceiling fans in each room kept the air moving. If he had an air conditioner, he clearly didn't use it. The living room was cosy with a window looking through a handful of scattered trees towards the ocean and a door which took them to the deck.

AJ didn't notice any family pictures on the walls or shelves as she passed through the living room, nor a television set. Just an old, faded sofa and a recliner chair.

"Wait out there, miss. I'll make some tea."

AJ drank tea occasionally, not because she liked it – she much preferred her beloved coffee – but because it reminded her of her grandparents, who, like many of their generation, drank tea for any reason whatsoever. 'Feeling down? Let's have a cuppa.' 'Celebrating a birthday? I'll make some tea in the good china.' 'Aliens have landed? I'll put the kettle on, expect they've had quite a journey.'

Tea always brought a smile to her face and, despite the balmy Caribbean weather, felt like the perfect introduction to Marleigh Smith, a man nearing a century on the planet, and their best hope of unlocking the mystery of the Blade of Calcutta.

37

GONE

1704

On our second morning after leaving Kingston, the rising sun revealed a fierce battle erupting to the north-west of our position. The captain had me look through the spyglass and I confirmed one of the ships was a Spanish galleon. The other flew the St George's Cross of England.

"Is it navy or privateer, Wil?" he asked with some urgency.

"I don't think it's a ship of the line, sir, but we're still too far away to be sure."

Rochefort paced back and forth as we sailed closer. He sent me up to the crow's nest with the spyglass to have a better look and warned me if I dropped it, I'd better not come back down. I tied a piece of twine around it and tucked it into my waist with the tether secure to the belt. Chances were the brass tube would slide from its leash if it fell, but it made me feel a little better as I scrambled up the rigging.

The *Royal Fortune* was on a broad reach with the bow rising and falling as we crested the peaks, running at 45 degrees to the waves.

I held the spyglass as steady as I could and focused first on the English ship. I could now see a few men on deck, none of whom wore uniforms of the Navy. The ship was a small brig sloop, not much bigger than our carrack, but with many more cannons lined up on the main deck.

They'd taken several hits from the galleon, one of which had blown a section of deck to pieces at the base of the main mast, and another must have hit them farther forward, below the main deck, which had consequently collapsed under the weight of their cannon. Bodies lay strewn about, and survivors struggled to man the remaining guns.

"Privateer, sir," I yelled down. "Badly damaged already."

Captain Rochefort looked up at me, along with the rest of the crew, who were getting excited for battle.

"And the Spanish ship?"

"Merchantman, but they have a full gun deck, sir. At least six a side."

"Come down, Wil," he shouted with a wave. "Angle across the starboard side of the sloop, Mr Crowe. We'll use them as cover and fire once we clear them."

"Aye, sir," Vin confirmed and cut a few more degrees to starboard with the English ship now no more than half a mile ahead.

"Prepare the cannons, boatswain!" Rochefort yelled and the men frantically went to work loading our six guns with the powder and balls they had at the ready.

As we closed in on the battle, the English sloop took two more hits, one right at the waterline and another shattering more of the decking. I realised neither ship had moved since we'd made our approach. They were both sitting dead in the water, trading blows. A single cannon fire from the sloop severed the main mast of the galleon, sending the heavy wooden spar, along with its yards and rigging, crashing to the deck and across the helm.

I turned my attention back to the sloop, which was now quickly taking on water. "She's going down!" I yelled, and I'd barely finished the words when the ship dipped its shattered midships below the ocean surface, its back broken. The bow and stern raised simultaneously, spewing the few remaining men into the sea along with sails, rigging and chunks of unidentifiable wood.

"To port, Crowe! Turn to port!" Rochefort screamed and Vin cut the wheel, heeling the *Royal Fortune* over on its starboard side as the ship cut across the stern of the quickly sinking sloop.

"What are you doing, man?" Hinchcliffe yelled at the captain.

"We're no match for their cannon!" the captain shouted back.

"For God's sake, we can finish them!" the boatswain yelled, flying up the steps to the quarterdeck. "We're here to fight, not run away."

"I'll not sail us into certain death, boatswain. Now heed my orders!"

Hinchcliffe stood inches away from the captain, and both men glared at each other.

"Prepare to fire starboard cannons!" Vin ordered, and the two men whipped around. "This will work, sir," she added.

Hinchcliffe shoved the captain aside and ran down the steps, barking at his men to prepare the cannons.

"What are you doing, Crowe?" Rochefort asked, the sting having left his voice.

"You'll see, sir, no time to explain," she replied and swung the wheel to starboard as we passed 100 yards off the Spanish galleon's bow and cut at 30 degrees to their flank.

"Fire, Mr Hinchcliffe," Vin yelled.

The boatswain bellowed the order to his men, and our three starboard cannons boomed in unison. I staggered across the quarterdeck as Vin cut the wheel again, this time to port, and followed with a series of sail orders.

Wood splintered and men cried out in pain and terror on the galleon as all three cannonballs thundered through the hull and indiscriminately tore ship and humans to shreds. Our crew cheered and those not busy trimming sails or reloading cannons waved their cutlasses in the air.

"Now we tack back and run across their bow at an angle again, sir," Vin explained.

"They'll turn next time, and blow us to pieces, Crowe," Rochefort retorted.

"They're dead in the water, sir," she said, pointing towards the stricken Spanish ship now behind us. "They've lost their rudder and most of their sail. I don't see any forward-facing long nines and they can't get much angle from the cannon on their gun deck. The only thing turning them now are the waves."

Captain Rochefort's shoulders dropped as he took in all that he had missed as we'd approached the battle.

"I'm sorry, sir, I didn't mean to overstep my bounds, but I saw we had the advantage," she said as we began the laborious task of tacking back into position while the Spaniards scrambled to form some kind of defence.

"The shortcoming was mine, Crowe. You did well," he said with a sigh. "I wish I'd sold this ship in Kingston after all."

"We'll be fine now, sir," Vin reassured him. "We have plenty of time to pick the galleon apart until she surrenders."

Rochefort looked tired and as defeated as I hoped the Spanish would be. He forced a smile. "You'll be fine, Mr Crowe. For now. Just remember what I told you."

Before Vin could answer, Hinchcliffe, Dutch, and two other men strode up the steps and stood before us with cutlasses and pistols drawn.

"We don't run from a fight," the boatswain growled, "and we'll not take orders from a coward who would."

My heart leapt into my mouth and my blood began to boil. Rochefort had been kind to us, and I was sure we were about to see him cut to ribbons by his own men.

"Boatswain, running from a fight is only slightly worse than sitting down in the middle of one," Vin said firmly. "May I suggest we conclude our conflict with the Spanish before we turn on ourselves?"

Hinchcliffe spun sharply around and glared at Vin, then relaxed and nodded. "Fair enough. Are those guns loaded?" he yelled, returning his attention to the crew on the main deck.

"Thank you," Rochefort said once the men had retreated.

"Don't thank me," Vin replied. "It's my fault you're in this mess. I should've followed your order."

"They would have reacted the same way, Mr Crowe. We'd both be facing their wrath instead of only me. The error was mine in suggesting retreat."

"Well, we have a battle still to be won, and I'll gladly take your orders, sir," Vin said as she watched the galleon we could now see was named *Cielos de Oro* rig its remaining sail to rotate broadside to us as we close-hauled back into position.

"Hard to port and follow their bow?" Vin asked.

"The safer play would be to starboard, Mr Crowe. It'll put us out of range after the turn while we run downwind to attack again."

"That will also give them more time to recover, sir," she countered.

"*Audentes Fortuna iuvat,* Mr Crowe," he replied, and Vin cut hard to port.

"Ready the starboard cannons, boatswain," she called out.

"Fortune favours the bold," I translated, recalling the famous Latin phrase my mother had taught me.

"Indeed, lad," Rochefort said. "And your father is certainly bold."

I smiled in pride, and more than a little amusement, as I didn't consider my father to be in the least bit brave. My mother, on the other hand, was fearless.

The Spanish galleon was slowly spinning and running downwind as the stiff breeze filled its ragged sail. But we had full sail back on a broad reach and were gathering speed as we passed within thirty yards of their rotating bow.

"Fire!" Vin yelled, and our three cannons boomed once more.

The noise and concussion shook me to the core as our cannonballs ripped through the gun deck of the galleon.

"That should…" Rochefort began, but never finished.

I saw the puff of smoke from the main deck of the Spanish ship and heard an awful sound, like a butcher slapping a large cut of beef down on his cutting block. One moment, Captain Rochefort stood beside me, and the next he'd vanished in a hail of wood splinters. The single shot the Spaniards had fired from a smaller gun they'd turned towards us on the main deck had clipped the front of our quarterdeck and directly hit the man who'd been three feet from me.

I looked down at my arm and saw the wood shards and splinters embedded in my flesh, small red circles widening from many of the wounds. For a moment, I thought I was going to pass out, but I gritted my teeth and steadied myself with a hand on the helm.

"Wil? Are you all right?" Vin asked, my injuries hidden from her view.

I nodded. "I'm fine, but the captain… he's gone," I replied, still in disbelief.

Vin cut the wheel to port and sailed downwind from the bow of the galleon until we were out of range, then turned again to begin our tack back into position. Once she'd finished shouting orders for trimming the sails, she turned to me.

"Gone? What do you mean, Wil?"

I looked behind where I now saw the port side rail had a section smashed to bits. "He was standing right beside me, and then he was simply gone. The Spanish fired one shot from their main deck. I saw the smoke. I think it hit over here," I said, swinging around and pointing to the shattered deck in front of the helm.

"Thank God it missed you," Vin muttered, crossing herself. "But you're bleeding," she added, her voice losing its deeper tone.

"It's just a few splinters," I said hopefully, still too scared to look more closely. "Don't worry about me. Concern yourself with their deck gun. They were able to fire at a tight angle."

Vin looked at the wounded galleon with its rigging and masts torn to hell. They'd managed to rotate downwind but were now limited in their speed and manoeuvrability with no rudder control and little sail. Flotsam bobbed all around the battleground, some from the galleon and much from the privateer ship, which was now sitting on the bottom or still making its way down. The seas here were far beyond our lead lines for checking depth.

"Boatswain!" she called out, and the man scaled the steps, surveying the damage to the quarterdeck on his way.

"Where's Rochefort?"

"He's dead," Vin replied. "Hit by the cannon shot, which did this," she added, pointing to the scarred decking.

"I didn't realise they'd got a shot off," he said in surprise.

"A smaller cannon from the main deck, sir," I explained. "I was able to see it from up here over the smoke from our own guns."

"Doubtless we'll need to disable that cannon before they give up," Hinchcliffe said, squinting across the ocean at the Spaniards.

"Agreed," Vin replied. "So let's make this pass our last, boatswain. Aim the starboard cannons to converge on a point 50 yards out."

"That's mighty close quarters, Mr Crowe," Hinchcliffe said, shaking his head.

"It is, sir, but it if we get this right, it'll be the last shots fired in this contest."

The boatswain nodded. "Fine. What about that gun they're dragging around the deck?"

"You won't have to worry about that if I position us correctly, but have your men ready to drop the sails in a hurry. All but the foremast topsail."

Hinchcliffe's eyes narrowed, and he stared at Vin for a few moments.

"Time is against us, boatswain," she said firmly.

He nodded. "Fine."

"And boatswain," she added as he was about to leave. "When the cannons fix on their bow at 50 yards, fire on your call. Just make sure you time our roll to hit them above the waterline."

He grunted and jumped down the steps to the main deck, barking orders as he went.

"When did you learn all this?" I asked once he was gone.

"My father," Vin replied. "When we sailed on his fleet ships, he'd tell me the enemy was somewhere around us and ask what I planned to do."

"So you've practised this before?"

Vin scoffed. "Not exactly. We kept on sailing straight, but he'd use blocks of wood to show me the likely outcome of my reactions and what I should have done."

"Oh," I mumbled. "But this is a plan he'd shown you?"

"Not exactly," she replied.

38

CAIMAN GRANDE

Present Day

Marleigh took his time bringing tea outside along with an array of biscuits, refusing assistance on any level. He added milk and sugar to every cup before handing them out. Apparently, he had one way of serving Earl Grey, and everybody took it that way. Neither Reg nor AJ minded. Once he'd finally taken a seat and handed out biscuits, he appeared ready for conversation, so Reg let AJ take the lead as the old man couldn't stop looking at her.

"My name is AJ, and this is Reg..." she began.

"He your papa?" Marleigh interrupted.

"No, Mr Smith. Reg is a friend and we often work together."

"Doing what you say?"

"We both run dive operations here on Grand Cayman."

"Like the scuba?"

"Exactly," AJ replied. "Have you ever tried?"

Marleigh finished chewing a bite of a shortbread. Or gumming it into submission, AJ wasn't certain. The man didn't have many teeth left.

"Used to dive for lobster and conch, but that was just holding our breath, now, didn't have no tank. Stopped a few years back. They have rules about all that now, you know?"

"They do," AJ agreed, wondering at what age this amazing man had retired from freediving. "Keeps them from being hunted out of existence."

The old man sipped his tea then looked at AJ. "Ain't more lobster we need, it's fewer people."

AJ and Reg both laughed.

"I'm sure you've seen many things change over the years, sir," AJ said, aware that she along with the two men before her were all expats, although Marleigh and Reg both had their citizenship and she her permanent residency.

"Not much for the good," he said, staring off at the ocean through the handful of trees between his home and the iron-shore coastline. "'Cept that pub down the road. I like that place."

"The Fox and Hare?" AJ said with a broad smile.

"That's the one. I go most Sunday mornings for a good old English fry-up breakfast."

"We've been known to lift a glass there ourselves," Reg commented.

"So what brings a couple of scuba divers to my house asking about my family? Not trying to build some resort here and fill the shoreline with concrete, are you?"

"Nothing like that, sir," AJ replied. "Our interest is in your family from eight generations ago."

Marleigh looked at her for several moments with a blank expression. She began to wonder if he'd heard her correctly, or perhaps taken offence in some way.

"I'm old," he finally said. "But I never met none of them from that far back."

AJ laughed and sprayed a little tea out of her nose.

"That's just lovely," Reg said under his breath, and handed her a napkin.

"Sorry," she said, her cheeks blushing, but she noticed Marleigh had a wry grin on his face.

"How long they take?" he asked, looking at her arms.

AJ touched her forearm self-consciously, unsure whether his question was fuelled by pure interest or disapproval. "Each one took about 60 hours," she replied. "But I'd go to the artist's studio in Atlanta for two days at a time."

"They go all the way up?" Marleigh asked, pointing to her shoulder.

"Yes, sir," she replied, rolling her T-shirt sleeve up a little more.

The old man shook his head and rolled up his own shirt sleeve, revealing his forearm. "Came in one colour back in my day, and weren't long before it turned from black to green."

Reg leaned forward and studied the faded and blurred image, but he instantly recognised the warrior riding a winged horse emblem of the British 1st Airborne Division.

"Thank you for your service, Mr Smith," Reg said.

"Navy man?" Marleigh asked, pointing to Reg's arm.

"Clearance diver," Reg replied, rotating his forearm to show the slightly less green and blurred tattoo on the inside of his arm. It was a diving helmet with a crown overhead and vertical fish on either side. "Falklands."

Marleigh sat back in his chair, the wrinkles around his eyes heavily creased in thought. AJ and Reg sipped tea and let the man consider the situation in his own time. He finally spoke. "It's Marcus Smith you askin' about, then?"

AJ put her cup down on the saucer, worried she might spill it. "That's right. So, you know about him?"

The old man laughed, revealing the few teeth he still possessed. "He the only one in this family done anything worth talking about, best I know."

"We were told you may have family heirlooms passed down through your father," AJ said. "There's a book we're trying to track down, written by Marcus Smith's partner, William Crowe."

Marleigh nodded. "I have some boxes somewhere. Stuff I took

after my father's funeral back in England, but that were a long time ago. I may have known back then what was in those boxes, but I certainly can't recall anymore. I never had much to do with my father."

AJ picked up a subtle change in the man's voice. A hint of sadness, perhaps?

She spoke softly. "May I ask what happened between you?"

Marleigh's eyes wandered across the horizon where they lingered without a response.

"My apologies, sir. That was rude of me to ask."

The old man turned to her. "No, young lady, I don't mind the askin'. It's the tellin' I've always had a hard time with." He shifted in his chair and reached for his teacup, which was empty, so he set it down again. "My father was a good man until the war. The Second World War, I mean," he added. "My brother didn't make it home, and I was missin' for over a year. Best he knew. I was in a prison camp where the colour of my skin didn't make it easy, but I survived all they did to me."

Marleigh fell silent and Reg stood, taking the teapot inside the house to brew a fresh batch, leaving him alone with AJ. The old man didn't seem to notice Reg leave.

"One way and another, I wasn't good for much when I got out. Stayed in France a while. When I came home, my father took the losin' of my brother harder than his pleasure in seein' me. Least it felt that way at the time, but like I say, that prisoner of war camp didn't leave me much of the way I was before the war. The problem were likely me as much as him."

"When did you come here?" AJ asked.

"Went back to France for some time. Best part of twenty years, I believe. Never did settle or find myself an occupation I could stick to. Friend got me a job working on freight ships with him for a year or so, and we made a stop here back in 1965. Spent a day on shore leave, then told my friend I was staying."

"Just like that? You decided to live here?" AJ asked.

"Just like that," he replied. "Never seen nowhere quite like it.

Since the moment they unlocked that prison cell door in Germany, I felt like I was runnin' from something. Never could understand why, but I tried a lot of things to rid me of that feelin'. Some I'm none too proud of, if truth be known. That single day here was the first time I didn't feel that way no more. Figured I ought to have more days feelin' that way, so I stayed."

"How many times did you go back?"

"To England?"

"Or France," AJ clarified.

"Father's funeral is all," Marleigh said. "Stayed a week, but it woulda been less 'cept they only had one flight a week back then. This is my home."

AJ thought about the living room bare of family photographs and pondered how to phrase another delicate question.

"I never married," Marleigh said, saving her the trouble. "I'm guessing you were getting around to asking me," he added with a wry smile.

AJ tended to wear her thoughts on her face and had long since known a poker career was not on the cards for her.

"Kids?" she asked.

"None who's claimed me," he replied, keeping a grin on his face, which slowly faded. "Not sure what to do with the little I have when I'm gone," he said, looking at his modest home on land which had appreciated substantially over the past half a century.

"You have family in England," AJ said, as Reg reappeared with a steaming pot of tea. "We found you through your uncle's family."

The old man's eyes brightened. "Dare say it's time to look them up. If you two would get the boxes down from the attic, I'll take a look what's in them. If they haven't rotted away to dust, that is. I'll look for this book you were talking about."

"*The Bravest Captain*," AJ said. "That's the name. I'll write it down for you."

Marleigh nodded.

"Tea?" Reg asked, and Marleigh nodded again.

"I'm a rotten host havin' guests fix their own drinks, but thanks for makin' another pot."

"No trouble," Reg said, pouring tea into their three cups.

"I'm really sorry, but may I use your loo, please?" AJ asked. "That tea's gone straight through me."

"Of course," Marleigh replied, starting to rise from his chair.

"Stay right there, sir," she urged him. "I'll find it."

He settled back down, and AJ heard him asking Reg about his time in the Falklands conflict as she let herself into the house.

One door on the left led to what she guessed to be the single bedroom, so she walked through the opening from the living room into the kitchen, finding a door in the wall between the dining area and the bedroom. Behind the door was a small bathroom with another open door into the bedroom itself.

On the far wall of the bedroom, AJ could see an old map in a frame, edges of the paper torn and wrinkled. She couldn't resist taking a peek, stepping into the man's bedroom, where a double bed was neatly made. The map was of the Caribbean, and had to be either very old, or someone had gone to great lengths to make it appear so. A tarnished metal plate on the bottom of the frame read 'Taken from Goos' De Zee Atlas ofte Water-Weereld, 1666.'

AJ studied the map in awe, imagining what it had taken to produce the work back in the age of sail with such primitive measuring devices. The Cayman Islands on the Dutch map were but three small specks, marked Caiman Grande and the two sister islands simply Caimanes. AJ's jaw dropped, and she forgot all about her need to use the bathroom. She dashed out of the bedroom door into the living room and then made the two men jump when she burst onto the deck.

"I'm so sorry, Mr Smith. I swear I wasn't snooping about your house, but I have to ask you about the map in your bedroom!"

"She apologises a lot, doesn't she?" Marleigh said, looking at Reg.

Reg raised an eyebrow. "With good reason, a fair amount of the time."

They both returned their gaze to AJ.

"Is that a genuine antique map from the 1600s?"

"Best I know," the old man replied. "It was on my father's wall. I remember it from when I was a lad. Been hanging in there since he died."

"That sounds like a nice antique," Reg said, frowning at AJ. "But what's got your knickers in a knot?"

AJ beamed. "According to that old map, Grand Cayman is a wee bit north of Little, which means Crowe was never talking about Little Cayman. The maps he would have been working from in the early 1700s had the islands misplaced by latitude."

39

CAPTAIN

1704

With the galleon now pointing downwind, we were tacking on a beam reach, ready to cut back and come across their bow once again, or so I thought.

"Drop the sails!" Vin bellowed and turned sharply to port.

As the *Royal Fortune* turned, the sails began to luff, flapping loosely while the men furled them as quickly as they could. But we kept turning, until we were facing the *Cielos de Oro*, which was moving slowly but straight towards us, albeit slightly north. We, on the other hand, were stalling into the wind.

"What in the Devil's name are you doing, man?" Hinchcliffe shouted.

"Ready the cannon, boatswain!" Vin yelled in return.

The galleon was no more than 60 yards from us, and Vin cut the wheel again, turning us beam to the wind. And our opponent. The lone foremast topsail luffed and rippled as our bow slowly crept around with the last of our forward momentum ebbing away.

I was looking up when the cannons boomed, causing me to

stagger and catch my balance. The first cannon shot missed to starboard, but the other two converged on the starboard side of the galleon's bow, boring through the wooden ship, destroying everything and everyone in their path.

"Come on, come on," Vin groaned, looking up at the topsail as the crew trimmed it with the rigging to catch the wind.

Slowly it filled and began pulling us around until we were back on a beam reach enough to move away from the path of the galleon, where Vin turned downwind to outrace the Spanish and not give them a chance to hit us with their deck gun. If anyone was still alive to use it.

The pirates cheered and waved their swords in the air once more, most of them looking up at Vin as they did so. She turned and stared at the galleon we were now pulling away from. Their final remaining sail was being furled, and a bloodied man stood at the decimated bow, holding up a piece of white cloth.

Vin's shoulders slumped, and she let out a long sigh.

"Not bad, Mr Crowe, not bad," Hinchcliffe said, arriving behind us.

We turned around to where all the crew who were on deck had gathered at the base of the quarterdeck. Vin turned to port once again, beginning our tack to bring us alongside our prize.

"Looks like you got rid of Rochefort and made quite the bid for captain, Mr Crowe," Hinchcliffe said sternly.

"I have no desires for the position, boatswain, and I considered the captain a friend. I shall mourn his passing, sir."

Hinchcliffe sneered and was about to speak again when the crew began chanting, "Captain, captain, captain..."

The boatswain gritted his teeth and held up a hand to quieten the crew, who quickly fell silent.

"Show of hands," Hinchcliffe called out to them. "Who votes Crowe as captain?"

Now, the men were more hesitant, sensing they were coming between Vin and the boatswain, who could make their life hell.

"Do you understand our letter of marque, Mr Crowe?" Lefty

asked. "You were with Rochefort when he transferred our goods in the Admiralty Court, were you not?"

"I was," Vin replied. "But understand, I'm not seeking the position, sir."

"It ain't a matter of wanting, Mr Crowe," another man said. "We need someone who can read and talk with those toffs who run everything. I'd say you're the best we got."

Hinchcliffe stiffened, and Vin looked down at the deck. The men watched her as she contemplated our new predicament.

"I say again. Show of hands," Hinchcliffe barked.

This time, the men didn't hesitate, and a sea of hands rose in the air.

"Damn it," Vin muttered under her breath. "I have conditions," she said, looking out at the crew.

"Let's hear 'em," Lefty responded.

"Unless they resist further, there'll be no more killing here today. Enough blood has been spilled."

Murmurs and groans ran through the small crowd, but heads were nodding.

"Looks like that'll be fine," Lefty said, and no one complained.

"Same goes for any other prizes we take, gentlemen. I'll have the last say, and I'll not be allowing the slaughter of non-military men."

The grumbles were louder this time.

"You like these Spanish bastards or what? They'd spill your guts given half a chance," Dutch shouted. "We've all lost friends to Spanish and French blades."

"Military blades, not unarmed merchants, sir. These are my conditions."

"Hands!" Hinchcliffe yelled.

It was enough of a majority to not require a count, but it certainly wasn't unanimous. The boatswain, for one, hadn't raised his hand for either vote. Neither had Dutch and their little band of brothers.

"There you have it, Mr Crowe," Hinchcliffe said without any pleasure. "You're captain whether you like it or not."

Vin nodded, and the pirates cheered.

"Prepare to tie alongside, Mr Hinchcliffe," Vin said, using the chain of command.

The boatswain frowned, his intentions hard to read, although he left no doubt that his mood was foul.

"Aye, Captain," he finally said and returned to the deck, delivering orders to the men as he stomped down the steps.

We carefully approached the galleon and threw a line across once we were close enough. I could only see four or five Spaniards on their feet, and wondered how many souls had perished. The only men we saw from the privateer ship were floating face down in the water, their bodies already being tugged and dragged under by opportunistic predators.

As the exhilaration of the battle began to subside, the pain in my arm grew. I picked a dozen smaller splinters out, but the two largest were left, and I'd need a bandage to stem the bleeding once they came out. An event I was not looking forward to.

Vin took a look at my arm. "I thought I told you not to get in the way of cannonballs, Wil," she said, and smiled at me. "You'll live. Go to the captain's cabin and take any alcohol he has hidden there, and find the cleanest shirt we can tear into bandages as well. Then stay in our berth until I return. I'll patch you up when I come down."

I nodded, knowing she didn't want me to see the carnage on the other ship, or witness more brutality if the Spaniards tried something impetuous.

"Aye, aye, Captain," I replied, and she cuffed me playfully across the top of my head, grinning.

"I seem to be digging us a deeper hole to climb out of Wil, but climb out we shall."

"I know," I replied. "But where can we go now? Jamaica isn't safe. Even England might have word of our crime before we reach home."

She puffed out her cheeks and let her breath slowly escape her lips. "British America," she finally said. "We'll sail the Straits of Florida and sell whatever we have in the hold on the east coast of British America." She let go of the wheel as the men hauled us alongside the galleon, tying the two ships together. "British America," she repeated. "That's where we'll go, Wil."

I desperately wanted to go home, but that didn't seem possible anytime soon. At least her plan felt like a step in the right direction.

"Then British America it will be," I echoed, and went below as instructed, leaving her to deal with the Spaniards.

Once I'd gathered the alcohol and the cleanest shirt the unfortunate captain had owned, I sat on our cot and looked out the stern window. I could just see the battered stern of the galleon beside us and felt the waves knocking the two ships together.

I tried my best to think of anything other than the throbbing pain in my left arm and the loss of Rochefort. In a few months, the man had taught me more than my father had in fourteen years. Perhaps being killed instantly by the cannonball was a better demise than the fate Hinchcliffe had in mind for him, but it was little consolation for the loss I felt.

My heart filled with pride at how my mother had stood up to the boatswain, and her magnificent skill and determination in battle. She had earned her right to the captain's position, and the crew had rallied to secure her in the role. Except Hinchcliffe, who still clearly wanted the position for himself.

Fear brushed my pride aside as I relived the boatswain and his closest allies challenging the captain, ready to cut him down for the slightest of errors. Surely, that same confrontation lay in our own future. Hinchcliffe would find a way, a moment, a brief opportunity, to discredit Mother. I gritted my teeth and resolved not to allow that circumstance to happen.

There was much activity for several hours as whatever the Spanish merchantman had carried in her hold was transferred to ours, which was undoubtedly much smaller. When Vin finally returned to the cabin, I felt the two ships separate and the *Royal Fortune* leave under sail.

"Look at this cutlass, Wil," she said, laying the beautifully crafted sword on the bed. "I think it's from India. The Spanish captain told me they'd attacked an English East India Company ship in the Atlantic and taken their payload. They were heading to Havana, Cuba, to drop their stolen cargo and continue to their original destination in Florida."

I picked up the weapon and admired the intricate craftsmanship and sparkling jewels. Despite its ostentatious appearance, the cutlass was well balanced and functionally designed.

"It's incredible."

Vin took Mr Helms's sword from her belt and handed it to me. "Here, Wil. I can use the new one, so you have this. It's better you're armed these days."

I set the gold and bronze down and took the cutlass from her. I thought of Mr Helms and the lessons he'd given us, wondering what he'd think of us now. Pirates attacking Spanish galleons. I suspected he'd be a little disappointed, but I hoped he'd understand we were doing what we needed to do to survive and find our way home. Even if that turned out to be a new home.

"Let me see your arm, young man," Vin said, and I put the cutlass down, taking a seat on the edge of the cot.

"Where are we heading?" I asked as she examined my wounds.

"Los Caymanas for provisions, then British America."

"Really? The crew agreed to the plan?"

"They wanted to go back to Jamaica, which would take weeks tacking windward, so I told them I had a contact in British America who'd pay handsomely for our forced trade."

"And they believed you?"

"They complained about sailing through Spanish-controlled waters, so I told them if they were too scared, then by all means, we could return to Jamaica."

I covered my mouth with my right hand to silence my laughter, and as I did, she pulled the biggest shard of wood from my flesh. I was unable to stifle my scream.

"That was the worst one, Wil," she said with a pained expression as she poured neat rum over the wound. "The last one won't be so bad."

"Give me a moment," I panted, the alcohol stinging as much as the extraction hurt.

"All right, tell me when you're ready," she lied, and pulled the second one out.

40

BEER CANS AND BOATS

Present Day

It was nearing midday by the time AJ and Reg left West Bay and drove east once more, with the atmosphere inside the Land Rover remarkably more buoyant than it had been that morning. Under Marleigh's instructions, Reg had hoisted AJ into the tiny attic of the cottage, where she'd sweated profusely handing down four cardboard boxes full of stuff. What they contained, she had no idea, but Marleigh had promised to call them if he came across *The Bravest Captain*.

The old man hadn't set eyes on his father's belongings since the day they'd arrived on Grand Cayman back in the 80s. He'd shoved them in the attic and told AJ and Reg he'd rarely thought about them over the past thirty-eight years. Their questions over the book and the thought of his estranged family in England had prompted him to spend time going through them.

AJ hadn't been able to bring herself to press the urgency from their standpoint, but she had warned him about Pritchard, and told him to call the police if a stranger showed up fitting the man's description.

"Maybe Alpers discovered the map discrepancy, and that's why he came to Grand," AJ suggested as they bounced along the road, now clear of commuter traffic.

"Possibly," Reg agreed. "Although he might have simply needed fuel to get back to Jamaica. There would only have been a handful of people on Little in the 1920s and they'd all have relied on supplies from Grand."

They drove on in silence until Reg turned on Frank Sound Road and headed north across the middle of the island. AJ was buried in confused thoughts of what the thin evidence they had might mean. Diving the site again was still a ridiculous long shot, but armed with their latitude theory from the old map, she felt like their search had more purpose. Plus, Mrs Wright would certainly restrict the location in the near future, and there was no guarantee they'd be allowed to dive it with whoever she brought in to search.

"What does the hilt we found, or the bone for that matter, have to do with Crowe?" AJ wondered out loud as her mind churned things over.

Reg rubbed his scraggy beard-covered chin. "Could be artefacts from another period altogether, right? We're looking at history in broad strokes of time, but a lot can happen in twenty or thirty years. There's every chance the hilt, the bone, and Crowe's visit were all years apart and not connected at all."

"I suppose," AJ admitted, but she wasn't ready to believe it just yet.

The idea they'd found traces back to William Crowe's story was too romantic and exciting not to hold out hope. But without a copy of *The Bravest Captain*, they'd likely never know. Reg was right. Even if the artefacts could be dated to the turn of the 17th century, it was a long way from definitive evidence that any of it tied together.

When they reached the small parking area in the woods by the side of Queen's Highway, Reg parked the Land Rover and they gathered up their gear. Making a couple of trips back and forth along the overgrown, rocky path, they prepared for two dives without having to return for tanks.

Conditions were even more perfect than the day they'd set the Reef Balls. The wind was no more than a gentle breeze, the waves barely perceptible ripples rolling towards shore, and a handful of wispy white clouds dotted the brilliant blue canvas of the sky above. AJ couldn't see a single boat on the ocean. The East End dive operations may have been out that morning, but by now they'd be back at their docks preparing for afternoon trips.

It didn't appear as though anyone had been there since they'd dived from shore two days prior. No markers, keep out, or archaeological site signs were posted, so Gladys Wright was yet to bar anyone from diving. AJ and Reg hadn't called to ask, preferring to take the forgiveness over permission tack.

As AJ double-checked her gear, a sense of adventure overwhelmed her. Her brain knew that civilisation was no more than a few miles away, but alone on the beach preparing to dive into the Caribbean Sea in search of centuries-old evidence gave her a thrilling feeling of isolation. She imagined mountain climbers and explorers had to experience the same emotion, and she could see why it would be addictive.

The two divers waded into the water, taking careful, shuffling steps to keep their balance and send any stingrays out from under their feet. They surface swam to deeper water, angling north where they knew Reef Ball number seven was located. The visibility was so clear, dropping to the sandy sea floor 30 feet below was akin to descending through space.

The concrete dome had already attracted a plethora of fish life and the fresh grey surface had dulled in the two days since they'd last been there. Soon, organic growth would take hold and over the following few years, coral would begin covering the surface.

They finned out to the approximate spot where they'd recovered the bone, and began a search pattern from there to where the reef itself began in slightly deeper water. Once more AJ found the thrill of anticipation was soon replaced by the monotony of the systematic process necessary to cover large areas of sea floor. Reg operated the magnetometer while AJ swept in and dug down to recover whatever metallic object the device had detected.

Her net bag she'd brought along now carried more beer and fizzy drink cans, a lead fishing weight with yards of line still attached, and a piece of rusty angle iron. Reg signalled that he would start scanning along the base of the reef between number seven and the next Reef Ball along to the west, and AJ gave him an okay sign in return.

Her digging had ruined the perfect visibility, so she figured he wanted to work in clearer water. She checked her Teric dive computer, which showed they'd been down for 48 minutes and she had 1200 psi left of the 3000 she'd started with. Reg, being a big fellow, would have used more air and was probably well under 1000 psi by now. The deepest they'd been was 38 feet, so excessive nitrogen loading wasn't an issue, and they'd stay down until their tanks were nearly drained. It was an easy surface swim to shore.

AJ watched Reg move away, swinging the magnetometer back and forth, covering a six-foot-wide swath as he edged slowly forward. Between exhalations, she began hearing a faint drone through the water and guessed a boat was passing by. It was impossible to tell the direction the sound was coming from as the human ear is confused by the different timing of sound through water, but she could tell it was getting closer.

Ahead, Reg also paused and turned his head towards the surface. The deep-throated tone sounded like a good-sized diesel engine rather than a higher-revving outboard. AJ knew one of the dive ops at East End ran 46-foot Newtons with twin diesels, so it could be one back out for an afternoon trip. They'd know soon enough, as it would either pass them by or come to a stop at the Anchor Point buoy in deeper water to the east of their position.

The drone continued, getting louder, until it felt like the sound engulfed them and they both watched for a hull cutting through the surface above. When it finally appeared, the boat was bigger than a Newton, probably 60 feet long by AJ's estimate, with a single screw. The captain took the transmission out of gear while still over the reef and the two divers watched the propeller come to a stop, the engine continuing to throb at idle.

AJ shrugged her shoulders at Reg, who gave a signal to stay where she was. He set the magnetometer on the seabed and finned towards the strange boat, slowly rising as he approached. A second, smaller shadow appeared off the stern and the hull of an inflatable tender broke the surface. Its outboard motor whirred to life, and the little boat began making slow circles away from the bigger vessel.

Reg paused at 10 feet below and watched the tender as it passed almost directly above him. The inflatable, which was no more than 15 feet long, spun around and coasted back over Reg's position. The dive-masked face of a man appeared off the side, hanging over the round, rubber gunwale, scanning the ocean below. His eyes quickly saw Reg, searched for a few more moments until spotting AJ, then disappeared.

AJ knew right away something wasn't right about the situation. Reg signalled that he was surfacing and began finning away from the tender, so he didn't pop up right next to it. AJ wanted to wave him off, a sinking feeling in her stomach telling her all was not well, but Reg was focused on the two boats, and surfaced halfway between them.

The moment his head broke the surface, streaks flew into the water all around him. AJ watched in helpless horror as her friend and mentor struggled to fight his way beyond the reach of the bullets. She sucked in a gasp of air as Reg's head jerked, and a red haze wafted and swirled around his mop of curly hair.

41

STAY PUT IN A SAFE PLACE

Present Day

AJ finned along the bottom towards her friend, who was now clear of the gunfire but bleeding and breathing heavily, streams of bubbles venting from his regulator. Reaching him, she carefully inspected his scalp where it appeared a bullet had grazed him just above his left ear. It was a superficial wound but bleeding freely into the water, so she removed her bright purple Mermaid Divers headband she used to keep her hair from her face, and dangled it in front of Reg's mask.

He rolled his eyes, but nodded and slipped his dive mask off his head, allowing her to fit the headband, which only just stretched over his melon-sized noggin. Replacing his mask, he tipped it up and cleared the water with a long exhale and AJ winced at the precious air escaping.

Reg showed her his dive computer. He had 512 psi left. She showed him her Teric, which wirelessly read 961 psi. They both looked up and saw the inflatable moving back into position above them. Their bubbles breaking the surface were easy markers for their pursuers to follow. Like targets on their backs. The alternative was to stop breathing, which wasn't an option.

AJ reached to the sandy bottom and found two small pieces of limestone the size of marbles. She dropped them into her hand, then pointed at the boat above. Reg nodded, confirming it was Stone Pritchard - Pebbles - who had them pinned to the ocean floor. Reg then pointed to the hull of the larger boat still bobbing over the reef and tapped the little rocks in her hand, indicating where Pritchard was. He then made the classic finger and thumb signal for a gun. It was Pebbles doing the shooting.

They both dropped to the sea floor and Reg gathered up a few more rocks and sticks of dead coral. He began laying out their predicament, showing the boats, the shoreline, and the two of them. He calmly pantomimed several scenarios. They couldn't surface or walk out to the shore without being shot. They couldn't move away and surface anywhere else, as the inflatable was following their bubbles. If they stayed put, they'd simply watch their tank pressure drop to zero.

Reg glanced at his computer and AJ saw he was now at 440 psi. They could move shallower and save some air, but not much, or the bullets would reach them. AJ was beginning to think they'd have no choice but to take their chances with Pritchard's marksmanship. Shooting from a moving boat was no easy task, even in calm conditions. But if they didn't know where the divers were about to surface, that would make the shot even harder.

AJ looked at her own computer. She had 890 psi left. She frantically nudged Reg's arm and began slipping out of her BCD straps, keeping the regulator in her mouth. Reg watched her with a frown creasing his face. She pointed to him and then to her BCD as well as his, tapped his chest, and signalled for him to swim west along the shoreline. Reg threw his hands up and grunted into his regulator, asking what good would that do.

AJ tapped her own chest and indicated she'd swim to shore on a single breath hold, then call for help. Reg waved her off, signalling she'd be shot. She waggled her finger back at him and tapped her regulator, followed by his. Reg's eyes lit up, and she knew he'd understood. Her plan was risky as both boats had to take the bait, but on the assumption the men in the inflatable also had guns, it was more important for them to be drawn away than the big boat, whose draft would restrict how close to shore it could come.

Taking long calm breaths, AJ tried her best to flush her lungs of spent gas and replenish with new, pure air. She'd been freediving many times, but it had never been something she'd pursued beyond having fun. Her friend Nora could hold her breath for an incomprehensible amount of time, but AJ figured she'd have two minutes at the absolute limit. It wasn't like she'd be sitting on the bottom of a swimming pool doing nothing but sitting on the bottom of a swimming pool. She had to swim a hundred yards underwater until she could stand and run out.

AJ slipped the Teric from her wrist and gave it to Reg, who fastened the strap next to his own computer. Now he'd be able to see the air in both tanks. They nodded to each other. AJ took her last gulp of air from the tank, then relinquished her air supply to Reg, who began finning away, carrying her BCD and tank under one arm.

Closing her eyes, AJ did her best to relax and bring her heart rate down. She desperately wanted to look up and see what the men in the inflatable were doing, but the lack of engine noise told her they hadn't moved. If the man dipped his mask in the water again, he'd see her sitting where Reg had left her and realise the ruse. The more each scenario batted around her brain, the harder it was to stay relaxed. Exertion, fear, rapid heart rate, and panic, all used more oxygen and robbed her of time underwater.

AJ finally opened her eyes behind her mask and looked up at the inflatable bobbing above her. Reg was already a good distance away, zigzagging side to side, taking quicker, shorter breathes from her regulator, and exhaling each time he turned. The bubble streams were several feet apart as they rose to the surface and he was paddling the sand as he went, stirring up a mess to hide the fact it was only him. From the boats looking at the bubbles break the surface, it should appear as though two divers were swimming side by side.

Reg was putting on a stellar performance, but it was all for naught. Either the men in the tender weren't paying attention, or they'd already detected the plan. AJ couldn't stay still any longer. If she didn't leave for the shoreline, she'd be forced to surface for a gasp of breath right by the little boat.

Moving with practised grace and ease, AJ made her body as streamlined as possible and put her fins to good use in long, deliberate strokes, willing herself not to kick herself out of breath. The inflatable's engine started and the sound of its propeller grabbing the water now terrified her. Was it following her, or Reg?

The now familiar deep drone of the diesel also picked up, and the sound from the two boats seemed to consume her as she kicked towards what she had hoped would be safety. Now, there was every chance the tender would pull alongside and shoot her in the shallow water, or wait for her to pop up, her lungs completely spent.

Why were they trying to kill her and Reg? It made little sense to her oxygen-deprived brain. If they wanted information, they wouldn't get it from a pair of corpses. The hilt and the bone were back in town, so AJ and Reg had nothing worth taking. *Simply to remove them both from the picture?* That seemed extreme, even for a piece of shit like Pritchard.

He didn't need them both! If Pritchard was correctly assuming Reg and AJ shared the same information about the talwar, then murdering his ex-partner, and more formidable adversary, made life simpler. AJ would be an easy mark. The revelation hit her a moment before she realised the sound of the boats was fading. They'd taken the bait. With lungs burning and every instinct screaming for air, now only a few feet above her, AJ willed herself to kick closer to shore. Finally, she could take it no more and popped up, gasping.

Standing in chest-deep water, she sucked in air and turned to see the two boats now slowly following the twin bubble trail Reg was leaving. AJ swam towards the beach until her hands scooped sand at the bottom of each stroke, then slipped off her fins. For another ten yards she did the awkward water run, which felt like moving through treacle until she could high-step clear of the surface and stumble to the shore.

Tossing her fins and mask aside, AJ sprinted to where they'd left the spare tanks, towels, and the Land Rover keys, which Reg had hidden under a rock. She paused and looked out across the ocean, where she could now see the larger boat was an old trawler converted into a research and salvage vessel. It stayed over the reef, but the inflatable was closer to the beach, tracking Reg. She figured he was almost through her tank by now and switching to the little he had left.

Running barefoot over the rough and rocky trail through the trees, AJ winced and groaned, but tried to think what to do next. A police car from either direction would be coming from Old Man Bay or Gun Bay, both ten minutes away. The helicopter from George Town would take even longer by the time it was airborne. She had to buy time.

Her hands were shaking as she unlocked the door and fumbled for her mobile phone hidden under the front seat. AJ ignored several alerts for missed texts and calls from Marleigh Smith and dialled Whittaker's number.

"Good morning, AJ, how…"

"Sorry, Roy, no time to chat! We're at Anchor Point and Pritchard has Reg pinned under water. He's been shot and now he's running out of air. Send anything and everything you have available!"

"He's been shot?"

"It's not bad," AJ said, then realised how ridiculous that sounded. "I mean, the bullet only grazed him, but he's bleeding."

She could hear Whittaker barking orders into his radio, which gave her a moment to gather her thoughts. Hopping onto the front seat, she reached into the back of the Landy and rummaged through the gear, keeping the mobile trapped to her ear with her shoulder. In a mesh bag of spare dive equipment, AJ pulled out a regulator system, complete with first and second stages, plus a back-up reg known as an octopus. There was only one, so she shuffled out of the Land Rover, dropping her phone on the seat, and coiled up the hoses so she could carry them.

"AJ? Are you there? Hello?"

She realised Whittaker was back and grabbed the mobile before heading back down the trail.

"Hey, sorry. I was getting stuff from Reg's Land Rover," she said, out of breath.

"Are you in a safe location, AJ?" he asked.

"Yeah, I am. They have a big boat and a tender, which are both following Reg. He created a diversion so I could get out of the water."

"Okay, I have patrol cars on their way, a Joint Marine Unit boat, and the helicopter is about to go up, so stay put in a safe place where they can find you, okay? And stay on the line with me."

AJ panted and grunted as her feet ran over rocks and sharp twigs. "They can't miss them, Roy. They're the guys with guns on the only two boats in Bluff Bay."

She hit end on the call, tossed the mobile on top of the towels, and began fitting the regulator to one of the spare tanks on the beach.

42

A PUNCH ON THE CHIN

Present Day

With her fins under one arm, mask on her forehead, and dragging a tank in each hand by the valve, AJ struggled into the shallow, clear water. She waded in until she was chest deep, then let go of the tanks, which dropped to the sea floor. Slipping on her fins, she pulled her mask in place, then dipped under to gather up the tanks.

Purging the regulator, she popped it into her mouth and made sure her mask was securely sealed, as she wouldn't have a free hand for a while. Scooping a tank under each arm, AJ began kicking west, angling slightly out to deeper water as she went.

The set-up was precarious at best. Her only attachment to the crucial air supply was her own grasp of the aluminium cylinder, and buoyancy control was solely reliant on her lungs. The tanks were heavier than the surrounding water while they were full, but would become slightly buoyant as the compressed air inside depleted. That would be a problem, but not one AJ would have to worry about for some time. Her immediate concern was finding

Reg before his air supply ran out, forcing him to the surface and into Pritchard's gunsight.

The Reef Balls served as handy landmarks and distance gauges, although without knowing exactly where Reg had made it to, they did little more than give AJ comfort from familiarity. The farther she went, the more awkward the tanks seemed to become, and her fears grew as she began second-guessing herself. Had she missed him? Had he already surfaced? It was hard for her to look up, so if she missed anything on the surface in her field of vision ahead, it was possible to swim right below his dead body bobbing in the sun. The thought made her shiver.

Finning past another concrete dome, AJ could see the next one in the distance, staggered closer to shore. As she neared, a shadow moved around the sandy bottom, seemingly rocking back and forth. The clouds made shadows in this way, but they moved slowly in one direction as they crossed the sky. Pausing, AJ awkwardly rolled to one side and looked up, spotting the inflatable. Reg had to be close by.

She kicked harder towards the Reef Ball and, through the holes, saw movement on the far side. As she came closer, Reg rose from behind the artificial reef and gently finned towards the surface. He'd shed his BCD and tank but held his dive knife in one hand. She knew Reg had run out of air.

AJ dropped the second tank and hugged the one with the regulator to her chest as she kicked towards her friend, now 20 feet above her. He drove his knife into the inflatable hull of the tender, then continued stabbing at the rubber in different places, trying to puncture as many of the separated cells as possible.

The outboard engine revved to life, and the propeller thrashed in the water, launching the half-deflated craft forward. Reg pulled his arm back just in time as the metal blades shaved a few hairs from his arm. AJ reached up and tugged on one of Reg's fins, causing him to recoil and look down, bringing his knife to bear. She thrust the octopus regulator his way, and he snatched it up, purging the valve and sucking down air.

Streaks peppered the water around them once more and AJ watched a bullet hit Reg's shoulder, then fall harmlessly away having lost its velocity through the dense water. They both kicked for the bottom and hung to the side of the concrete dome while they recovered their breath, and AJ checked Reg over for further damage. He brushed her away, then raised a questioning hand, tapped her, then pointed to the sea floor. *Why are you here?*

She frowned back at him and was about to figure out how to sign *You ungrateful bugger,* when it dawned on her he had no way of knowing she'd called for help. Making the universal phone gesture, she whirred her finger in a circle for a police siren, then pointed to the sea floor. Reg's expression softened, and he sat for a moment, a light waft of blood still leaking past the headband.

The drone of the diesel engine picked up, and they both instinctively looked to the surface. Two figures were swimming towards the bigger boat. The moment the men climbed aboard, the trawler's prop churned the water, and the boat swung away in the direction of the open ocean.

About a hundred feet to the west, the inflatable hung in the water, its outboard below the surface, kept buoyant by one or two cells of air that Reg hadn't punctured. They looked at each other, and AJ figured they were both wondering if it was safe to go up.

Reg held up five fingers, pointed to the sea floor, and then to the surface. AJ gave him an okay sign in return, took a long pull of air from the regulator, then dropped it and swam away. She retrieved the extra tank, swimming back to Reg and setting it in the sand next to them. Reg looked from one tank to the other, realising she'd swum all the air they could possibly need from shore without a harness or BCD. He reached over and gently gave her a playful punch on the chin, followed by a wink.

Pearl would thank her profusely for saving her old man, but that gesture was likely the only time Reg would say anything himself. They'd go back to their mischievous banter where Reg would claim he'd had it all under control, and AJ would say he was dead meat until she saved his arse. It was how their relationship worked and AJ wouldn't have it any other way.

From the family holiday on Grand Cayman nineteen years ago, when Reg Moore had taken her scuba diving for the first time, she'd felt a trust and kinship with the gruff old sea salt. He'd been the one to set her up in Florida where she could learn the business and gain experience teaching and guiding. He'd given her a job on the island when she was ready, and together with her parents, helped her launch Mermaid Divers alongside his own business.

'Thank you' was just a phrase often frivolously tossed around without true meaning, so while it was still important to say the words in many situations, a gentle punch on the chin and a wink meant far more to AJ.

A drone of a different pitch reached their ears, and once more they looked up and waited for a hull to appear. When it did, they both recognised the underside of the DoE's boat they'd worked below for a day earlier in the week. Once the boat slowed and stopped a short distance from their location, they rose from the sea floor and eased up to the surface, where once they were absolutely sure there were friendly faces, they dropped the tank so they didn't have to fin to stay afloat.

"Are you two okay?" Casey shouted from the bow as she waved directions to her co-worker at the helm.

AJ and Reg both gave her an okay signal in return.

"I found an ancient artefact down there, so I thought I should bring it up!" AJ yelled back, nodding her head towards Reg.

He just shook his head and grinned.

43

A STRAY HAND

1704

My wounds had scabbed over by the time we moored in the bay off the north coast near the east end of Los Caymanas. My arm didn't ache anymore, but itched like the devil, and I prayed the mosquitoes wouldn't add to my discomfort. We would only be here long enough to restock our fresh water and to cook and salt the meat on the beach. Several fires already burned as the hunters brought turtles to our cook, who sweated profusely over the food. We still had plenty of provisions aboard from our last visit to Kingston, but the journey to British America would be farther and longer than we'd previously prepared to sail.

The next day, heavy rains throughout the morning completed our fresh water needs but drowned out Cook's fires. The weather had moved on by noon and with steam rising from every surface as the scalding sun reappeared, the fires were restarted with dry wood, and the process continued.

Approaching sunset, Cook declared he'd either grilled or smoked enough damn turtle meat to feed us till the grave. I hoped that wasn't true from either way of looking at it, but Cook was given to exaggeration. Vin declared we'd depart the next morning with the falling tide and the boatswain prepared the cockboat to kedge us to deeper water where we would use the wind to depart the island.

Having stayed on the ship, I'd been spared the ravages of the biting insects and found the bay to be a beautiful spot. The crystal-clear water revealed the colourful reef below us and turned a brilliant turquoise over the sandy shallows. I enjoyed watching the turtles swim clumsily about, surfacing every so often for a breath of air. Some of the crew fished from the bow and brought aboard an array of exotic creatures, only some of which we dared to eat.

Preparing to dine before the sun finally disappeared, Vin retired to her cabin to wash the salt from her skin, having helped bring the meat aboard. I helped Cook slice the fish he'd grilled whole above the fire, and set out the daily rations of tack, before heading below myself. After wrapping Vin's chest, I splashed fresh water over my face and arms, and hurried up top with my stomach grumbling and ready for the food I'd helped prepare.

When Vin returned from below deck, she carried a bottle Rochefort had hidden away in his cabin, which we now occupied. I'd found four when I'd searched for alcohol to treat my wounds.

"Here, boatswain," she said, thrusting the bottle into Hinchcliffe's hands. "A taste for each man to send us on our way."

Hinchcliffe eagerly took the brandy, plucking the cork with his crooked teeth. He reached out and grabbed the captain.

"Here, take the first pull…" he said, his hand missing Vin's arm and sliding across her chest.

The boatswain reeled, handing the bottle to another man and spitting the cork across the deck. "In the name of all things holy!"

Vin took a step back, and I froze on the spot. For a moment, Hinchcliffe stood with his mouth agape, and I prayed he'd take a drink and figure he'd been mistaken.

But fate was done dealing us a fair hand.

"Remove your shirt!" he demanded.

"I'll do no such thing, boatswain," Vin responded, "and I'll ask you not to place a hand on me again."

The crew were now on their feet and crowded around the drama unfolding. Here lay Hinchcliffe's last opportunity to back down before he definitively challenged the captain of the ship. Once he crossed that line, there would be no turning back; the matter must have resolution.

"Remove your shirt and prove yourself," the boatswain persisted, crossing the line without hesitation.

"What's this all about?" Lefty asked. "What does the captain have to prove?"

Hinchcliffe sneered. "The captain knows. Now remove your shirt or I'll remove it for you!"

Vin's hand dropped to the hilt of the talwar, hanging from her belt in its ornately decorated scabbard.

"I don't need to prove anything to you or anyone else aboard this ship. I proved myself in combat, boatswain, after which you all insisted I captain the *Royal Fortune*. You'll stand down and my discipline will be fair, or we shall clash blades."

My heart leapt into my throat. I couldn't believe after all we'd been through that a stray hand across Vin's bound breasts had given her away. My hand fell to the hilt of Mr Helms's cutlass, and I kept my eyes on Hinchcliffe and him alone. I had no idea what I, a fourteen-year-old lad, could do against the pirates if a fight ensued, but I resigned myself to dying alongside my mother with sword in hand, putting up my best defence.

Hinchcliffe slowly drew his cutlass, and my knees went weak. Vin followed suit.

"So be it," she said and took up a stance I recognised from our lessons.

The boatswain began moving to her right, and the crowd backed up, forming a circle. Jeers, murmurs, and shouts echoed all around in the dimming light. I heard several men call out wagers on the outcome, and Lefty refuse them.

Vin let the boatswain step in an arc around her position,

pivoting her feet as he went. Hinchcliffe didn't appear to take any particular stance, but I could tell he would move quickly when he chose to. As his back passed by me, I willed myself to lunge, driving my cutlass through his ribs, but my feet stayed planted. I knew it would be a coward's blow and one which would guarantee both our deaths at the hands of the crew. For all their dishonesty and deviousness, they still had codes of conduct, especially when it came to fighting amongst themselves.

Hinchcliffe swiftly lunged, thrusting his blade at Vin's right shoulder, an awkward move to defend without leaving her body open. Instead of deflecting his blade, she dipped and twisted her shoulders and shuffled left, whipping her blade across the under-side of his right arm. The man growled in pain, wildly swinging his cutlass to fend off further attack.

Vin now moved, keeping her stance as she shuffled her feet around her opponent. Everyone now knew Vin was not an easy mark for the pirate, including the boatswain, whose arm dripped blood across the deck as he pivoted. He'd underestimated her once. He was unlikely to be that reckless again. I hoped the slash in his arm had weakened him enough to even them up in strength, an advantage he'd held moments before.

"Come on, yer lying coward," Hinchcliffe spat. "Stop dancing like a woman and fight."

I cringed at his turn of phrase, but he was yet to reveal why he'd challenged Vin, and I prayed she could silence him before he did. Perhaps confidence in his hasty conclusion after brushing her chest might falter as she fought like a man.

Hinchcliffe growled and slashed the air before him, doing little more than tiring himself, but the crew yelled and encouraged him, eager for an entertaining fight. Beads of sweat flew from his face and long hair as he slashed again, but this time Vin stepped in, knocking his cutlass away with her blade and following through with the hilt into his nose.

He roared and swept his own blade back up, but Vin sprang to her right and dropped the talwar low enough to fend off the blow.

The move threw her off balance, and with blood spewing from his nose, Hinchcliffe lunged forward in a fit of rage, raising his cutlass over his shoulder and slicing it down across Vin's torso. The tip brushed her shirt, slicing the fabric open before she planted her back foot and jabbed her blade into the boatswain's right shoulder.

Losing control of his right arm, he dropped his cutlass to the deck and staggered backwards. The crew yelled and screamed, unintelligible as to who was rooting for whom. Vin stepped forward and prepared for the final blow when I howled.

Vin stopped in her tracks. Someone had dragged me forward by my hair and held a knife to my throat. The crowd fell silent.

"Drop it, Crowe," Dutch said, and bared his rotten teeth as he pressed the dagger against my skin.

"Finish him, and string up this dishonourable scum," I shouted, which bought me a blow to my head with the butt of his knife.

"This ain't how we do things," Lefty said from the crowd. "They was duelling as the code allows. Taking the lad ain't right."

The crew shouted and commented in unison, making it impossible to decipher their support.

"Right or wrong, I ain't letting Hinchcliffe die by the hand of this molly toff! Drop that cutlass or I swear I'll open up your boy's neck."

Vin let the talwar fall to the deck.

"No," I muttered, sure we were now both bound to die.

My mother looked at me and I could see she also knew this was true, but just as I'd been willing to sacrifice myself with her, she was equally prepared.

Hinchcliffe staggered forward and picked up the Indian sword in his left hand. Several of the crew, including Lefty, rushed forward to grab him and I screamed for her to move, but we were all too late.

The boatswain thrust the talwar into my mother's midriff, driving it upwards. She took one step back and fell to the deck as Lefty and the other men seized Hinchcliffe. I struggled against Dutch's grip, the knife drawing blood on my neck.

"Let the boy be," I heard a man growl from behind us, "or I swear you'll be run through as I live and breathe."

Dutch let me go, and I ran to Mother's side. Her chest heaved and blood ran freely from the wound in her stomach. I pressed my hand to her open flesh, and she groaned. Her hazy eyes settled on my face for a moment, before her body went limp in my arms.

I turned and glared at Hinchcliffe. The men held him and had taken the jewelled sword from his hand. I stood and drew Mr Helms's bronze-hilted blade.

"Let him go," I demanded.

The men released Hinchcliffe, who stood before me, bleeding from his right arm, shoulder, and nose.

"Pick it up," I told him, pointing the tip of my cutlass to his own cutlass on the deck.

He hesitated, teeth gritted and eyes full of hate.

"Defeat me and you'll live," I said.

The boatswain shook his head. "They'll not let me live."

I looked at Lefty.

"If that's your wish, lad," Lefty assured me.

"It is," I replied, and pointed to the sword once again. "Now pick it up, damn you."

Hinchcliffe considered his options for a moment, then reached down and clutched his cutlass in his right hand. He tried to raise the blade, but his arm wouldn't respond, and he winced in pain from the effort. Turning, he looked at Lefty.

"Yer slaughtered the unarmed captain with your left. Now you can fight the lad the same way," Lefty said.

Hinchcliffe took the sword with his left hand and held it up at a defensive angle across his body.

Though saturated with rage, I knew I needed to think my way through the following few moments. Mr Helms's lessons flooded back to me, and with deep breaths I cleared a path in my mind, sensing my muscles relaxing. My opponent was wounded and fighting with his weaker hand, but I couldn't make the mistake of underestimating a man duelling for his life. Especially a cold-blooded sadist like the boatswain.

I whipped my blade against his, testing his strength. By his expression, I could tell he was surprised how easily he blocked my blow. The crowd groaned and murmured, sensing the fight would be more one-sided than everyone had thought. I slapped his blade in the other direction, using minimal effort as I had the first time. The crew's shouts and jeers picked up, and I watched the flicker of hope spark in Hinchcliffe's eyes. He sensed I was weak, a young lad whose muscles and stature were no match for him, even fighting left handed.

"Cut him to pieces, Hinch!" Dutch snarled, and the boatswain's eyes lit up a little more.

I shuffled back a few fearful inches and watched Hinchcliffe's jaw clench. He swung his blade with all his might, sure he'd easily knock my block away, leaving me defenceless. Stepping in, his eyes widened when his cutlass swung away without contacting metal. I plunged Mr Helms's blade below the boatswain's ribcage and drove it home, the hilt stopping against his torso. My forward momentum continued, and I drove him backwards, with the crowd parting until he hit the gunwale and I toppled him over into the water.

The crew went silent, crowding around the side of the ship, watching Hinchcliffe's body splash into the ocean and float on the gently ebbing surface, bathed in the orange light of sunset with a dark haze spreading around his lifeless corpse. I wasn't sure whether they would now turn on me, but I didn't care. I pushed my way to my mother's side, where Lefty joined me.

"I'm sorry, lad," he said, putting a hand on my shoulder. "But you did the captain proud."

I nodded. I'd prefer her to be alive and ashamed of me, but that wasn't to be. Both my parents were dead. One I'd hated and died by my own hand to save the other, and now I'd witnessed my mother murdered before me. So much violence on the heels of a young life filled with love and peace.

"Help me move Mo…" I caught myself, although now it surely didn't matter. "The captain, to the cockboat. We're going ashore."

"You'll find no shortage of hands to help you, lad," Lefty replied.

"Two is enough," I said. "They'll drop us at the beach and row back."

Lefty looked down at my mother's body. The corpse of the captain they all knew as Vin Crowe. "We'd be honoured for you to remain with us, lad. I dare say you'd make a fine navigator."

"I wish you safe travels, Lefty, but we'll be staying here."

Lefty sighed. "I hope our paths cross again, lad. It's been a pleasure sailing with you both."

I nodded. Our time on the *Royal Fortune* had been an adventure, but it had always been a means to an end. Fate had spoken, and decided our end to be on this island, a great distance from our home. In that moment, my pain of her loss was overwhelming, and I couldn't imagine leaving without Mother at my side. Making everything possible. Making everything all right.

"What about 'im?" Lefty asked, pointing to Dutch, who now looked terrified with a sword at his back.

"I honestly don't care," I said, as Lefty helped me lift Mother's body.

Lefty looked at Dutch, then to the man holding him. "He wanted to be with Hinchcliffe. I say let him be with Hinchliffe."

As we rowed towards the beach with my mother held in my arms, I heard the screams of a man being torn apart by the sharks, drawn to the blood of two men in the water.

44

QUEEN AJ

Present Day - one week later

AJ sat on a folding chair under a pop-up tent on the beach at Bluff Bay. In the chair next to her, Marleigh Smith listened intently with his eyes closed, his wrinkled brow creased. Reg stood with one hand draped over the tent frame, staring off into the distant horizon as they both listened to AJ reading from sheets of paper.

The frantic texts and messages Marleigh had sent while Reg and AJ had been underwater fending off Pritchard told her he'd come across a copy of *The Bravest Captain* in the first box he'd opened. He was terrified to turn a page in fear of the three-centuries-old binding coming apart. Sharing the same concern, AJ had brought Gladys Wright into the loop immediately, and Marleigh had willingly surrendered the first print edition into her care.

Seven days later, the three of them were learning the contents of the pages together, as excavation took place 20 yards away between the tent and the road. Another, larger tent covered an area carefully cleared of trees and brush where a small archaeological team methodically continued their dig, now in its fourth day.

As AJ read the words written in the style of the era, the faces of the characters began taking shape in her mind. Young Wil, the narrator of the story which seemed fantastical in parts, was forced to go from a boy full of adventure to a man drowned in tragedy. The mother he adored. Truly a brave captain and a fearless woman during a time when such boldness and tenacity were neither expected nor welcomed by the dominant sex.

AJ's voice wavered and cracked as she relayed William Crowe's words, describing Davina's demise at the hands of boatswain Hinchcliffe. She faltered altogether at the mention of the cutlass with a bronze hilt, with which William, a young lad of only fourteen, sought swift justice and revenge. AJ looked up at Reg, and they both remained speechless for several moments.

"We found it, Reg," she finally stuttered.

Reg nodded, and Marleigh rested a hand on AJ's leg, giving her a gentle squeeze.

"Continue," he whispered.

AJ cleared her throat and took a deep breath before finding her place on the page and reading on. In his text, Wil described taking his mother's body ashore, then watching the *Royal Fortune* sail away from Los Caymanas.

He went on to say how the pirate ship was never heard of again, and that he believed he would die alongside Davina, alone on the island. Two weeks later, having survived on fresh water from rain and turtle he'd caught by hand, an English merchant ship came by to re-provision. Suspicious at first, the captain finally agreed to take Wil aboard, and he earned his fare home by working as part of the crew.

In England, he'd faced accusations and scandal surrounding his father's murder, news of which reached his homeland around the same time he did. Apparently Duck and Gordy briefly pursued the reward, but the case never made it to court. Wil told the story of how Davina, tired of the lord's abuse, had saved her son's life by taking Montgomery's. Davina's family assigned their barrister to the case and, mired in a lack of evidence to suggest other than William's word, no formal charges were brought.

Towards the end of the book, William talked of his good friend from Salt Cay, Marcus Smith, who arrived in England shortly before the work was published. Marleigh was visibly touched by the mention of his ancestor and the three fell silent for several minutes until Gladys Wright called from the excavation site.

Reg helped Marleigh to his feet, and they slowly made their way up the sloping land from the beach. He was amazingly nimble for his age, but the rocky terrain was difficult, and Reg and AJ carefully supported the little man all the way.

Gladys and the two archaeologists wore white Tyvek suits and nitrile gloves, but she pointed to an area under the tent which apparently she felt was far enough away not to contaminate the dig. Once they reached the spot, AJ could see they'd made a rectangular hole the size of a human being, around three feet deep.

Facing west and looking into the length of the grave, she could see the bones of a skeleton had been partially revealed, the skull at the far end from them. Resting along the length of the remains was the tarnished outline of a cutlass which appeared intact. The priceless Blade of Calcutta.

The reality of staring into the open grave of Davina Crowe was overwhelming. A brave woman who'd taken her son from the clutches of an abusive father, disguised herself as a man to earn a place amongst the crew of a pirate ship, then rose to the role of captain. She paid the ultimate price at the hand of a deceitful and hateful man while trying to do nothing more than take her son home.

Tears fell from AJ's eyes as she looked at the remains. Lovingly buried by Wil Crowe more than three centuries ago, the grave had weathered countless storms, and thankfully dodged the march of progress and construction. She felt guilty, as though they were invading the woman's peaceful resting place, but she also wanted to see Davina buried in a more appropriate spot. Honoured and remembered. Taken home, as she had tried to do for her son.

AJ made a mental note to look into finding their living descendants and enquire about a grave for Davina in the family cemetery near William. She recalled Buck mentioning he'd contacted family members. When all was said and done, she didn't know if there'd be any financial reward for their discovery, but if there was, AJ decided she'd contact Simon Morris. As she stared at the remains of Davina Crowe, she could already picture a bronze sculpture of a gallant woman wielding the talwar. The perfect monument for the original gravesite.

"Excuse me for a moment," she said, and stepped away from the tent, earning a disapproving look from Gladys.

It took several rings before Buck Reilly answered her call and greeted her. "I was just thinking about you," he said, and she really wanted to reply with 'What are you wearing?' but the timing didn't feel right. And he might take her seriously.

"We've found her," she whispered.

Gladys had given them all strict instructions about secrecy and forbidden them from taking pictures while the excavation process took place, but AJ felt Buck had a right to know.

"Seriously?" he replied, sounding stunned and excited.

"We're not supposed to tell anyone, so please keep it to yourself, but yes. I was looking at Davina Crowe just before I called you," she said, her voice cracking slightly. "She's incredible, Buck."

"And..?" he asked.

"He buried it with her," AJ replied. "She's clutching the Blade of Calcutta to her chest."

"Have you any idea how big this discovery is, AJ? I mean, cover of *National Geographic* big."

AJ groaned. "I'm not having much fun with the press lately, so I think I'll let the Cayman Islands National Museum bathe in that glory. Besides, I only found what's left of Wil Crowe's sword. The archaeologists took over from there."

Buck laughed. "Can't say I have better luck with the press. But make sure you lay claim to this discovery. It all started with you finding the bronze hilt and figuring out the latitude discrepancy."

"I'm just glad that wanker Pritchard didn't get his hands on it," AJ seethed, picturing the man desecrating the grave just to steal the talwar.

"I can't tell you how happy I am your marine police caught him," Buck responded. "Have they said what they're going to do with him?"

"They're talking to the Bahamian authorities about that murder case you mentioned," AJ replied, still whispering. "With the pictures we have of his disguise he used here, a witness they have now says they can ID him. I think he'll be extradited."

Buck laughed again. "Best not mention my name around the Bahamians, but I'm glad the bastard is finally getting what he deserves."

"I'd better get back, Buck. I can call you tomorrow with more details. I just wanted to let you know and thank you for your help."

"Anytime. And congratulations. Just don't let them call you Queen AJ."

She wasn't completely sure what he meant, but she said goodbye and ended the call.

When AJ returned to the tent, Gladys was explaining that despite their find matching William Crowe's description from his book, it would take months to authenticate the remains, as well as the sword. AJ barely heard the words. There was no doubt in her mind who she was looking at in the grave. She had similar certainty that the bronze-hilted sword she'd found in the water belonged to Mr Helms and had been the weapon Wil Crowe used to kill Hinchcliffe. The bone could well belong to Dutch or the boatswain, but in truth, AJ didn't care either way.

"Do you reckon Crowe really believed he buried her on Little Cayman?" Reg asked quietly.

AJ wiped away the tears which were trickling down her face again. "I'd like to think he knew exactly where he was. Davina navigated them here, and he made no mention of seeing or passing Cayman Brac, which they certainly would have done to arrive at the north-east of Little."

"Don't suppose we'll ever know for certain," Reg replied.

"If I buried my mother with a sword worth a fortune, don't reckon I'd tell anyone where that was," Marleigh said. "Wil Crowe didn't intend nobody to be digging up his mum."

"It feels weird, doesn't it?" AJ whispered. "But I hope Wil would be okay with us finding her."

"We found another item of interest earlier today," Gladys said, walking over and pointing to a table where several mud-covered objects rested in stainless-steel trays. "Needless to say, most of what we stumble across is discarded junk, but this is unique."

She pointed out what appeared to be a heavily rusted, curved tin with a stopper.

"This isn't my field of expertise, but after a quick search, I believe this may be an army issue canteen."

Reg leaned closer and studied the object. "World War One, that is. I had one when I was a kid. My grandfather brought it back from France with him."

AJ looked at Gladys. "Can I pick it up?"

The museum director pointed at a box of nitrile gloves at the end of the table. "Put those on, and please don't..." she mumbled a few incoherent words, then finally finished with, "Please don't do *anything* to it."

AJ wriggled her sweaty hands into the gloves, then carefully lifted the canteen, feeling how light it was. How it hadn't rusted to nothing seemed a miracle, but somehow it had survived. She turned it around in her hand, looking for any kind of identification marks. Gladys's stare felt like a laser beam locked on her every touch, and rightfully so, as AJ had a strong urge to rub a little more dirt away on the concave side below the top.

"Okay, time to put it down," Gladys ordered firmly.

AJ rolled her thumb across the surface, pushing away years of grime, and as Gladys took a step her way, Reg held out his arm and stopped her.

"What've you found, love?"

AJ gently brushed the surface to reveal three letters stamped into the old metal. C.M.A. She looked at Reg, aghast. "Christopher Michael Alpers."

Reg grinned. "The poor bugger was this close, and probably never knew it."

ACKNOWLEDGMENTS

My sincere thanks to:

My incredible wife Cheryl, for her unwavering support, love, and encouragement.

My family and friends for putting up with me.

My talented fellow author and friend, John H. Cunningham, for loaning me his cool Buck Reilly character. Check out *Graceless* and *Timeless* for more fun between Buck, AJ, and Nora..!

My editor Andrew Chapman at Prepare to Publish for his consistently excellent work and sage advice.
Gretchen Douglas for her eagle-eyed proofreading.
My advanced reader copy (ARC) group, whose input and feedback is invaluable. This group pushes me to be a better writer, for which I am eternally grateful. It is a pleasure working with all of you.

The Tropical Authors group for their magnificent support and collaboration. Check out the website for other great authors in the Sea Adventure genre.

Shearwater dive computers, whose products I proudly use.
Reef Smart Guides whose maps and guidebooks I would be lost without – sometimes literally.

My friends at Cayman Spirits for their amazing Seven Fathoms rum… which I'm convinced I could not live without!
Reef Balls for their permission and guidance with using their products in the story. Check out the great work they do at www. reefballfoundation.org
The Central Caribbean Marine Institute (CCMI) who I mention in the book for the wonderful work they do for our ocean environment. Find them at www.reefresearch.org

The Cayman Crew:
My lovely friend of many years, Casey Keller.
My new friend, the incredibly talented photographer, Lisa Collins of Capture Cayman.
Chris and Kate of Indigo Divers.
Diane Davidson for allowing me to drop her into the story in a fictitious role.

Above all, I thank you, the readers: none of this happens without the choice you make to spend your precious time with AJ and her stories. I am truly in your debt.

LET'S STAY IN TOUCH!

To buy merchandise, find more info or join my Newsletter, visit my
website at
www.HarveyBooks.com

If you enjoyed this novel I'd be incredibly grateful if you'd consider
leaving a review on Amazon.com
Find eBook deals and follow me on BookBub.com

Visit Amazon.com for more books in the
AJ Bailey Adventure Series,
Nora Sommer Caribbean Suspense Series,
and collaborative works;
The Greene Wolfe Thriller Series
Tropical Authors Adventure Series

ABOUT THE AUTHOR

A *USA Today* Bestselling author, Nicholas Harvey's life has been anything but ordinary. Race car driver, adventurer, divemaster, and since 2020, a full-time novelist. Raised in England, Nick has dual US and British citizenship and now lives wherever he and his amazing wife, Cheryl, park their motorhome, or an aeroplane takes them. Warm oceans and tall mountains are their favourite places.

For more information, visit his website at HarveyBooks.com.